MW01227961

LEGEND AND LEGACY

By

Gold & Janell

Copyright © 2022 by Goldenmindspresents

All rights reserved.

No part of this publication may be reproduced, distributed, or transmitted in any form or by any means, including photocopying, recording, or other electronic or mechanical methods, without the prior written permission of the author, except in the case of brief quotations embodied in critical reviews and certain other noncommercial uses permitted by copyright law. For permission requests, write to the author, addressed.

Part Two Coming Soon

ACKNOWLEDGEMENTS

We would like to thank our family, all of our supporters, and a special thank you to our sisters: jas, bay, keke, quay, and amaris for the moral support during the time we needed you all...

Special Thanks To My

Editor: Calvarydiggs

Cover Designer: Mnsartstudionew

And

Book Formatter: Foysal Rumman

www.fiverr.com/foysalrumman?up_rollout=true

Table of Contents

Prologue 1

Chapter One 13

Chapter Two 22

Chapter Three 33

Chapter Four 39

Chapter Five 62

Chapter Six 81

Chapter Seven 93

Chapter Eight 108

Chapter Nine 127

Chapter Ten 134

Chapter Eleven 140

Chapter Twelve 150

Chapter Thirteen 158

Chapter Fourteen 172

Chapter 1 183

Chapter 2 195

Chapter 3 207

Prologue

Young Hustler, Old Rules, and Young Player

♪♪shout out to my Miami and St. Thomas connect I never mention your name, I promise respect death before dishonor, correct? That's what you promised me since the foreign leagues along with, if we stay strong we can get paper longer than Pippin's arm...♪♪

As Grand Man and his right-hand man, Murder Marley sat at the kitchen table of Grand's son mother's house, counting a vast amount of money in different denominations. Jay-Z blared through the speakers professing to his past and present street team that he would never change. "I plead the fifth when it comes to the fam, I'm like a dog, I never speak but I understand." Grands 11 year old son, loyalty came rushing in the kitchen rapping along with the song.

Grand looked up from the pile of money smiling at his little nigga. "What you doing up, Loyalty?"

"I was sleep, but I heard my favorite song. Loyalty said innocently hoping his pops wasn't mad at him for rushing in the room on him while he was handling business. "What up Uncle Marley?"

Without breaking his concentration from the cash Marley said, "What you know nephew?"

"Can I have $100?" Loyalty asked about to grab a seat.

"It's a school night." Grand spoke in a firm voice stopping his son in his tracks. "Go to bed loyalty," He said Counting out $1,000 in small head 20s. "Here." He handed his son the small stack.

1

Loyalty grab the money and dropped his head walking down the hall back to his room. His pride was hurt. He wanted to stay up and chill with his pops and Uncle Marley. Instead of going all the way down the hall, he stopped around the corner so he could listen to Grand and Marley's conversation. Soon as loyalty was out of earshot, Marley started to rap with his mans. "Say, hundred grand why you be holding my nephew like that? You know he just attracted to the allure of the game."

Grand pulled a rolling paper from the yellow 1.5 tops packet and breaking up a bud of dro inside of it. "Sho you right. But dig, Marley, I'm raising bosses, not gangsters. If the streets is all a person know, then the streets is as far as that person can go. School will give him other options. You can't sell dope forever."

"I can damn sho dig that." Marley agreed passing Grand his zippo. "Fuck we been in this game since the 80s. I remember when we used to be running to cars in the Nolia, trying to get off two for the five powder packs. I don't see no stopping in this cycle, Grand what about you?" Taking a deep toke of the smooth marijuana smoke, Grand took a break from counting the money. His fucking thumb was cramping like shit. Did you take care of that with them busters over in Davis Holmes?" He asked skipping over Marley's original question to ask a question of his own.

"I couldn't catch that crumb snatching ass nigga, Kat, but the rest of them fools, Marley paused shaking his head. "The newspaper is the last thing they will ever miss. Because just as sure as this money is green, at breaking news, their face will be on that TV screen."

Grand nodded his head, puffing on his joint satisfied with the answer. "Good. I don't want it to stop there. I want every hand, every head. If you find out a muthafucker looked at them bricks- I want his eyes, ya dig?"

"You aim and I shoot." Marley stated seriously.

Pondering on that statement for a minute, Grand rubbed his chin. Even though he was frustrated he was still thinking. One thought that kept recurring was what the fuck gave them small-time niggas from the other side the nuts to break into one of his spots, and steal 24 bricks from him. The fact that the spot was in their Hood didn't mean shit to him.

Grand was the heartbeat of the whole west side and his hood, Third Ward, was the heart beat of the hood. Outside niggas didn't even come on Magnolia Boulevard aka the Nolia. Much less try the head honcho. They really had the game fucked up and Grand plan to make them aware of that.

"Tommy, Tony, EJ... Chris, Kevin, Pete...Slim, Biggs, Fatboy... Shannon, Ant-Ant, Turtle... Sharron, Kerry, Karen... T-Roy, Black, Sheila..." Grand casually called out names in repetitions of threes.

Marley listened intently, storing the names in his mental Rolodex, as Grand checked them off by the coolness of his tone, you would have never assumed that Grand was making a list of death. A list of people who was already dead, now all Marley had to do was close their eyes; the plug had already been pulled. It was about to be a real change in events. The clubs were about to be empty and the church's were about to fill up.

"Lil Tim, Fry and Stinson," Grand sat, finally concluding his, 26 name long, list, "I want to read about em."

Right in the middle of the conversation, the front door came open. It was loyalty's mother, Shayla, just coming in from work. Giving Shayla no more than a brief glance, Grand turned his attention back to Marley. It wasn't that Shayla wasn't attractive. Because she was drop-dead gorgeous. From the age of 13 until a couple of years in his twenties, Grand had paraded the 5 ft 4 inch, chocolate, perfectly shaped beauty around on his arm like Hood royalty.

But the time had changed with the mind frame. And now all they shared with each other was mutual respect and a child. Not only had Grand moved on, he had a wife whom he had another eight year old son by. Due to the fact their split was amicable, they were made on amiable terms. No matter what, Shayla was Grand's down ass bitch. They were from the same area went to the same elementary, middle, and High school together. Until Grand dropped out – for years.

Returning the gesture, Shayla didn't give Grand so much as a nod, throwing her pocketbook on the couch, heading straight for her bedroom. She was so tired, only thing that was on her mind was a hot shower and a warm bed. Grand didn't know how much she appreciated him for staying over watching loyalty during the nights she had to work. It didn't matter what Grand had going on, when it concerned his children everything else was put to the side. She couldn't do nothing but salute that.

Hearing his mother coming towards the hallway, Loyalty took off towards his bedroom, so he wouldn't get caught ease-dropping on his father.

Marley had left hours ago to drop the money off at the Stash House, Grand was still breaking down at the kitchen table smoking joints of dro, while in deep thought. Checking the time on his Motorola two way, he stubbed The Joint out and got up. It was time for him to head home to wifey, but first he had to let his young nigga know he was gone.

Soon as he cracked open his son's door, the Paid In Full portrait of Eric B and Rakim stared back at him. He still remember when he first bought the frame portrait at a concert in New York. That's back when everybody was really on their *cash rules everything around me,* shit. The real era of The Pimps, players, and hustlers.

"stop fronting, little nigga," Grand said sitting on the edge of his son's bed. "You ain't breathing soft enough to be sleep."

4

Loyalty saw no sense in trying to trick his daddy, so he came from beneath the comforter smiling. "You can hear a lion grumbling even when he is resting." He hit his pops with a line he once told him.

Grand chuckled. "You don't say. Why you ain't sleep? You know you got school in a few hours."

Loyalty came from under the covers and sat beside his pops. "The hustlers Howl at the Moon. I'll sleep when I run out of time, you dig?" He spit his pop game like he had it wrote down. Actually, he did.

"What's a hustler?" Grand questioned.

"A person who go and get it. No matter what it is, if he want it, he get it. There is no limitations to a hustler. It's not even a stop sign at the sky. It's all go, go, go, go, - never slow down. Whenever a hustler go fast, that's because he thought it through before he started. Drop a hustler off anywhere, any place on God's green earth, he's going to triple his worth." Loyalty answered perfectly, remembering the words from the handbook Grand had wrote, typed, and paid to be binded in real book form just for him.

"Do a hustler only make money?"

"No. He also makes history." Loyalty was right back with the response.

"How does he make history?"

"By learning history. Familiarizing himself with everything that happen before him.

Grand went in his pocket and counted out five-hundred dollars in tens. "Add this with your other money."

Loyalty went under his pillow and pulled out two stacks of money. "Can I carry it all on me?" he asked trying to grip the two knots in his small hands.

"That's what I gave it to you for. Flex your muscle, little nigga." Grand knew a muhfucka would take their chances fucking with Chelsea Clinton before they fucked with his son; it was two-thousand and one, Grand was running the hood with an iron fist.

When it came to his kids, Grand's every move was calculated. Every step was another step towards the future. Some people might look at it as a dubious move to have his eleven-year-old son walking around with thousands of dollars. But every one move added up to two. It was a reason behind every move Grand made.

Loyalty put the stacks together and bounded them together with the rubberband. "Today I'm going to buy ice cream for my whole class and drinks for my whole gym class." Loyalty slid the stacks back under his pillow.

"Why is you going to do that?" Grand asked loyalty, really wanting to know the logic behind his actions. "You know out of the whole crowd there will be a hater within the group."

Loyalty balled his face up and shrugged his shoulders. "If you ain't ready for the enemy then quit. That's what you taught me. Forget the haters I'm doing it so they can talk about it."

"So you going to waste your money on people who don't like you?"

"Daddy, what's forty-fifty dollars. I'm looking at the bigger picture. I'm building my reputation. Everybody who go to school with me is from around the way. And the ones that don't will still be around me in high school. The ones who are not from the hood, they can take my name to their hood. That way I'll be there without going there, ya dig? I know you can dig that." Loyalty kicked Grand's game with his own twist.

"You doing all that for reputation?"

"Why wouldn't I be-" before he slipped, he caught himself. "Nawl, I'm doing it for power. These are just my first steps. Reputation is the cornerstone to power."

Grand nodded in silent agreement. "What's the foundation?"

"Actions," Loyalty replied.

Standing up to leave, Grand went in his pockets and gave Loyalty another three hundred dollars - in big faces this time. "I gotta go. But with that money, buy your mother something nice."

"Can I come over with you, Mrs. Lola, and Legend this weekend?"

Looking at his watch, Grand said, "Is that even a question?"

"Nawl," Loyalty corrected himself.

"I'll be ready Friday night-"

"Me and Legend going to pick you up from school," Grand said cutting him off.

"Family first," Loyalty said.

"Now get some rest." Grand said heading out the door. "Family First."

Young Legend sat up at two in the morning watching *How to be a Player* with the volume down. He wasn't trying to get caught up by his mother- especially not watching the same movie she'd took away from him. No matter how many times he'd seen the movie, he still was captivated by the way Bill Bellamy finessed the females.

Hands down he was a true player. Legend wanted to have a lot of girls just like Bill Bellamy. Only thing he planned to do different was not lie to them. He wanted to have a lot of girls without having to trick them like they're the only one. He'd already learned from the movie, women didn't like to be lied to.

Legend was only eight now, but when he got big, he planned to be smooth as silk and a player like Wilt Chamberlin. Already at the tender age of eight, he had the girls in his third grade class going crazy. Even the fourth and fifth grade girls couldn't get enough of the little dark skinned boy with the hazel brown eyes and silky hair, who wore Ralph Lauren Polo, Nautica, Tommy Hilfiger, and Izod every day of the week.

Being a PRO in the staying up late department, soon as he heard the creek in the hallway floor, Legend cut the T.V. Off and dove in the bed all in one motion, he was not about to let his mother catch him up again. He wasn't with all that punishment stuff, but his mother definitely was. He held his breath trying to play sleep.

Grand tossed his Avirex coat on the Italian leather couch. He was ready to lay it down, but it was a must he checked in on his youngest son before he took a shower and cuddled up with his wife. This was the other side of Grand's life. In this world he wasn't a cold-blooded King Pin. He was a small business owning family man, who was striving to be successful. His wife - Just like everybody else in this different world – didn't know anything about what he really did for paper. They had no idea that it was drug money that paid for his car wash, barber shop, or his soul food restaurant. And believe it or not, Grand found more happiness in the world he had to strive to make it through. Yeah, the money he had in his other world was a nice cushion, but he was exhausted from the life. When he first started it was exciting along the way he got a thrill from the cash, but now all he got was satisfaction from the financial security that the game allowed him to offer his family. He was getting too old for all the energy it took to stay on top of the game. He was thirty-one years old, it was time for him to put his toes in the air.

In due time, Grand thought as he opened his son's door. He leaned against the door frame and looked over the décor of his son's spacious room. The little nigga had more stuff in his room than

Loyalty. And that wasn't out of favoritism. Loyalty just asked for less. Everything Legend seen, he wanted it.

His two L's. They both symbolized his two worlds, Loyalty was Grandman the hustler and Legend was hundred grand, no shorts, no change. The only difference between the two was, Loyalty knew of both his worlds, whereas Legend only knew of one. And Grand planned for it to stay that way. If it was one thing he wound change if he could, it would be raising his boys in separate homes.

No matter apart or together, Grand think, they will both have the best and more long as my brain work. Staring at the gold framed portrait of the legendary, Notorious B.I.G, he could of swore the deceased rapper winked at him. The many joints of dro had him tripping. Taking a few seconds, he admired the portrait Legend begged him to buy. And no matter the six-thousand dollar price tag, Grand got his eight year old son, the picture of Biggie posted up in his signature gold link Jesus head chain, along with the multi-colored Coogi sweater he made famous, and to top it off, he had a hand full of fucking cash, with the Versace shades on. Real Player shit.

"I'm going to tell your mother you been we watching movies," Grand said laughing to himself at the irony of both his sons playing the same game."

"How you knew?" Legend was still hiding under the cover.

Grand sat on the edge of the bed. "The front of the VCR.

The numbers still rolling. You gotta tighten up, young H.O. If it was your mother, you would've been busted."

Legend put his finger to his lips and said, "Shhh.. she might can hear you. I'm not trying to get in trouble. You smell like weed, daddy," he said sniffing the air.

"How you know what weed smell like, lil nigga?"

Grand pulled the cover off of legend. "Don't lay in the bed while a man is sitting on your bed."

Legend immediately sat up. "My bad," he said feeling ashamed.

Grand rubbed his hand over Legend's head. "Come on with all that. What was you watching?"

Soon as Grand took his hand off his head, Legend started rubbing his hair back down in place. "Man, you be messing up my waves when you do that." Legend shot a mug Grand's way.

"I was watching How to be a player. Don't tell mama," he said in a hush tone.

"Come on, lil Nigga. I'm a Carter. It make me feel some type of way when I gotta tell somebody the time," Grand replied seriously, not expecting his son to catch the metaphor. "What you know about being a player?"

"I am a player." Legend was dead serious when it came to that

player shit.

"What's a player?"

"A man of respect." Legend stalled trying to remember the rest of the answer. "A player is somebody who make his own rules. No matter the climate a player stay cool. Preez - Pre- what's that P word?"

"Pressure," Grand answered.

"Yeah that's it," Legend smiled, showing his missing front teeth.

"Pressure don't apply to a player. A player's word is always true. A player keep it clean, because dirt is for busters. A player-"

"How many rags do you shower with?" Grand cut in.

"Two." Legend held up two fingers. "One only for my face and the other one for my body. A player never wash his face with the same rag he wash his body with."

"When you take a piss, what you do afterwards?"

"I shake my ding- dong off in tissue and wipe the head of it off until it's no more drops coming out." Legend replied.

"Why you do that?"

Legend rubbed his hands together. "Because a player ain't about to be walking around with drips of Pee-Pee in his underwear."

"Why? Because he don't want the girls to know?" Grand asked.

"Nawl. A player make moves out of natural habit. He do what he do, because that's what he do. The girls just like what he do." Legend beamed with joy. He had been trying to get that line down packed, every since he got to that chapter in the players handbook his pops wrote for him to study.

Unlike Royalty, Grand couldn't give Legend stacks of money when he passed his once a week verbal pop quiz. That was the fucked up thing about Legend's world. He could not flash that cash like Loyalty, without raising red flags. Plus he was really too young. Grand would just buy him something fly. That Lil Nigga now he love some clothes, Grand thought.

"Loyalty will be over this weekend. We got to pick him up from school Friday," Grand informed.

A smile instantly spreaded across Legend's face. "For real!?"

"Can we pick him up in the fast car?"

"What's the name of the fast car?"

Legend thought for a second. "Grand National." although he knew the correct name of the car, he didn't know the actual name was really 'Grand National.' He thought that meant 'Grand' for his pops name and national for the name of the car.

"You still ain't told me how you know what weed smell like." Grand re-questioned.

"'I only smell it on you. I told somebody I wanted to smell like you be smelling when you come home late, and they told me, I can't smell like you, because you be smelling like weed." Legend admitted leaving names cut.

"Who told you that?" without the answer, he already knew Loyalty was the only person that would tell Legend something like that.

Legend shook his head from Side-to-side. "I'm a Carter, pops. It make me feel some type of way when I gotta tell somebody my name."

He Suprised Grand by flipping his metaphor back on him. Grand couldn't do nothing but smile. "Go to sleep before you miss school. He said standing back up.

Legend dove back up under the cover. "Never! I'll see you tomorrow. Family first." Unlike Loyalty, Legend loved school.

"Family First." Grand exited his son's room.

Chapter One

Two- thousand- thirteen

Tish placed her palms flat down on to Legend's well toned chest and leaned forward with her small feet planted firmly on the black thousand thread count Fendi sheet. She stared him directly in the eyes, as she lowered herself down his long thick dick.

"Oh Gaaawwwdd..." She moaned softly from the initial dolt of pleasure.

Legend sunk his fingertips in the soft round ass cheeks of the Maliah Michel look a like, that at the present moment had his dick in a vice grip between her pussy walls. Damn this bitch trying to make a nigga cum asap, he thought as Tish gyrated her body tack up his thick shaft.

"If I knew this pussy was this good, I would of been pulled up on you." Legend spreaded her ass cheeks and pushed a Molly capsule up her asshole. Leaving the words for the talkers, Tish smiled seductively and pushed back, causing his finger to slide straight inside her asshole. She wiggled a little before dropping down hard on his dick.

"Fuuuuccckkk..." she screamed at the top of her lungs when that dick hit her back wall. Felt like that long motherfucker was trying to get inside her stomach.

Getting straight to it, she begun to ride him like he was the horse on the Ralph Lauren Polo Logo. She went up and down in full speed, causing the sound of her pussy juice popping to echo throughout the room. Tish had sweat dripping between her breast and the aroma of sex filled the air.

"That's Right, ma. Pop that pussy for a real nigga." Legend said arrogantly as he inhaled the O.G. Kush deep into his young lungs, then he reached out and plucked the ash into the black-custom made marble ashtray that sat on the all glass nightstand. Leaning back into the fluff Fendi Pillows, he put the blunt back between his lips while he slapped her ass cheeks with his right hand. When she started twirling her hips like she was hula hooping he almost last his cool, and choked on the smoke he was holding in his lungs. "Stop holding back, daddy." Tish whispered in his ear after leaning forward placing her chest flat against his. This was her favorite position to ride a dick in. She knew men went crazy when experiencing this "Thang" while hearing her exotic moans up close and personal. To add a little more seductiveness into the mix, she stuck her tongue inside his ear.

Just when Legend thought he had the situation under control, he felt a pair of juicy lips take his left nut sack to meet a very warm, moist, and luscious tongue. Almost instantly he nearly lost all his will power and bust all in Tish, as Daphane sucked on his balls.

On a mission to please, neither one of the beauties showed the slightest sign of letting up. "This gotta be life." Legend mumbled with the blunt hanging from his lips.

Daphane pulled Legend's dick out of Tisha creamy Pussy and licked from the bottom of his cream coated dick slowly Savoring the taste of Tish's sweet Nectar making her way to the tip of his dick. "Mmmmh." She purred as she wrapped her pouty lips around the head of Legend's dick. DaPhane placed her Long torque along the back of the nine and a half inch dick while she bobbed her head up and down making exaggerated but seductive slurring noises. Going further down, she took his dick in her mouth until it touched the back of her throat.

"EeeeRRR." She gagged at first, but she came back up a little and Re-adjusted her tongue so her throat would be prepared to accept the dick head. Trying it again she eased the dick down her throat until she was able to tickle his balls with her tongue at the same time. No longer able to take being left out of the action, Tish crawled off of Legend and got up under Daphane pulling her pussy down to her mouth, she illicitly started to lick Daph's clitoris. As she Flicked her tongue at Daph's swollen clit, she patted down on her clitoris. Done with the teasing, she Pulled Daph's clit between her lips and used her Freehand to tickle DaPh's asshole.

"Ooohh-. My- My-..Fuuuuuucccccckkkkkinnn…Ooooo." Daph's screamed out as she felt her bigasm building up. She dropped her Pussy down into Tish's mouth and started grinding back and forth. She used her hand to Jack Legend's dick up and down.

"Open your eyes, PaPi. This is your show. Watch me do my thing." Daph demanded in her Sensual Puerto Rican accent as she poured Molly all over his dick, after coating it with a layer of saliva, the powder would stick to his dick. This time she went at that dick like her name was Rebecca and her hair was blonde.

"Come on, Papi. Give me my prize." Daph locked eyes with Legend as she French Kissed the head of his dick while speaking Spanish.

I'm definitely fucking with these bitches again, Legend concluded laying back watching Daph' drink his cum. He couldn't help but to smile at the grandness of his situation. At the tender age of twenty years old, he was living a life many people only dreamed about. There were so many People that Would kill for his lifestyle and here he was only living for the memories right now. But he could do that. His pops was the most successful businessman in the whole City. His Future was secured like Fort Knox.

Legend pulled himself from beneath the freak show and said, "That's enough for one night."

As if they didn't care whether he was a part of the movie or not they continued to shout the scene as if Legend was only an extra. Tish and Daph locked into each other like crabs in the sixty-nine

Position. Legend stood at the edge of the bed and watched the show in amazement before walking out the bedroom, so he could take a shower.

An hour later, Legend sat at the black marble table that was trimmed in white Patterns, with No shirt on and a Pair Louis Vuitton denim jeans falling on a fresh pair of – twelve hundred dollar-Jay-Z blue paten leather Louie kicks. He was slumped in the chair, still feeling kind of drained from the two hour 'Trey Play' with DaPh and Tish. Thanks to the hour he spent under the Jet shower head, he was slowly coming back to life.

Now refreshed and kind of focused, he held a thick wad of dead Presidents in his hand, with a blunt clutched between his index and middle finger, The Potent smoke from the O.G. kush was wafting through the bills as he thumbed through the check.

He Paused for a second and wiggled his thumb. "I should of been counted this fucking Paper." Legend said to himself as he concluded the count of the First bundle OF Money. He placed the blunt between his lips, as he Wrapped Rubber bands at the ends of the stack. The smoke rising toward his face causing him to squench one eye trait-way closed like he was trying to imitate Popeye the sailorman.

"Thought you said that you didn't sale drugs." Daphane said from the doorway with her hand on her hip catching Legend by surprise. "I don't." Legend replied without breaking his Concentration. Three thousand and four hundred, three thousand four hundred and one, he continued his count not bothering to look up at DaPhane. He wasn't even trying to hear Daph's lecturing Right now. It Never failed, every time she seen him with large sums of money, she Went to inquiring about his dealings with drugs.

Daph rolled her eyes and sat at the edge of the table." And you still insist on lying to me after I just walked in on you counting a table full of money, with a large bowl of weed in front of you. She shook her head. "You're a pathetic liar." She said turning her lip up at Legend, but he wasn't paying her any attention.

"I never once denied the fact that I get money or that I smoke weed. But a drug dealer? Man Stop I like living good, Not Working hard," Legend retorted.

"I told your lil dumb ass about calling a grown man a liar" he briefly glanced up at a now dressed Daph. The P2I Skinny Jeans were hugging her curves so perfectly, it was causing Legend's dick to brick up. "Where Tish at?"

"Who the fuck you calling a dumb ass? You're the one a dumb ass, if you're willing to risk everything you've worked so hard to accomplish, just for some extra money." Daph retorted getting pissed off at Legend's ignorance.

"Man shut up. Ain't nobody risking shit," Legend snapped back. "Yo you really a fucking hypocrite. You do drugs. Preach to your supplier about selling drugs, not me." He put the money down on the table, taking a brief break, so he could roll him another blunt.

"Correction: I smoke weed and POP Molly recreationally." Daph said getting offensive. "And FYI, just in case you haven't noticed - I been getting my stuff from none other than, Legend Carter!" She pointed out with a cute smirk on her pretty face.

"Okay. If you wanna say I sell drugs, because I done sold a couple grams of Molly and a little weed cut out of my Personal Smoke sack." he shrugged his shoulders. "Cool. Go right ahead. I'm not the only one who do that on campus. and you really a dumb head if you don t think Pure MDA is a drug." he said throwing a rubber banded wad of money at her being Playful.

"Fucker!" she giggled throwing the money back at him. "But on the real. Let's be honest Its twenty thirteen, who in College don't POP Molly?" Daph asked trying to support her claim.

"I'ont pop Molly, I rock Tom Ford, " Legend replied seriously.

"Shut the fuck!" Daph hissed.

"You always got a slick comment. But that's exactly what i mean. You got to be selling real drugs. Because the lifestyle you live and the money you spend, canst be Justified by a little side hustle on campus. Nawl, you got to be moving the real deal."DaPh boldly insinuated.

"You wear thousand dollar heels and you drive a seven series BMW. I think you selling drugs." he flipped it around on her, so she could see how easily she could fit inside the same stereotype.

"Boy stop! You already Know my Parents take care Of me.

Don't even try me like that. You think I'm Playing, but I really think you're selling them white people that Cocaine." Daph told him with a serious expression on her face.

"What? Why you over there smirking? I'm being so serious with you-" Daph couldn't understand why legend was lying to her. He was letting the fact that she was born with a silver spoon in her mouth fool him. She might've been spoiled, but she wasn't no dumb bitch.

"Let it go, ma. I don't I don't sell no cocaine. My people take care of me too. This house, the cars, my clothes - my parents paid for it all. All I got to do is stay in school." Legend never involved people in his business, but DaPh was getting on his nerves. "And this money came from me selling my 1970 Pontiac Lemans." he added still seeing the curiosity in her eyes.

Daph rolled her eyes. "Whatever you say. I guess your POPS support your addiction to smoking O.G. by the pound too. Hmm. Any way what you got planned for the weekend?" She asked changing the subject.

"Ain't no fucking telling. That's the advantage of going to school in your hometown. You don't have to travel to go home," Legend stood up and started putting the bundles of money inside a leather Louie Knap sack: "what you getting into?"

"I don't even know. I'm not even trying to go way back to Chicago Just to come right back in two days. But my little sister want me to come home. What should I doooooo?" Daph whined stretching across the table.

"Haha. You hell. Go home. Remember, family first. There isn't shit going on down here" Legend stood over the trash basket, that was already full of blunt guts and the plastic wrappers that the Optimo cigar, splitting another Cigar down the middle with his thumbnail.

"I know, I know. But my allowance account won't get refilled until the twenty-fifth. That's like two weeks away. My daddy already talking about I need to get a job, because I'm spending too much money. If there isn't nothing going on down here, why don't you come with me?" Daph asked fake pouting, sitting up pulling her BCBG baby doll T-shirt down.

"Don't worry about the money. I'll fuck with you on the ticket there and back. You better get a job before your pops spank that ass." Legend sat back at the table and started twisting a bud between his thumb and index finger, causing the weed to fall inside the open cigar crumbled up.

"Imagine that- ain't nobody spanking this ass but you. And why you avoid my question?" she asked noticing the way he dodged answering her invitation.

"Come on, ain't nothing changed. If you was looking for a dude, I'm still not yo' guy." he retorted nonchalantly, as he exhaled a thick cloud of smoke out of his mouth, only to inhale it back up his nose.

"'Get over yourself, you KNOW I don t want No guy! Just cause I invite you out of town with me don't mean I'm on no getting booed up shit." Daph said one thing out her mouth, but in her heart it was a different feeling.

Although Daphane had been a full blown lesbian since her junior year in high school, she couldn't deny the magnetic attraction she had to Legend, It was never in her plans to come way to Carrollton, Georgia with the intention of following her education, and ending up falling in love. Never in a million years did she think she would get caught back up in the emotions a man created in a woman. But sometime shit just happen. And the day she bumped into the six feet one, one hundred and ninety five pound dark chocolate beau, with the hypnotic swagger, the first day of her freshman year at the University of West Georgia, it was one of them rare occasions of something that just happen.

And nearly a year later, it still was one of them things that just was happening.

Of course she loved women and enjoyed the instant openess that came along with being in a relationship with one. But sometime she really did yearn that masculine touch. She even missed being able to go out with her significant other and not attract stares and slick comments. She wasn't blind though, She knew there was nothing in this world that would make Legend settle down with her -or any other woman. He made that crystal clear.

"That's so Not you, ma. Get out your feelings." Legend said seeing right through her facade. He knew now Daph felt about him, she was cool and all but that relationship shit was all the way out the question, DaPh was a model type chick and she had a head on her shoulder. But she was after what she would never obtain his heart.

"I'm not in my feelings, you're just so fucking insensitive to other's emotions." Daph went in his bowl pinching out her blunt.

"Other people's emotions don't have shit to do with me. Emotions are a personal thing. I don't deal with my own emotions. Fuck I look like dealing with another person's feelings? He nonchalantly retorted while putting the Flame to the end of the freshly rolled blunt.

After pulling the smoke into his already overcrowded lungs, he looked into Daphs hazel brown eyes. "Come on, babe. Don't look like that. Trust me, just have fun and enjoy the moment. I'm not the hubby type. I told you from day one, I ain't shit and when it comes to relationships, I ain't got the patience." he rubbed his wavy hair. "Shit." he mumbled.

"If I wasn't already this gay bitch, you'd make a bitch hate dick and go gay. FOR Real, FOR Real. I don't see how a straight bitch deal with you. ON the real, I don't understand you, you'll make a woman feel so comfortable but you're so cold at the same time. You're a cold ass nerd." she said looking him directly in the eyes. And like a real man, Legend never broke eye contact.

"Nobody deal with me. I told you, I'm not Mr. Right. I'm Just that nigga that'll make you forget about when will he Show up." Legend said being truthful.

"'Why did you decide to fuck with me after you haven't fucked with a man in four years?' he asked trying to make a point.

"Why not? You're cute, I'm nineteen away at college- Fuck lets have fun. I'm young, wild, and free." she exclaimed telling the half-truth.

"Exactly. You don't look at me and think picket fences and baby carriages and shit I'm telling you this cause I fuck with you. Yeah, we have casual sex, but you're my friend. In a crazy way, I care. Not in the way you want, but I do care. Don't lose focus. I'm not that guy." Legend stood up putting the straps of the knap back over his shoulder. "Why you tell the other girl to leave?" he asked referring to Tish, as he walked down the hall, leaving Daph sitting at the table.

"Legend, Legend, Legend, you must don't know, women love Mr. Wrong just as much as they love Mr. Right maybe more." Daph mumbled as she walked out the front door.

Chapter Two

I know this fucker not about to fuck this bitch while my girl laying up in the hospital in a coma for his ass, Legacy was completely caught up in the vivid story about Heatless and Shuntric, she fucked with that 'Heartless Vendetta,' but the sequel "Empty Chest vengeance" had her flipping the pages on her I-Pad in anticipation for the next word.

The new young street author, Arièus Potts A.K.A. A.P da Dons, had came into the book world with his sexy gritty street love stories and fucked the game up. The way he painted the picture so rogue, but so beautiful at the same time, you'll mistake him for Jean-Michel Basquait. His stories was so vivid, you'll start speculating can how much of the story was false.

"Damn, Heartless you had me doubting you for a minute there." Legacy breathe a sigh of relief seeing that it was only a dream he was having. Man, I got to put this damn I-Pad down and handle my business, she thought looking at the half a block sitting on her passenger seat.

Despite what she knew was best, seconds later she was back caught up in the next line only thing that purled her away was the ringing of her I-Phone 5.

"Ugh! Right when I was getting to the good part. They need to add an "I'm Reading app." Legacy laid the I-pad in her lap and grabbed her phone.

'Money' the caller I.D. Read. And that wasn't anybody name either.

"'Talk" she immediately answered.

"I'm about to pull up, sexy." The man on the other end of the phone advised.

"Koo. I'm in the Lexus." Legacy disconnected tempted to pick the I-Pad back up. But the car pulled beside her before she got a chance to grab it, so instead she hit the locks, so her customer could get in the car.

"What's the business, Legacy?" the dude asked as he got in the car and closed the door.

"Cocaine." When it came to business, Legacy played the game like a poker player. "That's the whole sixteen-five, right?" Legacy passed him the tightly packaged half a brick. "'Fuck you sweating for?" This nigga was acting all nervous and shit.

"That molly mean." he replied wiping his forehead. "You already know this the whole check." he put all three of the stacks together and put a large rubber band around it before handing it to Legacy.

"That's what it better be." Clumsy ass nigga, coming to re-up geeked on the Molly, legacy thought in disgust. "When you ready for another package, get at me." Legacy put the money in the center console and hit the button to start the car.

"When you going to let me take you out, shawty? " he asked with one foot out the car.

"You can't afford the plates I eat.

"She put the car in gear, anxious to get back to her loft, so she could read her book in peace.

"All you got to do is name the place, I got you." he kicked it as if his pockets was so deep his hands get lost looking for all his cash. Even if he didn't have it, for the walnut brown dime, he would come up with it.

"Come on, dude. You damn near thirty and you taking care of yourself, your five kids, and your baby mama off a half block. Baby boy, what I look like going from Filet Migon to Hamburger Helper. Next time you come at me like that, I'm going to put Triple up on it." Legacy wasn't interested in dude in no type of way, and he knew that. Hey, every dog wanted his day. He just was barking up the wrong tree.

"If that's how you feel." he replied lamely, bitching up at the mention of Triple's name. Nobody wanted the kind of problems that young menace would bring. He stepped out the car with the half a brick tucked under his shirt.

"Duck couldn't even come back at a bitch." Legacy said to herself as she pulled out of the carwash Parking lot.

Legacy swerved in and out of traffic bumping the new K. Michelle song "V.S.0.P." Now that she had made all her drops she could let her hair down and enjoy the way the wind blew through her new Pixie hairstyle. She was totally in her own world as she pushed the Lexus coupe down Maple Street.

"We got too much history, Very special." Legacy sang out loud as she sat at the red light. It was such a beautiful day, she was contemplating on going to the pool and getting a couple laps in Maybe that's just the place I should go to get some reading in, she thought, looking out her driver side window just as a 1970 convertible cutlass pulled up beside her with the top down.

"Now I know what they means when they say. I got an old school harder than your new school. I got to have that car." she vowed to herself.

Sitting beside the old school that was painted Denver Nuggets blue with the yellow pinstripes, she felt like her 2013 Lexus was a Ford Explorer, The twenty - three inch But Nicks sat perfectly under the growling machine, she nodded her head in approval of the deep lips on the chrome rims. The door handle sparkled along with the Rims as if they were cut from the same material. The crest velvet -

same color blue as the paint- interior was trimmed in the same yellow as the pinstripes.

Just when she was about to roll her window down to inquire about the price he wanted for the car, her phone started to vibrate in her lap. She checked the screen; it was her mother. "Fuck." She knew she had to take the call. Legacy got one glance at the dark skin driver, who was coolly bobbing his head to the music with his eyes hid behind some Gucci Aviator shades and a blunt clutched between the same hand he was holding the steering wheel with.

"Damn!" Soon as the light turns green the bird drop down and roared up the street too fast for her to follow behind him without speeding. "Hello."

"Young lady watch your mouth." She sighed, riding along with the lunch. College traffic. Thank God, I don't have classes today she thought. I just seen this car I want it so bad. But the driver left me at the light. Legacy wine like the spoiled 20 year old she was.

It didn't take nothing for her to transition back to her real world. The extra life she was living, was being live All In The name of Love. She could only imagine what her mother would do if she was to find out, Legacy was running the streets dealing drugs for her incarcerated boyfriend.

And it wasn't no small-time shit either. Legacy had been flipping triples money for 16 months and she was already at to Bricks, starting from the quarter key triple had left at her Loft one night.

When triple first got locked up and presented the idea to her, she was reluctant. How could she sell drugs? She didn't know the first thing about drugs. She didn't even know who to sell the stuff to. She was born and raised in the suburbs. Now if it was weed, Molly, or some kind of prescription pain pills, she would be able to get off that easily. Everybody in the college campus was doing that stuff. But that wasn't the case. Triple was talking crack cocaine.

Eventually Legacy gave in, only because Triple's freedom depended on it. Triple had gotten pop on some very serious charges which he told Legacy he didn't do and with a public defender he was sure to spend the rest of his life in prison. With the love of her life in the balance, Legacy threw caution to the side and did what she had to do.

From behind the walls Triple made it easy for her. He sent the clientele her way and protected her through the same force- his reputation. Triple coached her on the beginning steps of the game. He only gave her what she needed to know. Nothing more. Anything extra would be him losing control.

Triple just didn't know that he created a beast. Legacy was a natural at the hustle. Before long she was moving to her own beat. Creating her own path. But she still was using Triple's brand. She didn't know how he did it, but he instilled fear in niggas from afar.

But no matter how much it thrilled her, the game would stop soon as she paid Triple's lawyer off. That was the promise she made to God.

"What car do you want now?" her mother asked, cutting into her thoughts. "We just bought you the Lexus for your birthday. You're really getting like your father with this car obsession thing."

"It was an older model convertible with rims on it." Legacy responded turning into the drive thru at McDonald's. She was famished.

"What do you want with that kind of car? A lady don't drive them oily themes. Where are you at anyway? You better not be near that Westside." Her mother was so green, she thought the only place you see cars with rims on them, was in the hood.

"Them cars is not oily mother. And noooo I'm not on the west side. I just left campus. I'm grabbing something to eat, then I'm heading home. What you got going on?" Legacy hated to lie to her mother, but some truths hurt it worse than the lie.

Outside of the fact her mother didn't agree with her relationship with triple cross, they were best friends. More like sisters instead of mother and daughter. Out of her 20 years on this Earth, her and her mother had only argue once. And that was when she started fucking with a young street do at the age of 16.

Although she was completely obedient when it came to her parents, when it came down to them telling her what type of guy was right for her - she went insurgent. She wasn't about to let nobody deter her happiness. She understood they wanted the best for her. And all that was noted, but at the end of the day it was her life.

Now that she was in college and showing her parents, she could maintain her own life and not lose focus, things had gotten a little better they still refuse to accept her boyfriend, but they stayed out her relationship, still praying to God that Legacy what comes to her senses. No matter how acceptive if they become of her decision, hanging in the hood was still a no-go.

"Honey, Nothing really. These people working on my last nerve at this daggone bank. After I meet with this next client and complete his portfolio, I'm out of here. You want to check out that new Italian spot downtown? Her mother asked.

"Can I take a rain check? Class got me exhausted. I think I'm going to lay up and read all weekend. Next week we got to sit in these long-ass seminars and listen to some rich know-it-all tell us how to get rich. Hold on, mother. Legacy roll her window down.

"Yes, can I have a chicken salad? Yes, that'll be all." She went in her change purse to get a few dollars. "Mama?"

"I'm here." Her mother answered. "A rain check? I guess so. What you reading?"

"Oh. I'm reading 'Empty Chest Vengeance'. That book got me swooning. I want to marry Heartless." Legacy half joked. Just like her, her mother had a real passion for urban literature. But this was the same woman who despised the street, but she loved Street books. She just didn't get that.

"You're still reading that? Girl that book so full of suspense. What part you at? Her mother asks ready to gossip about her favorite pastime.

When he had the dream about grudge fucking Nadia. If I would have really- I'm tripping. I'm talking about if I. I meant, if he would have really did that, I would have hated heartless." Legacy indulge in the gossip as she put in Miley Cyrus on her iPod. She has adjusted the volume as darling begin to play.

"Ump.I forgot you were a part of #TeamMoonk. Who do you think killed Pinky? I think Heartless or that devil boy, Say No More did it." her mother replied.

Legacy could picture the look on her mother face when she had to mention Say No More or Heartless name let her mother tell it, they were the devil in the flesh. It was so crazy how a book could be so omnipresent, it seemed like real life.

"And you on #TeamBella. You got to rap for the Cougars, don't you? She teased her mother. But come on Mama you don't read too many A.P. da Don Books not to understand the way his characters think. Heartless ain't making no peon move like that. It wasn't messy enough for say no more to be responsible for it."

"So who did it? Text you the expert on this type of stuff. Please enlighten me. Her mother said.

"All right check this out. I'm not saying Heartless won't do that. But he understand the position he has been forced to play. His main focus is his wife right now. Plus he the patriarch of his extended family, so his shoulders are heavy. He not exposing his true troubles. He's grinning and still bearing it. He know he's a made man. The move he's been making from day one, was all to ensure he made it to boss status. He not going to downgrade himself. Now it's the same thing with say no more. He know that he is the closest thing to heartless it's just like Jay-Z and Memphis Bleek. Why the fuck Bleek going to stress when Jay is up? No reason to. But say no more got a different logic. That fool just do it for the thrill. He addicted to the street in the worst way. So he'll do it just to do it. But-"

"Love will, storm." Her mother cut in.

"Exactly say no more than fell in love with love. He's so off balance by the new field, it's hard for him to do anything other than try and figure out these new emotions. You need to reread the book. You missing out on a lot. Legacy smacked her teeth.

"Man, just tell me who did it. Her mother snapped.

"Lil Coolie made the mess oh, so heartless made him clean up his own mess. He could have got it done another way. But he had to let him correct his own mistake. Dim the type of lessons a boss will teach his protégé." Legacy gave her mother The Rundown. She might grew up in the suburbs, but her mind was a little more acute than her mother when it came to thinking like a street person. Mainly because she never turned a blind eye to it. She might not never been there, but as much as she read and watch documentaries about the street, she was on point.

"Giiirrrlll and That made perfect sense. You remember when they was at the Heat game? Heartless had told Cooley he had to handle that with pinky kids. Uh uh uh. I just started on one of his new books 'Streetz Raised Me.' Put my nose in that thing. I bet this his best book. Her mother said in excitement.

"That's the one with Lil BOB crew in it? I already bought that '2Hearts1Beat,' Asking through it. I'm dying to read it. That's why I got to knock this one out but look mama doll, I got to let you go. Toodles." Legacy line was beeping and this was a call she couldn't miss.

"All right Bella- dang why keep calling you that? But I love you." This was her mother's fifth time calling her Bella (the female Queen pin in the Heartless book series). It might was a mistake with her mother called her that. But if she would of pay more attention to the things she adamantly ignored, she would see the Bella in the real life Legacy.

"Hello." Legacy quickly clicked over without responding.

"You have a collect call-"

"Yes, I accept." Legacy said cutting off the jail automated recorder. She was three anxious to hear her boo voice.

"What up LG?" the gruff voice came over the line, barely audible over the background noise.

"You baby boy." she said cheerfully. "What you got going on TC? Legacy asked calling him by the nickname she had given him.

"You know me, baby girl. Really just coolin, waiting for these white folks to come on with it. How you holding it out there in that cold world?" Triple Cross asked his main chick.

"Fuckin' with a whole lot of snow. But I got this heat on me, so I can melt a brick plus one, ya dig." Legacy used a little of the lingo she had learned from one of A.P's books to tell Triple Cross she was moving two bricks of cocaine. Her memory was so good, she used the lingo word for word.

"I dig. What Paul Pierce for a shovel?" Triple Cross asked talking in code, asking her, was she paying thirty-four thousand a brick. He was smiling on the inside and how game tight his baby girl was getting. Then he started frowning at the realization he never gave her that much game about the streets. He knew Legacy came from a different side of the fence, and he always respected that. The only reason he had her moving weight now, because he'd got knocked on a murder and an armed robbery and he was in desperate need of lawyer money.

What's a jack boy and end that life you only acquired fear not love. Although it was better to be feared than loved, you paid the price for that when you was out of sight. Especially in jail. Yeah, niggas might shoot you a couple hundred to keep you straight while you was in there. But helping you get out of there? Please! For what, so you can take from them again? Yeah right.

The saying was true; there was no honor among thieves. So Legacy was the only person- we have the only loyal person, triple cross had on his team. He respected it though. But, boy, when he beat this case, he thought. The streets was going to feel his pain for real. He hoped the streets could accept the punches the same way he was accepting them. Because he was about to put the worst kind of pressure down. He had to push the thought of legacy and another man out of his mind before he snapped.

"Now and just for the record I love you. Turn Michael Jordan backward. And it's clean. But look everything good on the business. Talk to me. I miss you. Have you got your visitation back yet? I need to see you." Legacy held the phone to her ear with her shoulder, as she got her bags out of the car.

"I miss you too." He replied. "Fuck no. I've been trying to get at the Corporal, who took my shit. He's supposed to come back today. Where you going to send me some more pictures? Where you at? You at home?" Triple Cross was trying to come up with another excuse to tell Legacy, why she couldn't visit him. He's been using the visitation restriction excuse for three months now. Yeah, he was crazy about Legacy, but he was a true player by heart. He had to stunt on these bustas on the cell block, by having a different bad bitch come through every visitation day. Hands down, Legacy was his baddest and most beneficial check. But you know a man going to be a man.

"I got you when I get out of class tomorrow. Me and Jazzy went to fusions last week and was all the way turnt. I just pulled up at the house when you was calling. Man, I'm going to call that fuckin' dude myself. What time he come on?" Legacy walked through her loft, kicking off her stilettos and slinging her bags on the bed. She was so hungry, she was about to go in on the chicken salad. On the phone and all.

"You have one minute left." The automated voice warned.

Saved by the Bell, Legacy thought, ready to pig out on the salad.

"Nah, you ain't got to do that. I got him. Look umma call you tonight. I love ya, pretty eyes. Remember, LG, it's better to be feared than loved hear it if you love too much, they'll see you as weak.

Jus-" Before Triple Cross could finish the phone hung up.

Legacy lay her phone on the couch beside her and wasted no time going in on the salad. She guessed she would shower and read until triple cross called back.

Chapter Three

"The call party did not accept-" the automated voice informed Triple Cross for the third time in a row. "Bitch ass niggas. We'll see how they feel when I touch back down." Triple Cross mumbled to himself. "I just wanted them niggas to keep the same attitude." he slammed the phone down after the third nigga from the hood screened his call.

Triple cross left the phone hanging off the Jack as he started making laps around the cell block day room. This jail s*** for the birds, he thought as he looked around at the environment he was temporarily stuck in. This shit was killing him softly. He hated to be in a position where he had to depend on another nigga. He knew niggas couldn't wait to get the ups on him. That's why he played for keeps every time. Any time Triple caught a nigga down bad, he left him down worse. Fuck what you thought.

At the age of 21, Triple Cross was labeled a menace to society. Not only by the law, but the street as well. Shuffle had been in the robbing game since he was 13. And as he got older the more vicious he became. Triple cross was a real robber. He blew money to take it again.

Most people assume niggas turned to the take game because they wasn't hustlers. Well that was far from the truth. When it came to Triple Cross. He was born from a couple of old school hustlers. His pops ran spot and his mother ran a coke trap that could get a nigga crazy paid overnight. He was a hustla by birth. He started out hustling. Late nights & early mornings in the Trap was his first love.

But just like a bitch who quit her day job to start the night shift at the local strip club; he love the fast paper. He had seen it first-hand, you could hustle a whole year and never profit 20 bands because of all the extra shit that came along with the dope game. But you could kick in one door or lay one nigga down and take a sucker off for 50 or 60 bands in 10 minutes- no sweat.

Now that he'd experience the flip side of the game, it had taught him two valuable lessons. One: no matter if you got it from a caper, you still got to stack that lawyer paper. Two: No matter where you commit your crime at, who you commit your crime on; the streets was still watching, and a Niger will tell the whole movie before they became a scene. But it was all good; it was the first step a man take that determine whether he learned from his previous mistake.

"What's good, Triple Cross?" A neighborhood hustler named, Virgil greeted when he walked past the stairs, where a bunch of other cats from the hood was posted up.

"Not a muhfuckin thang. Triple responded. Virgil was one of the few Hustlers that triple had spared. Mainly because his pops Houston Wildwood triples pops before he got killed.

"I hear that. You heard about that fool Big Tank?" Virgil pulled a roll cigarette out the pocket of his orange and white striped shirt.

"Hell yeah. That's fucked up Big Boy went out like that." Triple Cross really wasn't into showing emotions, so he shook the image of his big partner laid up in a casket out of his head. Real niggas only cry when babies die, he thought lighting his camel off Virgil scroll up.

"I'm trying to tell you. Take me in the street, not my sleep. But C.I.P to the homie." Lil Tre-Loc Added throwing up a bunch of gang signs.

"Umma get up, fool. I got to try this phone again before we lock down." Triple slap hands with Virgil and a couple more of the cats before walking back to the phone wall.

For some reason, soon as he snatched the phone off the jack, images of the day he first met Legacy flashed in his head. Not dialing a single number, he just got caught up in a four-year-old daydream....

It was 2009 and young triple had just turned seventeen, so you know he was feeling himself on some grown man shit. Plus he had just scored for his first 20 bands a couple of days prior. You got to know his head was blowed (no homo) and his chest was on swole.

Triple swerve his freshly painted box Chevy in the QuikTrip parking lot. In a rush to grab a pack of camels and get back out the store, he just jump out the car and rush in the store. The driver door was left wide open and T.I.'s new CD "Paper Trail" was on full blast.

"I'll take your broad. I'll fuck your bitch..." Triple swaggered in the store still humming along to the song that was playing.

"Look you need to take your car and get it the fuck out my way." Triple heard a soft feminine voice say from behind him.

Triple turned around ready to blast whoever the fuck was trying to check him. "Who the fuck you-" Goddamn, Triple's whole game plan changed when his eyes landed on the green eyed bombshell standing before him. She had to be the baddest bitch he'd ever saw. "The keys in the car, move that muhfuckah."

"I'm not moving your car." The young girl snapped back, rolling her neck and eyes at the young thug. "You should know better than leaving a running car, behind a line of parked cars. Someone could steal your car."

Triple could tell by the way the girl talk oh, she wasn't from around the way. Plus he'd never seen her before. And that was rare because Carrollton was only so big. He would have at least heard of her. She looked to be around his age, so she would have most definitely her up him.

Triple walked off on the hazel brown dime piece when she made that crazy ass comment. He knew she wasn't from around the way, talking about he should know better. Everybody new triple was young, wild and didn't give a fuck.

"Aye, Let me get a pack of Camels." Triple told the cashier digging in his Robin Jeans pockets looking for his fake ID. "Keep the change," he told the cashier, sliding the ID and a $20 bill across the counter.

"Thank you," The cashier said.

When Triple step out the store, the green-eyed girl was sitting in a new model Maxima looking pissed off. Yeah, she is square, Triple said, strolling up to her driver side window.

"I'm about to move my car." Triple said leaning in her window. "You got to tell me your name first."

"What would I tell you my name for? I don't even know you." She snidely retorted.

"I'm trying to get to know you. Why the fuck you think I'm asking you your name?" Triple asked.

"Don't talk to me like that. And get out of my car like that." The girl turned her neck to the side. She was putting up a good front, really and truly she was feeling the young thug doubt dude. Mainly because his swag was foreign to her. Out of her 16 years, this was the first time she's ever been close to a street dude.

"My name is Triple Cross," he surrendered now can I know your name?"

"What kind of name is that?"

"My name. You wouldn't understand the concept if I explained it to you. Why you being all stiff on a nigga? I just want to know you." Triple turned his Thug button down and got on his player shit. He already knew, with a girl like the green eyed I'm in front of him, he had to put something up under her to make her slide.

"You wouldn't know." She said letting her guard down. "My name is legacy. You happy?" Legacy smile.

Triple pull his phone out his pocket. "Give me your number."

***

"A Triple! A Triple!" The loud voice screaming out his name snapped him out of his reverie. He looked towards the voice with a menacing look on his face. "What the fuck?" He snapped.

"My bad, my nigga. They calling you through the vent. Tattoo said, they just came back in from detail. They got your shit." The dude replied.

"Iight. Tell him, get that shit down here. I'm on the phone, bruh." Triple finally dial the number. "Triple." he said when the automated voice requested his name.

"Your call was answered, but positive acceptance was not given by the call party."

Just like before, the call wasn't accepted. Triple said 'fuck that shit' and pulled up on his little hood bitch that was pregnant with his first child.

"This call is subject to monitoring and recording. Thank you for using Securus."

Unlike them phony ass niggas, his bitch accepted the call off RIP. Bitches keep it realer than niggas. Triple slid down the wall and got comfortable on the concrete.

"What's up baby daddy?" Tasha purred sexily into the receiver.

Triple kicked one of his legs out. "What's going on in the hood?"

Same ol. Same ol." Tasha sighed. "You know shit don't change in the Nolia. You need some more money on your books babe?"

"Hell yeah. Aye, Fat Trav gave you that check for me?" Triple asked.

"Man, your boy on some bullshit. I'll sell pussy up and down the whole third before I keep chasing them bum ass niggas."

"Bitch, I'll kill you." Triple replied seriously. He didn't give a fuck about the bitch. But she was pregnant with his son and talking about selling pussy. This bitch done lost her fuckin' mind.

"Damn! I'm just playing with you. But your people playing games. They stressing they fucked up." Tasha told him.

Triple knew them niggas wasn't out there hurting, but he still asked, "Is they fucked up?" Just on the strength.

"Come on Slim. You know these niggas out here checked up. Every one of them. They think it's over with for you, since you don't got indicted." Tasha gave it to him Raw and Uncut.

"That's how the game goes." Triple said taking the cold shoulder like an ice cube. He was silently thanking God, that he was smart enough to leave that quarter key at Legacy spot that night after he caught LB for eleven bands and a quarter key. When he made that move he wasn't even thinking about hustling. More than likely he was going to give that work to one of the same niggas who was shitting on him. But, hey! All was fair in love and war.

"Is they going to give you another bond?" Tasha asked.

This was another thing Legacy didn't know. After Triple's tenth month he had caught bond. Although, the DEA had revoked it after 3 days- that's when he got Tasha pregnant. Legacy with steel flip out. In her mind, triple had been down 16 months straight. Shit, fuck them 3 days, Triple felt the same way. Only thing he got accomplished was getting Tasha hood rat ass pregnant.

"Play in your pussy for me. I know that thang wet." Triple wasn't about to waste his breath on that stupid ass question. He much weather get a memory to jack off later.

Chapter Four

"Chow call!" Someone announced for the 96 man dormitory as the sally port door started clicking. "Loyalty, they just called chow." Loyalty's right-hand man, Gunna advised stepping in Loyalty's cell, putting his state shirt on. "You ready."

Loyalty stood in the mirror brushing his hair. "Hell yeah. Who working J building?" He asks putting the brush back in his locker box. He went under his pillow and grab his shank (homemade knife) putting it on his waistline. Although he didn't have any beef going on, he still refused to go anywhere without his strap. This was prison where personalities clashed and chrome met chrome.

Loyalty was way above the petty bullshit. It was a known fact, Loyalty was about his paper. But he was defiantly about that life. He helped his own. That's how he get in to respect in the roughest level 5 prisons for the past 7 years.

"Mrs. Tillman in the booth and our dude working the floor of J-2. Everything look mafia, right? Here put my phone up." Gunna lay his Fusion 2 touchscreen on the bed as he finished tucking his shirt in.

After they made sure everything was on point, they mobbed out the dorm side by side. Loyalty kept his eyes on everything while appearing not to be paying attention to anything.

"Loyalty, what it is lil bro?" A GD who loyalty had been doing time with since he came in the system at seventeen, asked when him and going to walk by the group of GD's posted up in the cut.

"Steady Mobbin fool. What y'all got going on, Bug G?" Loyalty stopped and dapped his nigga up. Gunna kept pushing. He was on a mission.

"Shit. Laying on my gangsta to send this gas out of G-1. You still ain't got a phone?" Bug-G asked.

"Hell nawl! That fuck ass nigga Debo caught me slippin again. I got two bands for a phone." Loyalty said.

"That bitch Debo don't play. I thought when he made Captain he will fall back. His fuck ass be on it like a regular officer. I got some watch phones on deck." Bug G told him.

"Oh yeah? What you want for one?" Loyalty asked. He looked towards J-building to see where Gunna was at. Seeing him on the green gate hollering at somebody in the hole, he knew he was stalling for the right moment.

"Give me three-fifty. That's just for you." Bug G said.

"Say no more." He slapped hands with Bug-G. Umma get up. I got to holler at these fools in G-2 before they clear the walk.

Loyalty walk the short distance to G-2 and started beating on the window trying to get somebody attention inside the dorm. "Aye bruh, tell Rude Boy, I said come to the window." Loyalty told the dude, leaning down talking through the bottom vent.

"I got you, bro. Aye, you got some ice for sale?" The dude asked Loyalty wiping at his nose.

Some ice cream, fool. Crenae. I'm trying to buy a gram. I got one fifty. The dude repeated.

"Oh, you talking about the crystal meth shit. Nawl, I don't fuck with it. You got to holler at them ESE's for that shit. Loyalty still couldn't get over the fact black people was running around snorting crystal meth. Niggas in prison would do anything to take the pain away.

"That's what's up I'm about to get Rude for you."

Loyalty stood back and turn his attention towards J-building again. "Damn that fool gone." Loyalty said to himself. He knew Gunna had to have the Pack, if he left him on the walk by himself.

"Whoa!" Rude Boy yelles, banging on the window to get Loyalty's attention.

"Mob life, muhfucka! Wazzam Don?" Loyalty asked squatting down to the event again.

"You, me, the mob. Wazzam? Where Gunna at?" Rude asked not understanding why Loyalty was on the walk solo.

"You know he met Papi on the dock. He had to get back in the dorm. Look, send the Iceman over there to grab this shit tonight. I'm about to get off this walk. My dorm leaving out the chalk the chow hall. 2LUV." Loyalty said putting two fingers to his forehead.

"Say no more." Rude Boy said and saluted back.

Loyalty turn on the heels of his black Prada shoes and strolled back towards the door with his hand stuffed in the pockets of his crisp white state pants with the blue stripes going down the side. He passed by the groups of gang members only offering a head nod this time. The kicking it was over.

"Loyalty Carter! Put your hands on the fence." Sergeant Lewis walked out of the dorm booth just as loyalty was about to enter the building.

"Iight. make sure you touch the metal. I got a pipe right there. Loyalty toward told her turning around to grab the fence.

"Boy get your crazy ass off that gate. That'll just make your day if I pat you down!" the cute brown skin Sergeant tees, slapping the count sheets against her thigh. Sergeant Lewis was one of the few countries holes who work at the prison who look like something.

"Just being around you make my day. The only reason I came out the door and was because I heard you was working in the chow hall. You know my situation too ugly to miss a beautiful moment.

"Loyalty flirted out of habit he put his back against the wall and kept his head turned towards her. He already knew how the game was. It was a bad bitch on the walk- the jackers was on the lurk.

In prison the jack game was serious. It didn't matter how much rank the whole had; she was going to get it. Loyalty wasn't the type of Jacker who would whip his dick out on a hoe anywhere he didn't even Jack on any female. She had to be with the move. And it had to be one on one we're only the female he was jacking off could see. But loyalty respected the Jack game. He rather a nigga to be pulling his dick on a bitch instead of being on that Elton John shit. If Sergeant Lewis wouldn't have stopped him, he wouldn't even be talking to her. Worst thing was to get caught up in that gun line.

"Uh huh. Whatever. Your little black ass always trying to run game. I hear-" Sergeant Lewis stopped mid-sentence. "Nasty muthafuckers" she hates looking over his shoulders rolling her eyes.

Loyalty already knew what that "nasty motherfucker" comment meant. That could only mean one thing. The snipers were out.

"Don't turn around. They over there jacking. Sick fuckers." Sergeant Lewis could use every curse word in the book. The facts still remain the same- she still hadn't got on that radio and called a cold. So she was eatting (watching them jack).

"Man, I'm about to go in the dorm." Loyalty said not trying to be in the line of fire. That's why it wasn't any bitches working on the South Side, he thought. These niggas some real animals. He wasn't with all that in the open jacking shit. Nigga got to be a player sometime.

"No, you're not. Hold up." Sergeant Lewis fake like she was about to get on the radio. "y'all better take you out nasty asses in the dorm before I lock you all the fuck up!" she screamed on the jackers to no avail. Everybody knew she wasn't about to lock nobody up. "Lil dick bitch." she turned her lip up still watching the two dudes bust inside from tissue.

"Good-looking, Sergeant Lewis. That ass super fat. I don't see how you walk in them tight ass pants. "The Jacker yelled walking towards G-building.

She shot both of them a bird. "Don't ever tell me you're about to walk off on me. You talk to me until I tell you to push." She joked with him.

"You know my conversation is money." Loyalty told her. He didn't know who she thought she was. Every time she seen him on the walk she wanted him to sit up and talk to her about nothing. She was the type of bitch who would have a nigga on P.I. (pending investigation) on the strength. Haven't dropped one pack. He wasn't with that sucker shit. Yeah, she look good. But working in a prison could do too much to an average bitch ego. No matter if the bitch was ugly, she would get too much attention. So imagine the attention a fat ass and a pretty face. Then on top of that, Sergeant Lewis with only 25 with rank.

But fuck all that big head shit. Loyalty didn't give a fuck, she knew what it was with him. Fuck all that attention shit; he wanted the digits.

"There you go. Why you always got to go there? Is that all you think about Sergeant Lewis acts catching an attitude.

"Hell yeah! What else is it to think about? I'm 24 with a life sentence. What am I supposed to be doing? Hiding behind a corner with my dick in my hand? I'm trying to get out on the street, so I can have you bounce that fat ass on this dick fo' real "loyalty gripped his dick through his pants.

Blind eyes could see, Sergeant Lewis was digging Loyalty. She sold it. See some people got it all confused when they started thinking just because a nigga was locked up a woman stop being attracted to the type of man she likes. If people would open their eyes they will realize the reason there were more women working in prisons than men was because they were after a man. They did say all the real niggas was either dead or in jail.

Sergeant Lewis took a deep breath and exhale. "Look I want to fuck with you. But you got to get move to the other side. It's too many eyes over here. And niggas ain't got shit going on, so they running their mouth as a Pastime. I'm not about to go out like the rest of these slow holes. They about to make me the Sarge over F-building and put me on night shift. We can definitely Rock then." She said looking down at the large dick print Loyalty was holding.

It was crazy how she seen dick all day, every day and never got turned on, but just being close to Loyalty her panties drench at the thought of licking all over his tall slender body. She wanted him in the worst way. But she was playing cautious because he was GF (Goodfellas Mafia Family) and it was a known fact that the mob stay and some crazy shit. And not just some normal prison bitches. Nah, they stay in the type of shit that shut the whole prison system down.

"Ain't nobody trying to play with you. We've been through this before." Loyalty knew ninety percent of every female officers that work in prison had at least one nigga they really wanted to fuck with, but was too scared to take the chance and break the rules. So instead of going all the way, they opted to tease and flirt.

"I know, I know. But I was only a C.O. 2 (second rank correctional officer) then. Now I can move around a little better. And this whole time I've been peeping the scene. Learning from these other hoes mistakes. Just get over there. I'm going to show you it's official. Do you still got a phone? "she asked seriously.

"I hear you." Loyalty stuff his hands in his pocket. "I lost my HTC last week. Deebo pussy ass knocked me off. I'm riding with my brother." Loyalty was keeping it real about what happened to his phone. But it was no pressure getting another phone. He was going to make her prove herself before he move to the north side.

"That's what's up. Just be patient. I got you. I'm going to get you something better. I'm going to be upfront with you. I want to be with you. And I'm not talking about no chain gang boyfriend/ girlfriend shit like these other females be on. Then soon after a nigga leave they get fired for bringing the pack to the next fly nigga on compound. I'm about to get you up out this fuck shit. You transfer oh, I'm right behind you. No matter where you go. "Sergeant Lewis have finally said the words that had been on her chest since she met loyalty 15 months ago, when he was working on her kitchen detail.

"I dig. But it's count time. We've been out here talkin 30 minutes. Niggas watch for that kind of shit over here. Now that she just changed the game up in the fourth quarter, loyalty had to switch up his game plan. He couldn't just be around her in the open anymore.

"Okay. But Count Me In, boo. "Sergeant Lewis hat drop that whole officer exterior. Loyalty had her leaning on the fence like the girl at the football game.

"Aye, Pat me down. I got a shank on my side. Write me a D.R." Loyalty was dotting every I. "Call the floor officer out here to help you." The art of war was deception.

Sergeant Lewis did just that. Once she had the dorm officer pat loyalty down, sure enough they found a 7 inch blade. "Carter, I should lock you up. Because I told you to give me the knife. You lucky I don't feel like letting nobody out of Jay building. Riley write him a Dr. Quotation she instructed the dorm officer, twisting hard for her new man.

"Damn, Carter. I thought you had her." The male officer said shaking his head. "Boy, what I'll do with that ass." he whistle watching Sergeant Lewis ass until she was out of sight.

"Fuck that police ass hoe." Loyalty spit on the ground. "I know you ain't going to write me up, bruh." he kicked it to the country officer who was semi cool.

"Come on, Carter. You know I'm not on all that police shit. I wouldn't dare write you up after how I seen you stabbed that boy up that time on the yard." The C.O. half joked.

Loyalty left him standing in front of the building and walked inside the door.

"Specs on Tom Ford, button-down Michael Kors, I'm always on like the refrigerator, um plug it in and you know it. The AP or that PK, where a Breitling when I'm bored…" Loyalty strolled through the dorm rapping the new Rocko song, pulling his shirt out of his pants.

"Say Loyalty!" Somebody call his name from the other side of the dorm. It was a young Muslim cat from Atlanta name, Sabir.

"Wazzam, shawty?" Loyalty asked standing on the middle landing up the steps, leaning on the rail waiting on Sabir.

"Aye, you got some more of that gas?" Sabir said standing at the bottom of the stairs.

"Yeah. What you trying to do?" Loyalty replied.

"I got a hundred and fifty dollar green dot. Fuck with me the mob way, nigga." Sabir said handing him the piece of paper with the fourteen digit green dot number on it.

"Don't I always fuck with your lame ass? You talking about about the mob way you better not let your Muslim brothers hear you talking about mob." Loyalty joked. But I got you lil bruh. Give me about ten minutes."

Loyalty Put the piece of paper in his pocket and continued to his room. Today was the beginning of the weekend, so the dorm was turnt up plus they had won inspection that week, so they had the flat screen and DVD Player for the weekend.

"Whoa!" Loyalty said as he shook the locked door three times, so Gunna would know it was him.

"Damn, broke ass nigga. That hoe, Sgt. Lewis had you on stuck, didn't she?" Gunna said when he popped the door with his phone glued to his ear.

"Bruh, that hoe just choose up." Loyalty closed the door back. "Told me she wanted to be with me and all type of cut the blue lovey, dovey shit. Oh girl talking about she about to get a nigga out and all. Where the shit at fool?"

"Right here. I been told you shawty was checking for you I could tell by the way she detour every time she seen you. You talking about she just cool with you, because you worked her detail. No wonder you been with the same girl all your life. You ain't no player Ha," Gunna fucked with Loyalty.

"I leave all that player shit to my brother. I'm the hustler." Loyalty retorted you frontin now. You know I don't play with them bitches."

"Yeah, yeah, yeah. But fuck all that." Gunna pulled the blanket back off of the bombs of weed and cans of tobacco.

"What's this?" Loyalty asked taking the duct taped bomb out. He really was talking to himself. He already knew what it was.

"That's half a bag of loud and ten cans. He said, her drop the other half a bag and coke on his next rotation. Let's hurry up and get this tape off. Gunna told the person he was talking to on the phone that he would call them back.

Loyalty put in his 'Gift of Gab' mixtape by Rocko and sat his CL-20 headphones in the window sil, as he crunk the volume up on his GPX CD Player. Going in his locker box, he reached under his folded white Ralph Lauren Polo t-shirts and get the four large Ziploc bags.

Gunna took the open razor and sliced through the tape, so Loyalty could do his thing with it once he had the tape off every bomb, he cut it up and flushed it down the toilet.

Off rip, Loyalty wrapped up two ounces and three cans and stuffed it in some Ziploc bags. That was for Rude boy and Haiti.

"Damn, let me see your phone to check this dot." Loyalty most forgot he still had Sabir check in his pocket.

"Your lil brother and wifey called." Gunna said giving him the phone.

Loyalty punched in the green dot customer service number as he fished through his pocket for the numbers Sabir gave him. He ended up pulling out six small pieces of paper- all with numbers and amount wrote on them.

"Damn who all gave me their money?" Loyalty mumbled as he loaded on the dots on his PayPal card. He'd just figure out who money he had later whatever they wanted, he damn sho had it.

"Aye, bruh, I'm about to hit this water. What you want to eat tonight? Gunna asked looking inside his locker.

"It dont matter. I got some chili, tuna, and summer sausages. You got some chips? Make some wraps and a Nacho kit." Loyalty sat down on the stool and took off his shoes, sliding on his Jordan shower shoes, so he could get more relaxed. "Where the blunts at?"

"I ain't no fucking cook, Nigga. Umma drop the shit off at the Chef room. Pay him some weed to cook this shit. The blunts in the back inside the saltine box." Gunna threw his towel over his shoulder and grabbed his knife briefs, soap dish and shampoo, before leaving out the room to give Loyalty a little privacy.

After putting majority of the work up in the spot, Loyalty kicked back, rolled him a blunt, and called his wifey.

"What's up, babe?" Jazzy answered on the first ring.

"You. What you got going? "Loyalty responded kicking his feet up on the stool.

Loyalty and Jazzy had been together- on and off- for nearly ten years now. Sometime shit was all good and sometimes shit was all bad, put for the most part they had an amazing relationship. Loyalty loved her because she was legal.

"Nothing really. Just waiting on my lil home girl from the college to pull up, we're about to go shopping. I called you earlier. Why you want get another phone? "Jazzy asked.

"I'm hiding from the world, I gotta get quite, so they can wander what the fuck I'm planning. Aye, you still be hanging with that green eye girl?"

"Man, I ain't trying to hear all that crazy shit. You better tighten up. Yeah, I still fuck with her." Jazzy replied.

"Who you talking to?" Loyalty pulled the phone away from his ear and sent his lil brother a text telling him to tap in. His lil brother was his go-to-man. Although they had different mothers and was raised a different way, they still was closer to each other than one another's jugular. Loyalty was a street nigga. And his lil brother, legend was a college kid. But no doubt they were cut from the same cloth, The sons of a hustler.

At times like this when he fell in deep thought about his lil brother, he started to wish he would of listen to his POP and took the good route and went off to school and played sports. But with him it was different unlike Legend, Loyalty was born and raised in the hood. He grew up on the side where you had to make yourself a boss. A nigga wasn't running around bragging on daddy money and flipping into your own money.

Loyalty's mother was the down ass hood chick and Legends mother was the square college chick who didn't know if the protects actually existed. Their father was the dope boy from the hood, who took what he had to acquire what he didn't.

Although Loyalty wished things could of been different, there was no regrets in his life, Fuck it, this was the life that choose him.

Only fucked up thing about it was, when his POPS found out he was fucking with the work, he gave him one warning to quit and focus on football.

Being young and ambitious, Loyalty continued to be insurrections and forced his Pops hand. Grandman disassociated his oldest son. At the time he didn't give a fuck about his daddy cutting him off. Why should he care? He was getting money, fucking hoes, had all the fly designer shit. Just on the strength of him being Grandmans eldest son, all the hustlers in the head showed young Loyalty love life was good. He was making his own way in the world.

But as the saying went: what goes up, must come down. Loyalty remembered the last time he seen his Pops before he caught his body.

The year was two thousand and six, and Loyalty was riding the wave of being the hoods golden child for the last two summers. Shit couldn't get any better for him. He'd just got plugged in with a big dog from the hood name, Uncle Sherman. Uncle Sherman was the man who stepped up in the spotlight once Grand Man Faded to black. So you know the money was flowing like ninety-two.

Where ever Loyalty went, the streets watched where ever he didn't go, the streets called for him. No matter how pissed off his POPS was at him for dropping out of school, Loyalty still idolized him. Every step Loyalty made, he made it like his POPS. He'd played the sponge for Fourteen years, now he was pouring out what he had soaked in.

Now I remind you, Loyalty's mother was Grand's hood chick, so you he handled a lot of his street business at her spot around young Loyalty. Till this day Loyalty still remembered the way Grand used to whip the yay with an egg beater. Like father, like son- he did the same thing. He remembered so vivid the times Grand and Marley would sit at the kitchen table for hours breaking down the work just to pass out to their young wolves that was a part of the team. Like

Father, like son- Loyalty built him a small crew of young lion's and kept his team fed.

On this particular day it was a Sunday and the sun was beaming. The block was bursting with activity due to the fact one of the big homies had just touched down from doing a dime. Loyalty was cruising around the block in his black cutlass, sitting on some black twenty two inch GFG rims with the T's out the twelve's had the trunk rattling.

"Black with the black rims/My shit the hardest/ Crazy off set make that bitch look retarded/or should I say bowlegged/ Just excuse me if I sound kind of big headed..."

Young Jeezy pumped through the six twitters, talking that real street talk. Loyalty dropped the gear shift and pressed his low top all white air forces down on the gas pedal, making the four-fifty four small block holler. He leaned up on the wheel with both his hands gripping the top, while rapping along with Jeezy.

As he was coming down the fourth street end of High Street, be slowed down when he seen a group of females walking we Robert Hendrix. Good thing he had some good Shocks, because the way he made that last minute turn his rims would of scrubbed Loyalty pulled up beside the group of sexy young females.

"Gretta, what up?" Loyalty asked the baddest one out the whole crowd.

"What's up, Loyalty? You better step driving so fast you aint got no license." Gretta flashed her perfect white smile.

"Drive for me. When you going to give me some play?" Loyalty wanted to fuck with Gretta in a major way. Him and his main girl Jazzy- was on some beefing shit, so Loyalty was free to do what the fuck he wanted to do. He wanted Gretta, but she kept trying to play him on some too young shit. He knew that was all a front. Plus he knew her having a little boyfriend from the hood played a part in her resistance.

"Boy, you know I ain't fucking with you like that. You straight with all them lil girls you got going crazy over you. Add me to the team and you'll be doing too much." Gretta teased, doing a little innocent flirting with the handsome young dude.

"I ain't straight until I got you." Loyalty drove slowly up the street maintaining the pace as the girls. "Just let me call you some time we can be friends, right?" he made one last attempt. They were at the top of the street, wasn't no way he was about to follow her around the block all day.

"Maybe." she said in her real pretty girl voice.

Just when he was about to respond, his pops pulled beside him. Coming off King Street- in a smoke gray quarter to seven with the top down. This was the first time he'd seen his POPS in two years. He was surprised to even see him on the block. But Grandman was that type of nigga; he never forgot where he came from. When he seen his thirteen year old brother on the passenger side his face lit up.

"What you know, Lil nigga?" Grand asked his oldest son. He hated he had to show his lil nigga tough love. But he tried to give it to him the easy way, Loyalty wanted it the hard way, so you had to let a man be a man.

"Taking it one day at a time, Ol' Head. How you? Loyalty tried to poke his chest out at the only living being he looked up to. He knew his father had heard through the grapevine about the moves he was making.

"That'll be your biggest mistake. Today doesn't mean nothing when you sitting beside the next fifty years. Dumb niggas only wanna last for right now, smart niggas only use right now to secure longevity success. Grand dropped a golden jewel on his son.

"Yeah, yeah, I'm getting money now, I'll be getting money then ya dig?!" Loyalty arrogantly boasted.

"Lil nigga when you're walking around with all the cash you own in your pocket, that doesn't mean you're getting money. That only prove you're barely getting by. I see you out here Putting ten-fifteen thousand in car. I heard about the spot you get in Magnolia Lake with Tracy daughter, Jazzy. So I'm figuring since you doing all that, you got to have at least thirty in your pocket and a hundred in your closet."

Loyalty was on the hush mouth. Grandman had just stripped him naked and exposed him. The fact that the twenty five thousand in his pocket was all that he owned, made it all the worst. He knew at the ace of seventeen he was going great in most people's eyes. And it was niggas on the block way older than him living the same way. But none of that mattered to Grandman. Loyalty was a Carter. The blood line of a winner.

"Big Giants make big statements. Let that shit go. I did it so you wouldn't have to. Get off that stoop and come sit on the throne. The sun shine on the King, then sets on the Prince you proved your point." Grand man waved the white flag trying to bring his son back into the folds.

"Young Legend! What up, lil bruh? You don't fuck with your big brother no more?" Loyalty addressed his lil brother, Ignoring his father.

"Come on, big bro. You know that's not true. Is that your car? I want to ride. Can I ride with Loyalty, daddy?" Legend immature mind couldn't even frame the picture that was being painted right before his young eyes.

"Tell your brother to pick the Family or the streets. Your brother is a drug dealer, Legend. You can't ride with him for your own safety." Grandman gave it to his youngest SON Straight up and down.

"Loyalty don't deal that bad stuff. He going to be a famous football player like Michael Vick. Tell him, bro." Legend said looking from one stone face to the other.

"Tell him to tell you the truth. Ask him what side is he on. Loyalty-VS- cove. He love the streets but a man is obligated to be loyal to his family. Now that the two have become oppositions, what side is you on? Loyalty-VS-Love. The final match," Grandman locked eyes with Loyalty. He knew he was wrong for throwing Legend in the middle. But he knew Legend was Loyalty's weakness. In war you played to win. He could see the conflict in his son's eyes.

"Niggas will betray you, women will disappoint you and money-money will always upset you. That I why we put family first because family will never neglect you." Legend repeated the phrase their father had burned in the mind since they were old enough to listen.

Legend knew something wasn't right. Their father had to be mistaken. No way Legend was about to believe his big brother had went against the grain. What do he need to sell drugs for, Legend thinks. Our father got money for real.

"When you want to know if a man is hiding something from you, don't search for the truth. Find his eyes. A man of respect eyes will never lie." Legend replayed the words his daddy told him when he was only nine.

Using that lesson Legend tried to lock eyes with his big brother. It tore him in two when his brother diverted his hazel brown eyes away.

"Let him be POPS. Loyalty never wavers. His family is out here too. "Legend said taking up for his big brother.

"Family first. Hit my line later, Young H.O." Loyalty told Legend and pulled away from the curb. I'm not turning my back on y'all. I'm just being my own man, Loyalty hoped his POPs and lil brother could hear his mental telepathy. Soon you'll understand

Legend. There was no doubt in his mind that his lil brother would grow up to be somebody. That's the way the cards was dealt.

All that night, Legend rode around the city. He was in deep thought. Niggas thought he was paper chasing before, wait till they see what he was about to do now. He was about to go crazy on the cash tip. It was a good thing him and his girl was broke up. He was all night like Wendys. He was about to get the money like it was something he understood.

And two months after that Loyalty ended up getting shot and caught a body. Some fool had took a sip of that "I think I can fuck with him Juice." One late night a nigga tried some old Compton shit and tried to car jack him at the red light on Bankhead. Like a true Carter it was till the death with him. So when the tool snatched him out the car he came up firing with that 44 bulldog.

The jacker got off one shot hitting loyalty in the chest when the police arrived, they were both sprawled out in the middle of the street. Loyalty was hanging in there the mask man was D.O.A.

The fucked up thing about it was, the person behind the mask was a nigga he had grew up with. Now he had a fresh case and no money. After the day Grandman called him out, Loyalty turnt all the way up on his hustle, when the incident took place, he was in route to the new house he'd just bought in Sage Hill for him and Jazzy (yeah, they were back together) He had his whole stash on him (a hundred and seventy-five thousand) along with fifteen bands in his pocket when the police found the half a brick of cocaine, they stopped asking him for justification for the money. Narcotics recovered, money confiscated. End of story. One day your up, the next day your down.

Grandman came and visited him one time when he first got bounded over from the hospital. He spoke to him like a man. He even attempted to take care of his legal fee's but Loyalty declined it. He had to stick to the script so he told his POPS, what was on his mind:

"When a man say something it's permanent. You gave me a choice. I chose. Now I gotta deal with the consequences. That's how the game goes. It was released right now, I'd be right back out there on the block pumping crack. You told me as long I continued to fuck with the work, you wasn't fucking with me and I respected that. You taught me to never respect a man who didn't honor his word."

"All ask is for you to never look at me no different than Legend. His life is different from mine. His eyes never witnessed the times you could stay up all night in the kitchen cooking crack. He never came home from school and the first thing he see is his father and mother, sitting in the middle of the floor counting a quarter ticket in drug money. He never seen you tell uncle Marley to put that chrome to a nigga dome, because he taking too long with that paper.

"I have. And you allowed me to see it you wanted me to see it. I grew up to be exactly what you wanted me to be what you showed me to be. Not who you tried to tell me how to be. Remember a father leads by example. I followed your lead, ol' head. You the one who gave me the blue print The Hustler's Handbook. You gave us two different books. Two different molds, Legend don't know, but I do. I always did. You gave him the player handbook. I'm what you made me nigga. A hustler."

"Legend seen the Grandman who came in with suits on. Always got a positive plan the businessman with credit cards and legal investments. The family man with political friends. Legend know dude I don't know that nigga. But you showed legend that side, so he would follow that example, we're both two different shades of you. We're all Carters. The realest niggas ever breed.

"Aye, ya seen how I cook that fuck nigga, Pops? I showed 'em. how a Carter Play" Loyalty ended it with a smirk. And Grandman smirked back looking at his son through the glass. If they never understood each other before, they did after that day.

Loyalty's ol' head, uncle Sherman paid his legal fees. And Grandman made sure he lived like the young PRINCE he was. Even though he had a top notch lawyer, the JURY still found him guilty of murder and gave him life. So he ended up with Life Plus Fifteen years. He had plead car to the fifteen for the trafficking cocaine charge.

Snapping back to reality, he realized, Jazzy had hung up on him. He looked at the screen and noticed she had sent him a text.

Black bastard you need to stop smoking so much, you done fell asleep on the phone, came!' Call me later, 2.

Loyalty typed her a quick text back and put the phone on the charger. He was about to call Legend, but he seen it was still around his class time. He'd call back later tonight. Hopefully he be around some bitches, Loyalty thought.

Loyalty loved kicking shit with his lil brother. Legend kept him alive. All that fly shit he wanted to do, his lil nigga was doing. The VVS pnky rings, Tom Ford shots, Michael Kors specks, losing Gucci Slippers in the Atlantic Ocean just to say fuck it and toss the other one in the ocean behind it. "Who give a fuck? Save the picture while it's in mid-air, just to brag on Instagram. The next day hit Collins and sneeze fourteen hundred on some Louie boat shoes.

And this lil nigga was doing all this without standing on the block. All he had to do was stay in school and he would freely live the the lifestyle of the rich and famous. Legend was the living proof that every nigga in college wasn't a square. Take away the fact Legend grew up in the suburbs and attended Private school, he was just as street as loyalty. And he didn't even know it. Grandman was his fucking POPS. Legend was his heartbeat. They were like Emory and Jay-Z.

God Please, Loyalty silently pleaded with his dear Lord. He needed to get the fuck out of this concrete jungle niggas looked at the material shit he had and assumed he was content with being in the bing. Fuck No! This shit was killing him more and more each day.

"One day, one day. Forever ain't strong enough to hold a nigga like me down." Loyalty mumbled to himself.

Being with a man in prison isn't hard. But it damn sure isn't easy. The emotional distress can be unbearable at times. Especially if you really loved the nigga that was locked down. That shit made you feel like you was doing the time also. Physically deprived and mentally entrapped. Then let's not forget the fact the same don't stop because the player been moved to a new field. Just because a nigga get put behind bars don't mean art the groupie bitches is going to disappear. You can cancel all that "at least I got my man to myself shit. One thing about a real official nigga, if he was that nigga on the turf; he was definitely going to be that nigga on the inside (Long as he still had some street connection) the same nigga who run the streets, run the yard. And a nigga get money on the yard just like he got money on the streets. Only difference is, on the yard the money came faster and more for less. One time Loyalty sent eleven bands home just off of cigarettes.

So you know a nigga kept his swag up. Now along with the same groupies you been beefing with since high school, you got some country back wood bitch, who lucked up on a prison job all over your man dick. And to make matters WORSE, she see him more than you do.

Now the flip side of all the long trips, lonely nights, and seeing them couples in the free world together who you love isn't purer than you and your dude) And let's not forget them nagging conversations with friends and family members about moving on. Now that was one thing that peeved the shit out of her. How can a person with morals and principles just turn your back on a person y'all took an Oath of love and Loyalty, to? That's what them disloyal bitches did ball with a nigga while he out, then soon as he got locked up they dissolved on that same nigga. That ain't how the game go. Fuck that. Till the bad get badder or the worse get worser real bitches stay down with their Don until the rocky road becomes smooth. Fuck all that jumping ship shit.

Okay, Okay. I got a little off the topic. You know how some shit can get you really riled up. But look, the flipside of it is the emotional fulfillment. That special attention. Hours and hours of mental banding. That's the advantage of being in a "Cold depth of space relationship.

It's a proven fact, that ninety percent of women didn't know their man mentally. Most women don't even know how it feel to be brought to a mental orgasm. Mental strokes of pleasure. The deepest love making known to mankind. When you are together, everything is mainly physical, yeah, the emotional is there, but you never go to deep on it. And just for the record: I'm speaking about a relationship with a street nigga. So you already know how that shit goes if you've been with one. You'll never know if that nigga really love you. But let him get locked up. You gone be like. "Wow!"

Somewhere in the midst of all the madness, sadness, loneliness, dry cry's, and brief spurts of contentness with the the fucked up circumstances - the end have to justify the mean. For Real, For Real.

"Fuck." Jazzy said out loud snapping out the stupor reading the black novel had her stuck in. "These books be having me sad as fuck." She laid the I-Pad dawn and got up to stretch her back, causing her perky thirty-four c's to press against the thin fabric of her UWG t-shirt.

Seeing she had a couple hours to burn before Legacy came through and picked her up, so she curled back up on her sectional with her I-Pad and dive back into the so familiar story A.P. da DON was telling in his street novel, "2 faces1tear."

Although the book was bringing her emotions out, she couldn't pull away from it. The story was so real she could of easily put her and Loyalty's face on the book characters, Heartless and Shuntric aka Moonk. She didn't care what nobody said, Arieus 'A.P. da Don Potts was the best at street love novels.

"I'm trying to tell you." Jazzy agreed with a part in the book when Moonk was telling Heartless what it was, when he finally made it to the county jail. "Niggas always talking that go on with your life shit." She shook her head and recollected on the time Loyalty had told her the same thing. That shit was just inscrutable to her.

How could a Nigga Just fix his mouth to tell the chick he been fucking, feeding, and splurging on for years to turn her back on you?

Fuck be wrong with these niggas? street niggas be kicking all this "No emotions" shit, but they do the most when it comes to emotions. They just be knowing when they were out they was sticking their dick in every Mary, Tammy and Pamela with a cute face and small waist. Soon as they get locked up, all of a sudden they start remembering all the fucked up shit they dove did to wifey over the years. All that "Go on with your life, I don't want to drag you" talk, Just to be his ass trying to run away from Karma.

But it was all good. Life had to be like this so you could speak from experience. You go through it to get through it. What was meant, will always be. What wasn't meant, would never be. That was the Physics of life. The way of the world.

Jazzy's phone started ringing alerting her to a new text message. She immediately opened the message when she seen it was from Loyalty.

"I'm glad I only fell asleep on you, instead of us. That mean we still got hope. Lol. I'll mob at you later. 2LUV."

She laid the phone down and smiled at Loyalty's charm. This was one of them moments where the pain was smashed by the brief smile. But the frown would be back. It always returned.

If it was just one thing she could do to bring Loyalty back home to her, she would do it. Even it she had to do some of the time for him, she would do it. Sometime she wanted to give up. Same time it got too hard for her. That was understandable, right? But she couldn't give up on him. Even if it took twenty-five years for him to make it back to her, she would just be waiting for a quarter century. Loyalty was her heart beat and Loyalty was embedded in her heart.

Chapter Five

The Perfect Pitch starts well before you step inside an elevator, a boardroom, or take center stage. Avoid being at a loss for words or leaving money on the table by mastering the "SP's" to the Perfect Pitch.

"NumbeR one: Preparation. Doing your research is a must. From the in's and out's of your industry to statistics on the problem your product or Service loans to Solve.

Number Two: Purpose. Now this is an important one. What does your service, product or business offer? If you are already in business, briefly note its profitability or impact if not, provide realistic estimates related to your business' Performance. Also include what you look to do going forward.

Number three : Potential, what is the problem your product or service solves? or better yet, what's in it for them? What does your consumer look to gain from your product or service? You and I both know, don't nobody want anything to do with it, it the outcome isn't income. "the small business expert said, causing the auditorium Full of college students to laugh and comment in agreement. She took a sip of water giving the class time to settle down before she continued.

"'Number four: Pace. It's not about rushing; it's about delivering a Pitch that's quick, simple, and to the point. Pace yourself, speak clearly, and speak fluently. I know we all want them instant results. But sometime moving fast can cause a blunder. So don't ever forget the most important thing is to take your time and make sure you be sufficient

"Number 5: Presentation Okay, ladies and gentlemen this is what you work for. This when you see if all your hard work was in vain or not. Look, don't freestyle or memorize a speech. Craft your pitch from a macro of what you want to say and condense it with bullet points to create a micro unscripted) message. The make familiar you are with the information, the less anxious and better focused you'll be in order to nail it.

"Now that, that is out there. Is there any questions?" the small business expert asked the class.

As the class erupted with questions, Legend sat at his desk with one earbud plugged in his ear; that was connected to his I- phone 45. He had the music playing the new song by EmiNem, "Rap cod: He had to check this song out. The internet was going crazy about it. Now that he'd heard it, he understood why the lyricism was so sick. Legend had to play it twice und put both earbuds in.

Dude is fucking insane, Legend thought as the sang went off for the third time. He pulled one earbud back out and set his Pandora back to Kendrick Lamar, "'Bitch don't kill my vibe" song, off his "Good kid M.a a.d city" album, as he took a couple notes on some good points he was hearing being made. Really and truly he didn't need this class, because if he needed any advice on business endeavors, he can go to the best business titan he knew; his father.

But sometime it was best to build your own nest, instead of getting everything from the nest. Legend actually was finding this class educational and beneficial. Besides the fact he was dying to smoke a fucking spliff, he couldn't sit in this one class all day. The fact he was sitting between two bad bitches, was an added comfort. Not that he would approach either one of them. That was not his thing. That could cause a misunderstanding.

When it came to the bitches, it was all about a fuck for Legend. Long as you set the female make the first move, you couldn't go wrong when you told them you was "Only looking for tonight. Tomorrow would come next." They either take it or leave it. Nine times out of ten, they always took it. Legend checked the time on his smoke gray G-Shock. Forty-five minutes, he took the other earbud out and decided to give the class his undivided attention for the remainder.

"Well the most important thing when investing in other people's portfolio is research. Okay, we have time for a few more questions." hands shot up in the air.

"Go ahead, young lady in the top row." the small business expert said.

"Would it be wise for me to rely solely on an investment adviser?" the young student asked flipping through her notes, making sure the question had not already been answered.

"I'm assuming you speaking in terms of selling an investment? The expert responded.

"Yes ma'am. I'm trying to think pass the right now, Just in case I ever invest in a stock company that bottoms." the female student replied.

"Is there anyone in here that can answer that question for her?" the expert looked around to see how many students would volunteer to help their peer. She was surprised when the dude she'd considered to be her non-attentive Student of the day. "Yes, help her out, music man" she pointed out the young student who'd had on earbuds majority of the class.

"No, that won't be a good idea for many reasons. Mainly because some investment advisers have a vested interest that doesn't align with your goals. And that can really cause conflict. Because your advisers could be hindering your progress, on the strength of their own ulterior motive. Best thing to do, is learn as much as you can

"Perfect example: at classes like this. So you can protect your own interest." the young male Student advised. The girl when tasked the question, was sitting right next to him. But he didn't address her,

64

he addressed the lady holding the class, because she counted him out.

"That was a very informative answer." the expert commended. "Did that help you out?" she asked the young lady who asked the question. She herself was completely impressed, with the answer the young man just provided. They had just provided some real crucial information that would save a lot of students from making bad decisions with investors.

"Yes, that just open my eyes. And potentially prevented me from making a detrimental mistake in the future. But can you give me a few more helpful pointers?" the young lady asked the expert.

"Of course. Music Man, okay I'm not going to call you that anymore. What's your name, sir?" She asked the young man she had nicknamed, "music man" due to the fact he was listening to music the whole class.

"Legend Carter." Legend replied, grinning at the gorgeous expert. Then he noticed the green-eye girl to his right cast a brief glance his way when he said his name. Probably done heard four or five of her friends talking about me, he arrogantly thought.

"Nice name." For some reason, she smiled back. "Legend can you provide her with a few helpful pointers real quick, and exit plan when dealing with bad investments?" the expert requested.

"Um... I'll try." Legend played modest. "One thing I would say maintain a clear rationale for holding a stock and periodically reevaluate whether the investment still fits your reasoning. If it comes a point at any time that you second guess your original judgment, pull out." he said addressing the green eye girl beside him that was asking the questions.

"Okay. Don't stop. Give me a couple more." the girl urged him on with a beautiful smile.

I know this chick not trying to flirt with me, by having me answer questions for her, Legend think. She just don't know, I'm fucking to real, he thought looking at the beauty before saying, "A way you could minimize surprises is by following the companies you invest and look out for significant changes, new management, acquisitions, or a new business model.

"Another thing is to recognize when you're holding too much on a particular stock. To stay diversified, I would suggest that no single stock account for more than five percent of your portfolio's equity assets. When it exceeds five percent, it may be time to sell it." Legend concluded pulling away from the intense stare the girl was holding him.

"Mr. Carter, I know we've over- extended our welcome. But your expertise is amazing, it's a shame you're not co-teaching this course. One last thing. Look, I know for those of you who have began building your nest egg while you're still in college, you're clearly aware the significant time horizon you have over someone starts postcollege.

"Mr. Carter can you tell them how to be strategic about managing their risk at an early stage?" the expert looked at her watch noticing they were thirty minutes over. But she was captivated by the expert knowledge the extremely handsome student - who couldn't be no older than nineteen or twenty -had in such a difficult field. The more she heard him talk, the more she became attracted to him. There was nothing more sexier than a man with intellect.

"That's easy, When you find an investment option that meets your needs, research it, evaluate it relative to all your other investment options, and invest in the one that gives you the most attractive profile.

"And be sure to investigate the company's consistency. One of the main reasons a person would sell is because the company-specific reasons you thought the stock either have changed or never materialized so be sure to invest in a deeply rooted company, who progress more than digress." that was it for today, Legend didn't give a fuck who asked the question -class was over with for him. He was about to go into a marijuana coma. He had to get the fuck.

"Okay, ladies and gentlemen it was a pleasure. But all good things must come to an end. Legend, can I have a moment with you before you vacate?" the expert dismissed the class. Immediately everyone got up simultaneously and gather their things.

Legend stuffed his books inside his Tom Ford knapsack, debating, whether or not should he stay and see what the lady wanted. He wasn't with all that staying after class shit. It was cool to talk during class, but when class was over. Class was over!

Just for the sake of a Potential Professional Connection, he decided to see what the woman wanted. Maybe she wanted to offer him an internship with her company. Before he got up, he noticed a piece of paper sitting on his desk, that wasn't there before. He opened it.

"I wanna taste your chocolate --! You fill in the blank. Col. 470-293-3781. AmbeR. I was the dark skin girl to your left. Not the question asker.

Legend smiled and put the note in his pocket. He wished it was the chick who had him answering all them fucking questions for her, But Amber would definitely do. He'd been thinking about hitting that juicy ass soon as she sat beside him.

"Oh, Legend give me one minute to put these papers in my briefcase." the expert said and bent over at the waist.

Legend's dick bricked up at the sight of the way her ass spreaded. It wasn't all that fat, but her spread was mean. "I don't have that much time though."

"Will you hand me that stack of papers right there?" she said looking over her shoulder, still bent over trying to situate her briefcase Legend didn't take his eyes off her ass, He wasn't trying to hide nothing, she could tell by the look in his eyes. Young boys, she grinned.

"These right here?" Legend's voice echoed now that they was the only two in the large classroom. "Yes." she stood up taking the papers cut of his hand. "Thank you." she bent right back over.

Legend knew she had to have on some thangs, by the way the tight slacks was cutting into her ass crack. Fuck all that, he stepped up behind her, pressing his dick against her ass and grabbed her waist. She was playing with the wrong nigga. If Legend didn't know nothing else, he knew women. What they didn't say verbally, they communicated through body language.

"Oh my God! This dick huge. What are you doing?" she asked in a voice that didn't match her body language. Although she was being hysterical, when she stood up she didn't pull away. Pulling away was the last thing on her mind. She wanted to press up on the snake in the young man's pants.

Legacy walked around campus with same of her sorority sisters, enjoying the sunny day. She really needed a quick excuse to get away, because she had some body on the way to snatch up some work. On the real, she wasn't trying to miss any more money. She'd already missed a sale for a nine, three -two ways, and a tour and a baby, while she was in that long ass class. But she wasn't tripping, because selling dope wasn't a career choice for her. This was all in the name of Love, she kept telling herself. Nothing more, Nothing less.Even though she was becoming hooked to living on the edge, she refused to lose focus. This was only for today tomorrow would come and be brighter. She wasn't a good girl gone bad, only a good girl doing bad. It was truly a difference so she thought.

"Ow shit!" Legacy said when she felt her phone vibrate in the back pocket of her Donna Karen skinny jeans. She knew that was her people letting her know they were at the meet up spot. "Look, I'll meet you at Z's. My phone is dying. I got to get my portable charger.

"Alright. Hurry up, girly. We know you can't miss the call from your boo thang." Her sorority sister, Tip said.

Legacy was so thankful this was one of them rare days, she were tennis shoes instead of heels. She was walking so fast she was on the verge of burning a hole in the bottom of her pink and gray Deions. But she had to get to that paper. At the same time, she had to keep a low profile and not arise any suspicion, because outside of all Triple Cross's Friends - No one knew she was pumping that work. This was one of the benefits of being from a totally different world than Triple Cross. Nobody on his side of the fence knew nothing about her, other than she was Triple Cross girl," she refused to let her people know about her extracurricular activities. Jazzy didn't even know.

Legacy got in her let and went up the street to the Krystal's, where her people were waiting. It was against her rules to meet anybody on the campus. Although she could come up with a thousand excuses why she was at the college. But she just wasn't doing that it was like bringing her other world into her other world. And it was mandatory she kept the separate.

Soon as she pulled into the Parking lot, she immediately spotted the person she was looking for. Wasting no time, she pulled her Lexus next to the white box chevy.

"Fool, what up?" Legacy asked automatically switching to her hood persona, borrowing a little more lingo from her favorite book character, Heartless, she looked around as she cuffed the sandwich bag with the two and a quarter in it. Seeing that the coast was clear, she tossed the bag in his window.

"Trying to get like you, beautiful. You still not fucking with the kid?" Young Sosa handed Legacy the brown paper bag with the stacks in it. He grabbed the sandwich bag that had landed in his lap and looked at it once, before putting it in the dashboard.

"If I didn't have a man, you could definitely get it." She said looking inside the bag. "This old and new, right?" Legacy asked referring to the money he owed her from the four, she had fronted him. Plus the work she had just served him.

"Hell yeah. Aye, why your man got you out here hustling, ma?" Young Sosa couldn't understand why such a beautiful woman like Legacy was stuck on a grimey nigga like Triple. But that was on her. He just wanted the money.

"Come on, Sosa. Please don't be no player hater. Ugh, that turns me off. Toodles boo boo." Legacy hated when niggas asked that. She didn't blame them for trying, but damn. They can save all that I can love you better shit. What the fuck make them think somebody got me out here? Like she was some dumb head or something. She knew what she was doing and why she was doing it. Yeah, Triple was the one who presented the idea and the means to her. But at the end of the day it was her decision.

When she got back on campus, instead of parking on the other side, she just pulled up at 2's (the college restaurant) Rolling her windows back up, she poured the knots of money in her lap. She took the rubberbands off the two large knots, and begin to count it up.

"Ain't no way forty-two hundred, this too many fucking bills, I know these niggas getting it in the trenches, but they need to bring bills when they re-up." Legacy complained out loud, as she thumbed through all the small bills, she had to get the money situated before she got back around her sisters. No telling when she'd get another chance to do it, once she got back with them.

She rubberbanded the bands, and put it in the glove compartment. That was going in Triple's lawyer stash. The other twelve hundred went in her purse. That was for her stash.

"Damn, my days of hustling is over with, after this brick." She said thinking out loud. After doing the quick calculation in her head, she realized, she was closer to having the paper for Triple's lawyer. Then she thought. Mind you when she started, she promised God, that she would stop when she had Triple's lawyer money. How much she had? She didn't know. But she knew she had more than enough she'd count it all up this weekend. For now, she had to get back to her girls. They had already started texting.

Legend's heart skipped a beat, when he inhaled his first burst of O.G Smoke in nearly four hours. The euphoric feeling caused him to lay his head back into the headrest, and close his eyes. Once the feeling of that first blast subsided, he crunk his car up.

Before he could put the car in gear, his phone went to ringing. He checked the screen, it was an unknown number. Usually, he didn't answer numbers, he didn't- know. But he made an exception this time.

"Run your mouth." he said with the phone held with his shoulder, as he put the car in gear with the blunt between his fingers.

"That is not the appropriate way to answer your phone." The feminine voice on the other end joked.

"That's why I pay my own bill, ya dig?! When you start paying it I'll answer it how you want me to." Legend retorted, as he rode around campus, scoping the bitches. He didn't know who he was talking to, but he was guessing it was Daph because she was the only female comfortable enough to call his phone checking him.

"Don't test me like that. I'm not one of them little girls. I'm a grown woman, I know how to take care of a man." the lady replied sexily.

With that comment, he knew it wasn't, Daph. That wouldn't have been her response. She knew Legend would never allow a chick to spend money on him. He didn't even sit on the phone with women for long period of time. That was that relationship shit.

"Iight,I won't. Who this?" Legend asked not feeling the guessing game.

"Touché. This is Quinn." this was the small business expert, who just taught the class. "I had to make sure you didn't give me the wrong number." She half- joked.

"That's not how I rock. I'm glad you called, so I could lock your number in. But look, umma call you back in like thirty. I'm about to grab something to eat." Legend told Quinn.

"Why you don't want to talk now?" Quinn questioned.

Legend couldn't do nothing but shake his head. After all the fronting she was doing when Legend had pressed up against her, come to find out, the whole reasons behind her asking him to stay afteR class, was because she was choosing, she went to telling him, how he just came at her like she was a slut, and all type of other shit, Legend wasn't trying to hear. From jumpstreet, Legend noticed the big rock on her finger. So knowing she already had a husband, there was only one thing left for them to do; and that was fuck. And that's exactly what her forty- three year old ass wanted a young nigga to knock the walls out that pussy. LegeNd usually dichit do the cd broads. But the fact, she had a body like lisa Raye, with long black hair, dark-smooth -skin and chinky eyes, had him wanting that Pussy.

"I just don't. Umma hit you back though." he replied nonchalaNtly.

"Okaaayyy. But don't call me. I'll call you. I'm about to meet up with my husband. When can I see you?" Quinn was eager to feel that thick young dick inside of her. It had been awhile, since she'd had the real deal. As of late, she found herself masturbating more and more, as her fifty-seven year old husband sex drive declined.

Just get at me. Find time and we'll get up." he disconnected without waiting for her response. He already knew Quinn thought, he was just a twenty year old, nerd with a little swag...she didn't the half.

Legend pulled to the bottom of the Z's and backed up in a parking space. He logged on to Twitter real quick to see what was going down tonight. As the page came up, he laid the phone in his lap, and railed another blunt before he went in the college hang out. Then put the blunt to his lips and lit it up. Grabbing the phone he scrolled down the screen to see what his "Tweeps" had going on.

"Just what I was looking for." he said when he seen someone announcing a kick back at one of the college apartments. This was a prime example of why he loved the college life. Fuck being in the streets. True enough, he had the swagger of a street nigga. But he didn't fake it like he was from the hood. He didn't try to act all gangsta and shit. He was just him. A Walé nigga with a Meek Mill swag. He fucked with the bitches, blowed the gas, got money, and kicked the shit. But don't get it twisted, he wasn't no emo-thug type nigga (shout out to the Panda) He was a Carter. The same type of nigga, as his Pops and brother, Loyalty. Player like Biggie, smooth like Jigga. Although he did what he did for his big brother, Loyalty and his little college hustle, he still didn't consider himself a drug dealer. How could he? He wasn't doing it for the money. It was Just a part of being in college. Well, maybe it was for the money.

The only reason he did what he did, was because he wanted his own stacks (to splurge with) yeah, it was cool to have the credit cards and all that. But every piece of money owned (even in his personal account) belonged to his parents. They never gave him in cash. Always plastic. He got whatever he wanted, whenever he wanted it, but he had a monthly spending limit on his black card given to him by his POPS) He didn't have to work. He had all the jewelry and fly designer shit. And still with all that, something was missing. He was born in the mid-ninety's, where a baby's first words are "High Life." He needed and hard cash in his pocket.

He needed the bankrolls. He wasn't willing to go off the grid for a little flash money Chris pops was rich like the owners of Cash Money. Just a little of this, here and there. Nothing major.

No matter how bad he wanted the extra shit, he would go without it all before he let his pops find out. Fuck that he wasn't about to end up like loyalty. The Loyalty kept himself above the water when he choose the street. Because he was from the street. Loyalty might not have had what he would have had, had he stayed up under Grand man's wings. But he had his own. That was all that mattered. And eventually he would have excelled to be on top of the game.

But that was no surprise. Loyalty was a Carter. There was no doubt in Legends mind, he will push himself through college. But maintaining the lifestyle like loyalty had? He knew that was beyond his means. His monthly smoking habit cost twenty fucking thousand. How the fuck was he supposed to maintain that without Grandman? He wasn't from the fucking hood, so he couldn't get out there and sell crack like Loyalty had. His college hustle didn't even make him enough to sponsor his shoe obsession.

Now the hustle he was helping Loyalty with, was what was really bringing the stacks in. Shit, Loyalty was in prison doing better than niggas on the street.

"Fuck that, I'm fucking with this Alpha Kappa Alpha kick back. I fuck with them chicks. Legend log off Twitter, once he seen the female sorority kick back. He knew their spot was going to be the spot to be at. He went through his contact list and tapped on loyalties connect number. He needed more weed and some Molly. He knew he could get off a couple grams of molly at the kickback. He could have missed out on the chance to make a couple bucks. Not that he needed it.

"Hello." Legend said into the phone wondering why it wasn't ringing.

"Wazzam, Lil nigga?" Loyalty responded.

"Aw fuck. I I didn't mean to dial your number. I was trying to call someone else. Your lame-ass must been laying on a call? You didn't even let the phone ring." Legend joked with his big brother.

"Lame ass nigga I called you. Man, don't tell me you out there on that Molly?" Loyalty joke back knowing damn well his lil brother wasn't on nothing but the OG.

"You got me fucked up. Haha," Legend chuckled. "Nigga, I just bagged this old broad, who was teaching our class today. She dumb bad. I might make her dance in front of the camera, and send it to you so you can see how I'm doing these bitches out here. And the broad husband supposed to be a millionaire." Legend bragged, knowing the type of shit his brother liked to hear.

"Oh yeah? Nigga I'm in prison and I got hoes bagging me. I just added the sergeant to my team, like its draft season." Loyalty shot back.

"You saying that like I'm out here choosing bitches. I choose clothes, shoes, and fast cars. Bitches choose me like a fourth grader at the bus stop playing bingo," Legend replied.

"Haha. You hell." Loyalty burst out laughing, thinking about the days when him and his friends use to scream *bingo* at their favorite car.

"What's good though, bro?" Legend asked shit, you know what's up?

"Loyalty replied. Say No More. I was just trying to call uncle Sherman, when you called me. He already ready for you?"

"Yeah, But he going to have two separate packages." Loyalty told him.

"Iight. I'll get at you when I get it like I said I was just about to snatch some more OG from him, so it should be in a minute. Go ahead and get Jazzy on standby she don't have any classes today. "Legend was al for handling the business for his brother, but he didn't hold the work for long periods of time. If it was just the weed, he wouldn't mind But Loyalty was getting cocaine and crack smuggled in the prison.

"I already know, you ain't gotta tell me that, I know how your lil scary ass is. But look on one of the packages, I need you to get one of your lil chicks - Never mind. I almost forget you got all them square bitches Umma send my lil bitch, Nia your way for one of them. I can't have Jazzy meet my sergeant hoe." Loyalty be forgetting his lil brother really cared about maintaining a drug free image.

"I get you, fool. Now get off my line. Family First." Legend said Family First," Loyalty disconnected.

Legend crunk the car back up and dialed Uncle Sherman number. He picked up on the second ring.

"Ol' head, what's good? Yeah, just got off the line with him.. I can come now... That's what's up... Put my normal order to the side...say no more... I'm on the way." Legend put the car in gear and sped out the parking lot. He'd grab something to eat later. He had to get the business out the way, so he could get everything wrapped and packaged in time for him to get ready for the kick back at Campus Quad.

Legend didn't know how the hell, loyalty was doing it-but he damn sho' was doing it. The fact loyalty had two mules (officers who smuggled drugs inside the PRISON) it was all the better, because they split the profit sixty- forty. Loyalty tried to give him a fifty-fifty Split. But legend turned down the extra ten percent.

Legend hit the road with money on his mind. He had to make a quick detour to his spot, so he could get the paper for his pound of OG Kush and the half ounce of molly. During school hours be only carried his American Express card.

"Girl, you know we going to shut the scene down. One of the Kappa's name, Ashley said, as they walked out of Z's.

"I'm trying to tell you. Alpha Kappa Alpha rock the spot!" another girl name, Bria said pumping one fist in the air, then the other one. She did a sexy sway, Pumping her right hand between her thighs when she went left, and her left when she went right next she bent over, Po king her ass cut, and started twerking while looking over her shoulder.

"Slut!" her twin sister, Dria said slapping her across her ass.

"Ouch!" Bria exclaimed standing up. "Hater."

"Who going to bring the alcohol?" Legacy asked.

"I already got some. You still got them bottles at your spot, Tip? "Ashley asked.

"Yep. Yep." Tip confirmed.

"Fuck all that. Who got the gas?" Bria cut in. She wasn't with all that drinking shit, she was from California, and she loved Cali bud like SNOOP LION.

"Shit, they got to bring the weed. Our spot, our liquor, our food. They got to do they part." Ashley said.

"Now y'all know, these broke ass college niggas is not about to SPONSOR the whole kick back with the strong. Maybe some bullshit mid. And I refuse to smoke that, we might as well put our chips together and snatch a little something. I'll even put most of it." Tip offered. Just like most of the females in their crew, Tip was another spoiled girl with financially stabled parents.

"Hell No! I'm about to go on Twitter and call these niggas out." Legacy knew they could easily snatch up a couple ounces of loud with no pressure. Even without her crews she could get a few ounces of loud on the faces from her people. But that would draw too much attention to her, because out of everybody, she was the one least expected to have street connections (Beside her boyfriend, Triple) she went on Twitter, Facebook, Instagram, and Tumblr and turnt up.

"What you post?" Bria asked.

"Fuck with the Illest bitches alive! Alpha Kappa kickback we got everything. But it's on the men to bring the herb. Remember real niggas blow strong." Legacy read off her post.

"I'm online now. On Twitter, these Q dog niggas swear they go come through." Ashley tapped in a hundred and forty characters and a few hashtags to find the competiveness.

"They swear they so turned. Tsk." Tip smacked her teeth. "I'm about to walk the whole campus with y'all." Tip complained.

"Quit crying. You always- oh shit, that's the car. Hey! Hey!" Legacy was jumping up and down trying to get the attention of the person who was driving the blue and yellow 1970 Cutlass vert; she had seen at the light about a week ago. This time the top was up and he was going so fast, she couldn't even make out the driver she wanted the car so bad, she almost chased it down when it kept riding pass.

"Legacy, no you didn't!" Ashley exclaimed. "You just went real groupie on us. Don't tell me, you fucking with buddy?" she stated seriously. They all stopped at the top of the hill up from Z's, awaiting Legacy's answer.

"What the freak wrong with y'all? I want to buy that car. I been trying to catch the owner for about a week now. How am I going to fuck with a person, don't know who? Who is he? I got to have that car." Legacy didn't know what they was on, but if they knew who dude was; they definitely needed to be telling her.

"He is not going to sell you that car. Stay away from him that's Legend." Bria warned her little sister away from the sexy, rich, heartbreaker. She already knew how hypnotizing his demeanor was. Bria knew for a fact, Legend had already fucked her, Ashley, and Tip. And not to mention the other Kappas outside their immediate circle. Right now, Legacy was the youngest and most naïve- so they thought- so it was their obligation to protect her.

"For real. Dude is a married woman's dream and a single bitch's worst nightmare-"

"But she'll swear she dreaming until the sun fades." Tip cut in. "There isn't a way you haven't heard of Legend. That's funny, I just noticed the similarity in you two's name. How cute Haha."

"They might be twins. Both of y'all do look like God took too much time making y'all fine ass's." Ashley said, causing everybody to burst out laughing.

"I swear, I never seen him before. But that's the smart ass fine dude I was telling you about. The one who helped me in investment class. I'm saying, who is he? What's so bad about him?" Legacy was so curious now.

"Nothing is wrong with him. He really a good dude. I don't see how you don't know him from here. Just like you only thing about it, he is only in for the Pussy. All and all he the coolest nerd in the world to kick it with. But soon as you cross that line-" Tip shook her head, remembering the brief fling she had with Legend.

"That arrogant black fucker is too smart for his own good. Haha. That's my nigga though. Now that's who be having that real Cali bud." Bria added.

"What he sell weed? And y'all know I grew up in the suburbs.

I know exactly one person from the hood. How y'all know so much about him and never heard of him?" Legacy asked.

"Legend is not from the hood. He's so suburban just got flavor. His family got crazy paper. Hell no, dude don't sell drugs. He smoke weed like a Rasta." Ashley said. "Oh…And we know him, because we all done fucked him." She added spilling the beans with a smile on her face.

"Nasty bitches." Legacy joked. They acting like this nigga was Casanova or somebody, she thinks. True enough, she loved Triple with all her heart and she would never cheat on him - But God damn, Legend was on the opposite of "No."

"Don't knock it until you try try it." Bria's twin, Dria finally chimed in. Everybody turned their head her way.

"What you mean?" Bria asked her sister.

Dria waved them off and kept walking. "Y'all bitches get off my clit. I did it before we made the pact."

"You sneaky hoe!" they all exclaimed simultaneously.

Legacy just shook her head laughing.

Chapter Six

Grandman jumped off the speed boat, his loafers landing on the dock with a thud. He took a minute before entering the building sitting at the end of the landscape. It was a must you collected your thoughts when you was playing chess.

Grandman brushed the few strands of lint off his Armani Exchange slacks. These young boys get too caught up in this movie star lifestyle shit, he shook his head, as he stepped inside the Kreoyle styled lounge that sat on an island off the Florida Keys.

"My main man, hundred grand. How's life been treating you, Ol' Head?" Grand's young connect, Cold El' Jefe, greeted soon as he stepped through the door.

"You know nothing but big steaks and shrimp plates, young lad. Come on, let's sit down. I'm not young as I used to be, my knees getting bad," Grand replied.

Cold escorted his ol' head to a private both where there was already a bottle of Ace of Spade on ice. "Bullying them corporate muthafuckers in them board rooms tearing up your knees huh? What's on your mind Ol' Head? I know you didn't come way to my humble piece of world for nothing. What you ready to get back in the game? Show these young niggas your jay ain't broke. I know the square shit wouldn't cut it for a true player. I got you a hundred right now. Twenty-two a key for you." Cold knew with his ol' head back in the game, he would easily be off four to five hundred keys a month.

"Young nigga, I'm keeping my hands clean, like they just been watched ya dig? Nephew, it's nothing about this game I miss. Especially since it's changing for the worse. You got to do more killing than hustling. These young niggas ain't got no morals these days. Plus they soft like hot butter. A little pressure and they going to tell on everybody from the boss to the runners.

"I ain't with all that sucker shit. You even tired of this bullshit. Look what you do. You stay held up on this little island, staying away from the world, because you know it's wicked. See I can't do what you do. If I was your age with no responsibilities, I'd sit around and slang keys and fuck bad bitches all day too.

"But on the real. I fuck with this worry-free life. Don't nothing change. I'm still in every spot, the latest drop, enjoying the same benefits of the game as you. Only difference is, the Feds can't fuck with none of my assets. I'm legit, ya dig?!" Grandman pulled out an imported Cuban cigar and clipped the end.

"Iight, I hear all that. I know you ain't trying to tell me to go legit. You know that's out the question. I've been moving bricks since I was 13 years old. You know how street niggas say, they going to die with their finger on the trigger? Well, umma die with a brick in my hand." Cold never known his ol' head to be on no preacher man shit. But they did say good living made a nigga soft.

"How you came into this game, Cold?" Grand asked a rhetorical question. He already knew Cold's story.

"Come on, Unc. You know what it is. A nigga fronted me five straight out the gate with this shit." Cold said speaking of the time his Haitian step-daddy gave him five bricks at the age of thirteen and told him don't come back home until he had eighty-five thousand. This was all after his step-daddy caught him and his cousin snorting cocaine.

At the time, Cold had never sold a nick of crack, let alone a brick. After being robbed for a brick, Cold took a half ounce of powder and traded it for a 38 revolver. It was history from there.

"Exactly. You came in a winner. A nigga gave you five bricks to teach you a lesson. And I respect that because you too smart of a young man to be on the fucking powder. But me? I came in this game moving gram and a half fifty slabs. That's after my pops died.

"I was doing that to feed my lil sister, brother, and the mother who would steal my rocks and smoke them all, not giving a fuck she just left all her kids hungry. See I was a loser, but I wouldn't stop until I became a winner, ya dig? And guess what I did? I became a mutha-fucking winner... but at the same time, I became a father." Grand paused at the thought of his oldest son who was sitting in prison. The mere thought was enough to break him apart.

"Cold, my little nigga in prison with a life sentence. Fourteen to thirty years before he come up for parole. I got all this money, all these connections, all this power, and I can't get my son out of the Bing. Why this shit not like the movies and books? Do you think I would have been different if I would've dropped that work on him? Where do you think he would be right now?" Grand asked Cold El Jefe.

"He wouldn't be in prison. You seen where he was going without you. Now imagine what he would have did you backing him. You forced him deeper into the streets. You can't expect the nigga to go from sitting on the block, seeing the hustlers and wanting to be the next big dope boy to being a college boy overnight."

"It don't work like that ol' head. You gotta give a mind time to transition. Sometime the picture is too big for the frame. Don't ever force the picture, it'll crumble. But let it go, ol' head. Remember what you told me, after I expressed regret over having my baby mama whacked? Actions are forever and you can never take words back." Cold didn't like seeing ol' head beat himself up about what happened to his son it was all a part of the life.

"You're right." Grand had a point he was trying to make to himself.

"For who I am today. To take over his seat, when he was no longer alive. He wanted me to be prepared to be who he was. He prepared me to be better." As Cold spoke, he dropped dry tears for the only father he ever had. His pops had been dead for four years now, and it still didn't feel real.

"Why did you follow the path he told you to follow? A boss makes his own way." Grandman took a shot at his young nigga's ego.

"He didn't tell me shit! He showed me! A son learns from his father. I made my own name in the streets of West Palm Beach." Cold tapped his chest with his fist. "After them first five bricks, he never gave me shit else. I made myself a boss. Then Pops died and he gave me one last gift...the Plug." No matter how advanced and wise, Cold was, he still was a ninety baby; respect was taking, not giving.

"So he gave you the means and the ends?" Grand was trying to ease his conscience.

"You can say that. But what it is? I know you didn't come all this way for a simple lecture. Okay, you told me, you wasn't back in the game, so you must be on early vacation. Let's go to London, ol' head. I need some new Louie loafers." Cold said changing the subject.

Right on cue, Grand's right hand man, Marley, walked through the door carrying two duffel bags. About time this nigga speed boat show up, Grand thought.

"Sorry I'm ate. All these fucking diamonds in my watch, it was hard to tell time." Marley sat the bags down with a smile. Cold looked at Grand in confusion.

"I need two hundred bricks. I know I can get a twenty-one a piece number, nephew. When I last sold a brick, it was going twenty to a street nigga. I was getting them from you for sixteen-five a brick. You said it yourself. You got to give a mind time to transition. My mind just ain't grasped these high ass prices yet. See you gonna die with a brick in your hand. Umma die with a egg beater in my right and a Pyrex in my left." Grand leaned back in the plush leather and looked at Cold.

***

Legend came flying down Colombia Drive in his two thousand and thirteen black on black Dodge Challenger, his twenty-two inch black Forgiato (aka Forgi's) tearing up the asphalt. He made the quick turn into campus quad, forgetting to put his signal light on.

Riding slow through the apartments, he changed the song on his I-Pod to "Forever Young" by Jay-Z, with his pinky finger because he had a half-smoked blunt between his thumb and index finger. He cut up the bass a little and evened out the treble, so the kickers in the drunk would vibrate perfectly.

Just as he thought, the AKA's (Alpha Kappa Alpha's) had brung the whole college out...plus some. They had people in the parking lot kicking shit. He crept through slow, looking for a parking spot. I'm about to park this bitch in the middle of the street, Legend thought, finding a parking spot just in time. He immediately whipped the machine into the spot, killing the ignition.

Legend put the blunt between his lips, as he strolled through his I-Phone SC. The light from the LED screen illuminated his face. The car was smoked the fuck out. But that was nothing new. He let the seat back a little and stretched one of his long legs out, and propped the other one up on the side panel.

Legend turned the phone sideways, and typed in a quick text with both thumbs. Once the text was sent, he laid the phone in the lap of his black denim Versace pants.

"Damn," he mumbled when the ashes dropped in his lap. He thumped the rest of the ash in the ashtray. He didn't bother the one in his lap. He already knew if he tried to brush it off, it would smear and leave a spot in his black pants. He'd just let it drop off when he got out the car. Reaching in the back seat, he grabbed the red Ralph Lauren Polo Sports back pack, and sat it on the passenger seat.

"Everything mafia, lil bruh." Legend read the text that he'd just received from Loyalty. Confirming he knew his people had got the Packages. Clearing the screen of the text, he put it on the digital scale and laid the phone on the center console. He went in his sports bag and pulled out a couple sandwich bags, and started stuffing them with OG-Kush.

"Fuck all that. I ain't selling shit." Legend said filling four sandwich bags up and putting the rest back inside the sports bag. He thought about the Tweets the Alpha's had sent out about "Real Niggas Blow Strong." Deciding to be a little extra, he called Pizza Hut and ordered twenty extra-large pizzas, along with hot wings and breadsticks. You gotta know, he charged that to his parents credit card

Legend put the quarter pound of OG in the plastic bag along with two bottles of Coconut Cîroc, fifteen boxes Of Optimos and ten boxes of white owls. Just when he was about to get out the car, he remembered the half ounce of Molly. He wasn't going to sell any of that either. He had to pull away from that dope boy impression people on campus was starting to form of him. He preferred to be the cool college boy who was partying on momma and daddy's money.

That shit, Daph had said last week about him being her drug supplier, really had got to him. He wasn't trying to fall in that category. He definitely had to switch the game plan up. He's seen too many dumb niggas get escorted out their dorm room in handcuffs. No way he was about to slip off the porch straight into the back seat of a police car.

Legend stepped out the car shaking his pants legs over his low cut black Gucci shoes, with the green, red and black writing going down the back. He slid the black, green and red cloth YSL belt through the loops. Putting the gray 3.1 Phillip Lim fitted zip up hoodie on, he closed the door after putting on the black Chanel frames. He put the hoodie over his head represent for my nigga, Trayvon Martin, he thought.

"What's good, Legend?" Someone called out from a crowd standing in front of the building.

Legend looked around, trying to locate the voice. But he couldn't place it with all the noise coming from the different crowds.

"Right here, Nigga. This J-Roc!" J-Roc waived his hand through the air.

"What's good, bruh?" Legend said slapping hands with J-Roc. Within a couple of seconds he was ready to pull away from the crowd. Legend didn't fuck with niggas. And it was way too many niggas in this crowd. J-Roc was a cool nigga. Legend had kicked it with him a couple of times mainly on some being at the same dorm room, at the same time fucking with the same group of hoes shit. You already know how that went. But other than that, it was nuthin'. J- Roc was on the football team, so his circle was the football team. Legend didn't rock with them fools, they was too turnt for no reason.

"Just coolin'. Trying to slide in something. I see you back in that batman muh-fuckah. I'm glad you put that drop up. Nigga can't get these hoes to stop talking about that drop. You know how to make it hard for the average nigga." Roc half-joked.

"I had to do something for the bitches. Y'all football niggas, the one that make it hard. I wish I had it to trick." Legend kicked the shit.

"Come on, swagg-nerd. I'm about to get on my nerdy. That's what the broads like these days. Umma get up though. I'm about to push up on these bitches, before they push up on you." J-Roc slapped hands with Legend and rushed off.

Legend proceeded towards the apartment where the kickback, was being hosted. He could already feel it; this was going to be one of them nights. It was a must he got some new pussy tonight. If he couldn't catch nothing fresh at the kick back, he still had Quinn on standby. That was just his backup plan.

Right when he was about to walk in the apartment, someone grabbed his arm knowing it could only be a woman, by the perfume, he spun around slow.

"Boo!" DaPh smiled, looking good with her hair in that Kim Kardashian up-do, she was killing them in a pair of Prada Pumps, tight jeans (Nine times out of ten, they were by a high designer) and a Alpha Kappa Alpha t-shirt, that was cut and tied on the sides, showing her flat stomach and diamond belly ring (Legend bought her for her birthday). The baddest bitches was always lesbians.

Legend looked his best friend/friend with benefits, up and down, checking her out. "Don't be doing that." Legend said puffing on his blunt.

"You lucky I didn't go upside your head. Why you didn't call me back?" Daph pushed him against the wall, and pressed her body against his.

"No signs of public affection." Legend pushed Daph off him playfully. Daph was his friend and all, but she knew he wasn't with all that touchy feely shit. "I didn't know you called though."

"Ugh, you irk me!" Daph hissed.

"'You fucking me tonight?" she asked, stepping out the way of a couple of people trying to get in the apartment.

Legend got a quick glance in the apartment, when the door was opened. Fuckin right, he thought. There wasn't nothing but bitches in the 'Partment but damn, it smell like a pound of Bobby Brown. I know niggas ain't smoking no shit like that, he shake his head, puffing on the O.G. Kush. It can't be no real niggas in the building.

"Hell nawl, I gotta fuck something new this whole week." Legend sat the bag on the ground, so he could get the lighter out of his pocket. His blunt had went cut.

"What you cuffin? I'm on the same mission. Let's get em down with the 'Trey Play'. I got a couple new bitches lined up." Daph offered. There wasn't too much, she wasn't willing to do for Legend. Especially when it came to feeling him inside of her. She hated when he wouldn't give her any dick. He just took advantage of the situation, because he knew, he was the only nigga she allowed to dick her down.

"I ain't fucking with you, Daphy Daph," Legend knew she hated when he called her that. He did it any way to aggravate her. "You know I fuck with you, I just ain't fucking with you."

"Whatever. Fuck you it's all good." Daph stormed off with an attitude she knew Legend was dragging her, because she had blocked him. When he tried to double back and fuck Tish again. But fuck that, she thought. He thought everything was supposed to go his way.

Watching DaPh's backside, he almost changed his fucking mind. Damn, what you doing that walk for, Legend think. Then he remembered what was on the other side of the door. "Another qualo, she love me tomorrow." he joked, imitating Tony Montana.

"I know you love it, when this beat is on/Make you think about all the niggas you been leading on/Get me thinkin about all the rappers I been feeding on/got her thinkin it's the same niggas that we been speaking on/ain't heard my album, who you sleeping on? You should print the lyrics out/ and have your bitch read along...

Dria and Ashley stood on the couch, with cups of alcohol, in their hand, turnt up as they rapped along with Drake's verse on ASAP Rocky's "Fucking Problem" song.

Ain't a fucking sing-along unless you brought the weed along/ Then ju- (okay, okay, okay...)/Then just drop down and get yo' eagle on/Or we can stare up at the stars and put The Beatles on/All that shit you talkin' bout is not up for discussion/I will pay to make it bigger/ I don't pay for no reduction

Drunk and crazy, some girls flashed their breast when Drake rapped about making it bigger." The crowd was already out of control, and Drizzy's feel good verses we're making it worser (in a good way).

"Where is Legacy at?" Tip asked looking around for her little sister.

"I think she went to the back. If she not back there, she might've went to Laysha's apartment, so she could talk on the phone." Ashley said.

"Campus police is going shut us down. There is a kick back down the hall too."

"This not a kick back. This a fucking party!" Tip yelled at the top of her lungs. "I'm drunk as fuck." She fell back on the couch.

Yeah hoe, it's the finale/my pep talk turn into

a pep rally/ say she from the hood, but she live

in southern valley/about to vacay to Atlanta, but she going back to Cali get your girl on my line/world on my line/the irony of fucking them at the same damn time/she eyeing me, like a nigga don't exist/girl, you know you want this dick.

As if on cue, the front door came open, and in walked that nigga who be having bitches eyeing him, like he didn't exist.

"Ill nigga alert! Ill nigga alert!" Tasha elbowed Dria, using their little phrase, they used for an extremely handsome dude.

"Where?!" Ashley shrieked looking around.

"Just came through the door." Bria said already knowing who her twin sister was talking about.

"Illest nigga alive alert!" Tip said looking Legend up and down, as he stood by the door talking to some other dudes.

"Stop it, Tip. We made a Pact."' Ashley reminded them of the pact they made to never sleep with Legend again - ever. Even as the words were coming out her mouth, it was hard for her to tear her eyes away from "God's gift to women."

"Do y'all got the paddle? Because I'm ready to take my SPANKS. I gotta get spanked by him tonight." Bria purred.

"Oh God! He coming our way." Ashley warned.

"Duh! We are the Illest bitches on campus. Y'all stop swooning," Tip pulled it together, and pretended she wasn't just clocking his every move.

"Man, the AKA's are definitely, falling off. Fuck y'all smoking in here? Twenty-Five dollars an ounce. I thought you said, 'Real niggas blow strong.' Because I swear it smell cheap as fuck in here." Legend teased them about the strong mid-grade weed aroma. He took a puff of his blunt filled with O.G. Kush and blew a cloud of smoke over their head.

"I guess there isn't any real niggas in the building." Dria said rolling her eyes.

"Aman." Bria added, copying Meek Mills, she looked Legend up and down seductively.

"It's definitely same bad bitches in the building." Legend grinned showing his perfect row of white teeth.

"So what's up, Nerd-boy? You sharing the strong?" Tip put her hand on her small waist.

"Yeah. I brung some shit for y'all kick back. It's not really much." Legend pulled the bottles of Ciroc out the bag first, handing one to Ashley and the other one to Tip. He pulled out the four zips of weed, and gave Bria, Dria, and Tasha a zip of O.G a piece. He put the last one in his pocket.

"It's cigars in the bag. And some Molly." Legend said taking five boxes of Optimo's out the bag. "I didn't give y'all this."

"And you talking about a little something." Ashley smiled at Legend, shaking her head. That's why she fucked with Legend.

He knew how to have fun. And she meant that in alot of different ways.

"Why you didn't bring any capsules? You'll have a bitch overdosing." Tasha asked.

"Ow, y'all wanna fuck the party up?" Dria smiled deviously.

"Hell no, we not putting the Molly in the Ciroc." Ashley shot the suggestion down before Dria could get it out.

"THE PIZZA MAN AT THE FRONT DOOR, ASKING FOR LEGEND CARTER!" Someone yelled over the music.

"You might as well had your own Kick back.

Bria said, looking at the pizza man standing at the front door with two stacks of boxes beside him.

"He too much." Tip said with her panties on fire. The smallest thing about Legend turned her on, like the way the words on the back of his Gucci shoes matched his belt. And the way the gray hoodie stood out from the all black, he had on, but at the same time it blended in with the whole outfit. Even the green and red stripes on the shoes, and the green and red stripe on the belt, blended in with the black and gray outfit.

Most women wouldn't even notice such small details, but she was a New Yorker; who wasn't a whore for fashion and style up there in the Big Apple?

Chapter Seven

While the party was jumping in the front room Legacy sat in the back bedroom, on the phone arguing with her boyfriend, Triple Cross.

"Why Triple? Whhyyy?!" Legacy hissed.

"Fuck you mean?!" Triple barked.

"That's what the fuck I'm trying to figure out." Legacy was really testing his fucking patience.

"Look, I don't know why you trippin'. I'm not doing shit. No matter how many parties I go to, I'm still faithful to you." Legacy tried to explain.

"Man, I'm not trying to hear that shit. You need to sit your ass down for real." Triple Cross warned.

"I'm in fucking college! What the fuck you expect me to do?! This my life. I'm not one of your little hood-rat chicks. When I go out, I'm not looking for dick. I'm just enjoying being young." Legacy screamed trying to get her point across. She honestly loved Triple Cross, but sometime he really was getting too controlling. He was so used to them disloyal hood chicks, it was hard for him to believe in her true loyalty.

"Don't make me get out and fuck you up, LG."

"You have one minute remaining." the recorder cut in.

"Look, I love you. And you really need to get your visitation fixed. We need to talk face to face." Legacy talking to Triple, but she didn't want him to call back. He was really in his feelings tonight, and that shit was stressing her.

"Remember what I told you. Make sure you put that money on my books in the morning. And when you going to give that money to my lawyer?" Triple asked.

"I'll put the money on your books on my way home tonight. And I got a meeting with your lawyer next week."

"Thank you for using Securus." the call disconnected.

Legacy got up off the bed and turned her phone off, she looked in the mirror and ran her hand through her freshly done Rockstar-shag do. She loved the edgy hairstyle, it really displayed her beautiful walnut brown face. So many times, she'd hear people say, that she resembled the singer, Beyoncè, beside the natural green eyes and the beauty mark under her right eye. When it came to the curves, Legacy easily gave the singer a run for her money, with her 34-24-40 measurements.

Legacy let out a deep sigh and slipped her feet back into her Alisha Hill bootie heels. She looked herself over one more time, making sure the stress wasn't showing on her face satisfied, she slipped the phone in the back pocket of her Victoria by Victoria Beckham Jeans. Soon as she stepped out the car, she was slapped in the face by the strong smell of O.G. Kush. She didn't smoke weed, but she was familiar with the smell from being around Triple Cross. I guess the real niggas came out, she smiled thinking about the hundred and forty characters she sent out earlier.

I tell da truuutthh/I keep a gang of bad bitches with me too

And we ain't never going back to what we used to do

I was gon lie to you but I had to tell the truth

The new Future song, "Honest" was pumping through the house speakers. That was the good thing about living in college apartments; you could party without the worry of your neighbor calling the police. Legacy walked around the room looking for her sisters. On the way from one side of the room to the other, she counted at least a dozen whack ass come on lines. People was packed in the apartment like a Mexican ride.

There they go, Legacy spotted her crew, sitting in the far corner with a table full of weed, Patron, and bottles of Ciroc. These hoes done turnt up out here, she wondered who had sponsored the kick back with all the strong. Had to be that white boy, Kyle, Legacy thought to herself, knowing none of them stingy ass niggas was the ones who blew bands for the kick back.

"Little sisteerrr!" Tip yelled when she seen Legacy walk up.

By the way she was slurring, Legacy knew she was drunk. "The party don't start 'till I walk in."

"Girl, we thought you had left. Aye, buddy you gotta move." Ashley told the dude that was sitting next to her and like a real lame, he moved.

"I was in your room, Damn, y'all got the Molly and everything. Who came through like this?" Legacy asked dropping in the spot next to Ashley.

"The dude who car you wanted to buy." Ashley hinted, not saying Legend's name, because there was people around who didn't see him give them stuff. She knew only their circle could decipher the message.

"Ooooooooh." Legacy said soon as she learned of the nerd's presence she started looking around for him. For what reason? She did not know. But she knew not to ask her big sister about anything concerning Legend. They were so quick to jump to Conclusions. When it came to the nerd for some reason, they started putting crosses up. She didn't know if it was because they found out he was fucking all of them at the same time. OR maybe they kept their distance, because after they found out, they found themselves still wanting him. Now, that's a laugh out loud moment-). Whatever it was, that was their business, out of habit she turned her phone back on.

"Ashley, I fuck with y'all." a dude said as he grabbed a blunt and a bud of a O.G. off of the table. He was about to pour a cup of Cîroc, but Ashley stopped him.

"Hol' up! All three of them bottles got Molly in them," she had to warn him. She wasn't about to lose her scholarship and end up jail for lacing nobody shit. Bria them thought it was a game. Ashley wasn't going out like that. Her momma would kill her.

Dude shrugged his shoulders. "I got my girl on the Molly, with her homegirl." he started rapping 2Chainz, as he poured a tall cup of dirty Ciroc.

"Alllrrrriiiggghhhttyy then." Ashley said rolling her eyes, putting up the 'L' sign with her fingers, as he walked off dapping like it was the seventies.

"Y'all out of control." Legacy shook her head, picking up her vibrating phone. Damn this some money, she stared at the screen debating rather or not should she ignore the calls he couldn't keep dipping out like that. She'd already did it twice today. Her sisters would eventually start thinking something was up.

"They about to crank up the beer pong table. You want to hit this Legacy?" Tip asked knowing damn well Legacy didn't smoke or drank.

"How I'm feeling I might smoke all this shit." Legacy half-joked.

"Daaammmmnnn!" Some girl yelled when she missed the cup at the beer pong table.

"Let me guess, he trippin' about the party?" Ashley already knew what it was like to be with a street dude. Her high school boyfriend was in prison, serving twenty years back in her hometown, Houston, Texas. But legacy was way stronger than her. She couldn't do the jail house relationship. Although she moved on, she didn't leave her ex-boyfriend hanging, she still looked out for him and sent letters and pictures.

Yes girl." Legacy responded, not really trying to talk about it. Her phone went off again. It was some more money.

"Fuck I might as well catch this lick. I ain't got shit but six ounces left and it's over with, she thinks. They won't think shit, but I'm creeping.

"You need to leave him alone. He so not your type." Dria added, she always found it odd, that square ass Legacy was in love with a thug.

"Speaking of the devil." Legacy held up one finger. "Hello." She answered pretending it was Triple Cross. She know that would buy her a little time.

"What's cracking, Legacy? You straight?" Black boy asked on the other end of the phone.

"Yeah. Aye, let me get away from all this noise." Legacy took the phone away from her ear.

"I'll be right back. I might need a blunt for real after this call. Haha." She giggled walking towards the front door.

"Black boy?" she made sure he was still on the line when she got to the parking lot.

"Yae." Black boy responded.

"What you trying to do?" Legacy asked getting in her Lex.

"Playing softball at four-o-clock." he said coding the request for four ounces of cocaine.

"You better be able to run a four-four, if you trying to play me." Legacy replied by telling him she was charging forty-four hundred. She had got so good at the lingo, it was starting to come natural to her now.

"Cool! Damn, this stop and shop on Stewart Street, don't ever have any Preach White Owls." Black Boy said giving her the meeting spot.

Legacy disconnected the call as she put her seat belt on. Before pulling out the parking lot, she decided to return the first call she missed.

"Face, what it do my nigga?" Legacy was back in her hustler persona.

"What it is what it ain't? I need one minute." Face advised her, he wanted an ounce of soft.

"I got you two-minutes for twenty-one seconds. You know that don't happen too often. Legacy gave him a deal. Two ounces of that flake for twenty-one hundred. She was ready to be off that work.

"Run it. I'm in the hood." Face informed her.

"Where about?" Legacy didn't go anywhere near the hood. She wasn't trying to get known. A lot of hood niggas shacked up with college chicks. One thing she had learned was that street niggas had photographic memory. Plus the drug task force had a precinct on the block.

"On the ball field." Face, said talking about one of the main dope strips on the block. He had to know that was a no go.

"Ching Chong store on Alabama Street, got the best fucking chili cheese fries on the block." Legacy hung up and push started her car. She had to hurry up and handle her business, she hated to miss a good party. And for some reason, she was trying to bump into that rude-ass, sexy nerd, who had rode by her earlier today, like she was some kind of hitch hiker. That shit there had her feeling some type of way for real. Spoiled ass momma's boy, Legacy pushed the nerd out of her mind and pulled out into traffic. I got my own check.

Sick of seein' sell out niggas/ married to these white girls/they can never be no friend of me/I just get my dick sucked/ nut in they mouth instantly/you feel dats what you need though/While you off at work or somethin' she fucked one of yo people/Now you want to kill somethin'/pull of you an O.J/If you ain't got the dream team then you ain't winnin' yo case

"Mmmmh." The girl moaned as she eased the dick in her mouth. Legend laid back in the leather bucket seats smoking a blunt with his hand on the back of the girls head. Souljah Slim was playing throughout the car and ol' girl was bobbing to the beat. His eyes was rolling to the back of his head.

"Oww your dick taste like chocolate, daddy." She slapped the dick against her juicy lips before licking around the head.

Legend didn't know who the chick was, but she was the best at what she was doing. He had bumped into her when he was coming back from the store, grabbing a box of Magnums cause he had setup a quickie with this bad red bone that lived in the same building as the kick back, but in an apartment downstairs. But hey, him and this chick went to rapping…and you can pretty much figure out what happen after that.

"Mmmh, mmmh, mmh." She locked her lips at the bottom of his large dick head and sucked on it like a blow pop. She pulled her mouth off the dick making a smacking sound.

"Humm, hum, hum." She giggled, noticing she had a trail of pre-cum running from her lips to his dick. She put his dick in her mouth, and cocked her head to the side, causing his dick head to poke her jaw.

"Fuck you look sexy as fuck like that. Can I take a picture of you?" Legend aske with the blunt hanging from his lips. He loved when a bitch looked at him with his dick is phone in her mouth.

"Hmm huh." She said with his dick head still stuffed in her jaw.

Legend grabbed his phone and turned the interior light on, so he could get a clear picture. "I got it." He hit the interior light button, turning the light back off with the blunt clutched between his fingers. "What you said your name was?" This bitch was jacking his dick and her hand job felt like her mouth.

"You never asked me my name." she smiled, dropping her head back into his lap. She was slurping on his dick, like she was trying to give his dick hickeys.

"Ooh fuck." Legend pushed her head all the way down, as he started busting in her mouth. This bitch was so amazing. She was swallowing the cum and sucking it out at the same time. On top of that, she was still going up and down on the dick. She was about to go for a second round, but Legend stopped her.

"What you don't want anymore daddy?" the blue-eyed Miss America looking white girl, asked frowning.

"Leave me please." Legend told her non-chalantly. She couldn't have been paying attention to the song that had been playing since she got in the car. If she had, she would've heard what Souljah Slim had said about white girls on "maintain."

"Dang! Just call me, please." The white girl put hr number in his phone and got out of the car. "Never know when you'll need a good blow job." She let the door down and twisted off.

Legend wiped his dick off with one of the wet wipes he kept in his dashboard. Since he had a little time, he wrote him a couple of blunts to fill his case back up.

***

Legacy pulled back up in the apartments bumping Miley Cyrus, "23." On the way back she had stopped by the liquor store and paid someone to grab 4 bottles of Ciroc for her sisters. She didn't drink, but just on the strength, she might turn up tonight. It was a celebration. She had made it in the dope game for sixteen months. No busts, no losses, never getting robbed, or nothing. She took it from a quarter key to a brick...And then she did crazy flips from there. Straight from the suburbs and college classroom- she put it down with the blocks. And she ain't never seen a block (a street corner). Although Triple Cross taught her this and showed her that, gave her the most customers and the connect- she eventually perfected her craft off of black author books. And she even built outside clientele and caught a better plug.

But unfortunately, her days of moving work had come to an end. It's back to my boring life, Legacy thinks, swimming, karate, and classes. No more excitement. I might as well start back kicking it with my momma on a daily basis. Legacy pulled into an empty parking spot, next to a black-on-black Challenger with some dark tints on the windows.

"This mutherfucker is so hard." Legacy whispered to getting out of the car, checking out the Challenger. It had to be the hardest car she'd ever saw...besides the nerd boy's droptop. She had to think of a way to get her parents to get her a tricked-out car. Or maybe she could buy her own with the extra drug money- that she didn't have to use on Triple's lawyer- she was going to have to keep it hidden from her people.

"This car I'm driving make you feel some type of way?"

Legacy was caught off guard when the Challenger door came up and a pair of black Gucci shoes hit the ground. If that wasn't enough of a surprise, her mouth dropped to the ground when the nerd pulled out of the car, grabbing the side of the raised his frame with a super fat blunt clutched between his fingers, and a black diamond ring adorning his pinky finger. He stood at full length and slammed the door closed.

"Thanks for your help in class today." Legacy didn't know why she said that, she couldn't think of a better comeback. And to think an hour ago she was anticipating this very encounter. What had she wanted to talk to him about? Cars? She couldn't even think straight. She hadn't paid close attention to him in class today. Why? She didn't know. Well, she did notice he was handsome. But at the same time she wasn't looking at him like that. Now that she had her all his notorious shit about him, she was curious to see what everybody else was caught up on.

Now that she was looking for it, she seen it. His swag was on point- his swag was definitely on point. From the way he wore his clothes loose (but not baggy) to the way his temp fade blended into his chocolate skin on the side of his face. Legacy ran her eyes over his chocolate skin checking for tattoos. When she see he had none, it surprised her. Through the strong weed aroma, she still could smell the Polo Blue. His hazel brown eyes were just too much to add to his perfect piece of perfection. Her heart skipped a beat when she noticed the black dot under his right eye... Just like hers.

"That ain't what you wanted to say. But you're welcome. "

Damn, Shawty look like Beyonce oh, he hadn't noticed that earlier. He was in such an off move then because he hadn't had a spliff in his paws. He wasn't studying nobody looks. Now looking at her face- her body was something he did check out earlier- he almost got lost in her green eyes. Them had to be contacts, he thought. He smirked when he noticed the beauty mark under her right eye. She got to be from Cali.

"What I wanted to say then? Since you know it all." Legacy leaned back on her car, sitting the bottles on the ground beside her. She put on a seductive smirk, crossing her arms across her perky 34 C's. Momentarily she forgot about everything.

Legend shrugged his shoulders. "I don't fucking know. I'm not a mind reader you know what you wanted to say. I just know it wasn't that." he retorted as he crossed his ankles, leaning back against his car.

"Watch your mouth when you talking to a lady, sir. But you got to know because I don't. Just tell me, what you think I wanted to say. I'll be honest, if you're right." Oh my God, Legacy. I know you're not flirting? She heard her conscience ask. She hadn't gave a man much opening in years. It's just a harmless conversation, she told herself.

"What's your name?" Legend didn't know why he asked her that. I'm trippin, he said to himself. She just gave me the green light to say anything, and I ask her fucking name.

She raised her eyebrows and smiled. "That's not what you wanted to say." Legacy teased flipping his words back on him.

"I'm not about to play this game with you. Obviously, you're scared to say what's on your mind. Where my car at?" Legacy was getting a thrill out of playing with Legend.

"Umma let you slide with that little slick comment. You really don't know who you talking to." Legend could tell from the jump that ol' girl was a tease. He wasn't even about to get caught up in that shit.

"What car? That's your car right there, isn't it? Or is that your parent's car?" he knew college girls hated to be put on blast about not having their own. He didn't care though. Shit, he hated to be played with when it came to pussy, so she could call it even.

"Don't try me. I drive my own whip. I got a pink slip for my car. Do you?" she rolled her eyes. "Anyways. I was talking about the blue and yellow car. The convertible." By habit, she ran her fingers through her shag. It was something about the hairstyle that made her run her fingers through it.

"You got a smart mouth. But I didn't know that was your car. It's parked at my house. I don't just have one car, you know? Like some people. Tell me your name." Legend said in a smooth but demanding way.

"Why you want to know?" Legacy smirked, still stringing him alone.

"You must got a boyfriend?" Legend was asking questions he hadn't asked a chick since middle school. Rather a chick had a man or not had nothing to do with hi. He was trying to fuck, not get married.

"No. I mean. Yeah- not really." Legacy was tripping. She couldn't even come up with an answer. "Why you want to know?" Not once out of four years had she denied Triple Cross, but here she was stuttering, like that Mystikal and Joe song. She tried to show a little attitude, but it was too late for that. The damage had already been done. Trying to play with Legend, she had played herself. She was starting to understand why her sisters warned her about Legend: they knew he was her type. And that was rare because he was really a nerd. But he had this street swagger without trying to act like some tough thugged out hood nigga. He would put you in the mind of the rapper Jay-Z. not looks, but the way he moved and his aura. And she could tell, he was just being him.

"My bad ma. I was just trying to make conversation. Just tell me your name." Legend seen the way her eyes changed, when she stumbled up on the question about her boyfriend. That's the main reason, when it came to women, he loved to go deep, but hated to get deeply involved. Women went through too many emotional changes. He was too young for all that extra emotional shit.

"Don't call me ma, that's not my name. Why is you looking at me like that?" Legacy had to check her emotions. She really was acting immature. She had no reason to be getting sassy with Legend.

He wasn't doing nothing, but being a man. And to be honest, he wasn't even coming at her. the way he looked directly into her eyes, did something to her, for real. Tell me your name then. "How am I looking at you? I was raised to look a person in the eyes when you talk to them, so you can see the lie before it came." He was also taught when a man asks something more than once, he went from being curious to being determined. Legend had asked her name three times already.

"What happened when only the truth comes out? Why not look for the truth? "Legacy was a whore for an intellectual conversation. She wasn't a talkative person by Nature. To her the only time a person should speak was when the words held value. Maybe that's why she wanted to bump back into the nerd.

"You don't watch for what's expected. You can't see the truth. You can only feel it." Legend went into his pocket and pull one of the blunts out of the case. He put the lighter to the tip and inhaled deeply, giving his lungs some more company.

"The line could be disguised as the truth. What then?" Legacy presented, just to further probe his mind. She was discovering he was just as nerdy when it came to psychology if he was in investment. Legend was the type of person who love to learn. Just so he could teach.

"You can't hide a lie. Unless you tell it with your eyes closed or diverted. Even then your actions will make the person aware of the lies. Truth is confidence. A lie is weakness. Can I know your name? "Legend asked again.

"Do you go with Daphane?" All of a sudden, Legacy remembers seeing this same black challenger at Daph's spot numerous times. And when she asks Daph who it was, she smiled and told her "just call him my boyfriend," But Legacy didn't understand it was only a joke.

"You a Kappa?" he knew she had to be. Nobody else would of asked him no asinine shit like that. That was the AKA's personal joke.

"Yep." She said proudly. "Answer my question."

"You won't answer mine. Why should I answer yours?" Legend pulled another blunt out the case.

"Dang, Snoop Lion." Legacy said when Legend sparked up another blunt of O.G. how the fuck you blowing O.G back to back like that, she thought. "You tell me. I'll tell you." She tried to reason.

"It don't work like that. You smoke?" Legend asked blowing smoke out of his nose.

"Drug free. Now tell me," she demanded.

"Where you from?" Legend asked.

"I'm not telling you."

"You must be choosing?" Legend grinned, smoke framing his face.

"Excuse me?!" she asked rolling her eyes.

"You heard what I said. You asking me about my relationship status and shit. It got to be a reason behind that." Legend said rubbing his chin.

"In that case you been choosing. You can stop. I ain't doing no drafting this season." Legacy slid one in on him then.

Legend chuckled. "Who you think you be talking to? The last thing I chose cost thirty-four hundred. You can say thirty-five since I let 'em keep the change. But I walked in them."

"I'm not trying to hear-"

"Legacy!" someone yelled her name, cutting off her rebuttal.

Simultaneously they both turned their attention towards the voice. Both for different reasons though. Legacy was trying to see who was misusing his name. He didn't like that. Plus Legacy sounded like a female name.

"Legacy, what are you doing out here with Legend?" Tip walked up on them with suspicion in her eyes. She didn't even know. She had answered his question. "Don't be out here trying to seduce my lil sister, Legend."

Legend looked at Legacy and smirked. That's why she looked at me like that when I said my name in class, he thought. "Your little sister choosing, Tip. She heard it was a new baller in town. She tryna fuck around." He joked.

"Come here, Legend!" Daph called out from across the parking lot.

Legacy looked at him, Tip looked at her…he got in the car.

Chapter Eight

Jazzy sat at a table in the back of the local library going over some papers for the test, she had coming up next month. She knew she had plenty of time to get prepared for the test, but since she had the free time, she decided to go ahead and clear some things off her schedule. She hated to be clustered with a lot of shit at the last minute. That could cause a real headache. She already had too much on her mind as it was.

Over the last couple of years, school had become her life. Ever since she entered college at twenty-two, she'd been going full throttle to get her degree. Not once growing up had Jazzy seen college being in the cards for her. Coming where she came from, most people didn't make it out of high school let alone college. Thanks to Loyalty that wasn't her destiny. Not only was he paying her tuition from prison, he had changed her life way before that.

Jazzy was an around the way girl. Born and raised on High Street. Her momma was a crackhead, so she was raised by her grandmother, who was the hood's candy lady. Her grandma was never a strict guardian, so coming up she had a lot of lead way. And you got to know, like every girl who led right in the middle of the hood's ghetto superstars, boys was her favorite pass time. She would be lying if she said she wasn't a little fuzzy growing up. Because she was.

But all that changed when she ran across young Loyalty. When she first met, Loyalty, she was fourteen years old, and fucking out of both pant legs, as the old folks would say. Being from the same hood and going to the same school, Jazzy and Loyalty already knew each other. Well, Loyalty only knew of her. That didn't surprise her, though. She was just a little real thin girl from the block back then.

She "knew" Loyalty, though. Every girl knew Loyalty. He was one of the "IT" boys out the hood. That's why it surprised her, the day he approached her.

Jazzy put her pen down and sat back and recollected back to the day she was connected with the person who would prove to be her soulmate....

The year was two thousand and four and it was a cold winter night. School was out for Christmas break, so you know the young freaks was out. Jazzy and her crew of young hoochies, was out trying to give up that coochie. Although Jazzy was the only one out the crew who body hadn't matured yet, she still flaunted her stuff, like her body was shaped like an S. The other girls might of had her fucked up body wise, but they wasn't seeing her angelic face and long thick hair.

With nowhere to go this particular night, Jazzy and her girls rode around listening to Destiny's Child.

"Y'all wanna go fuck with, Double Cross them?" Portia asked, at sixteen, she was the oldest, and the one who was driving. So she was kind of like the leader.

"Where they at ?" Amber asked turning the music down.

"He just texted and said they in the trap," Portia replied sitting at the stop sign waiting for their decision.

"Hell yeah, who all over there? I know Tez over there with them." Kendra said agreeing to the plan.

"I don't know who all over there. But you already know it's going to be a lot of niggas over there. Portia made a right turn, headed towards Molette Street, where the young hood boys was hanging at.

"I wonder if Slim over there." Jazzy asked, hoping he was. She'd been trying to get with him, since she had seen him at the football game in that Sean Jean jacket with the fur collar, plus the word around school was he had a big dick and ate pussy.

"Nine times out of ten, he will be. You know he call himself a dope dealer now. His dumb ass done dropped out of school." Portia rolled her eyes in disgust talking about her big cousin.

"All them dummies dropping out." Kendra added.

"Shit, if I was getting money, I'd drop out too." Jazzy said.

"Cause you're a dumb ass too." Amber joked.

"And I'll beat your smart ass." Jazzy retorted seriously, putting Amber on hush mouth.

"It don't look like nobody in that house." Kendra said when they pulled up to the bando.

"They in there. It's just boards over the windows. Look," Portia pointed. "Somebody coming down the stairs," she put the car in park, as a skinny man rushed down the stairs looking in his hand and balling it back up every two-three steps.

"Oh, hell no! I'm not going in no crack house." Amber said hysterically.

"I'm tryna tell ya'. Let me call this fool." Portia picked up her Metro Pcs and dialed Double Cross' number. He picked up on the first ring.

"I know you ain't fucking left." Portia snapped, hearing music in the background.

"Bitch, who you talking to? I'm still at the fucking spot. Don't be calling my phone with all that." Double Cross blasted back.

"Tsk. Boy fuck you. I'm outside." Portia replied. This was how her and Double Cross' relationship went: A lot of fussing, a lot of fighting and a lot of fucking.

"Man, I'm shooting dice. Bring your stupid ass in. Hold them dice." Double Cross said getting frustrated.

"Watch your fucking mouth, bitch." Portia knew Double would knock her upside the head, but that didn't stop her from talking. "We ain't coming in no crack house."

"This ain't no fucking crack house, dumb hoe. Is y'all coming in or what?" Double Cross responded.

"He said it ain't no crack house. What y'all want to do?" Portia asked her friend. Going in by herself was out of the question. "Who all in there? Because I'm not trying to deal with all them thirsty ass old niggas. They be chasing the pussy like it's a race." Jazzy smacked her teeth. They might have been hot in the ass, but they wasn't fucking nothing out of their age range.

"We're not coming in, if it's a lot of old niggas in there with y'all." Portia related the message.

"Man, this ain't no old nigga trap. Nobody in here older than seventeen. Man, quit acting like a dumb head. You know who the fuck I fuck with. Just take your stupid ass on." Double hung up in her ear.

"Fuck ass nigga." She pulled the mirror down, checking herself out. "Y'all ready? Ain't nobody in there, but the boys from our school. I guess this the dropout spot." She joked taking her seat belt off.

I came into this game/young and tall/gold mouth

Shot me a bill/I copped my first eight ball (aye, y'all fuck

niggas better get it together) I was focused/I knew what it took to get it/and I was fourteen working with a half a block, aye...

The strong marijuana smoke filled the air, and Corona and Red bull bottles was all over the living room floor, only piece of furniture in the room was a sofa, two recliners and a mismatched love-seat.

Judging by the looks of the furniture it was on good enough condition to sit on. Overall the room was clean.

fucking hoes, getting money/having twice the fun/But don't play with us, dog/we got twice the guns/and we was young, serving niggas that was twice our age/getting it, grindin hard, gettin twice the pay

Young Jeezy was blasting from the little boom box that was sitting on the cardboard box in the corner of the room. Even if you had a ruler, it would still be hard to measure what was beating the hardest: the trap or the little speakers. It was traffic coming through the spot, like it was I-20 west. The young hustlers played it like the '93 Chicago Bulls, and rotated the trap. When one scored, he passed the ball to the next player.

Portia, Jazzy, Amber, and Kendra all sat side by side on the sofa, watching the group of six boys on the opposite side of the room shooting dice and smoking weed. Everybody, but Portia was trying to decide who they were going to fuck. There were people in the spot, they hadn't expected to be there. There was even a couple of boys there who were still in school.

"Which one is you fucking with Kendra? Tez isn't here." Portia asked her, talking low. But she didn't have to worry about them hearing her, due to all the noise from them and the music.

"I don't know. I might kick it with Lil Tee. But we ain't going to be able to do nothing." Kendra said sounding disappointed.

"Why not? Your period must be on? I'm definitely picking Slim tonight." Jazzy could already imagine what his tongue was going to feel like on her young, hot pussy. There wasn't too many boys their age eating pussy, so she couldn't miss her chance to get licked.

"Man, my cousin over there. He be on some other shit. Dude be acting like he my daddy. I'm surprise, he hadn't told me to leave." Kendra couldn't believe her luck. Horny as one was, he had to be here. What the fuck he doing over here with all these 3 Ward niggas anyway?" Kendra think. He from High Street. But she already knew it was because her uncle Grand ran the block, and he was from the 3rd, so Loyalty had a G-Pass to go wherever he pleased. Just like her.

"Loyalty here?! Where he at?!" Portia asked forgetting all about Double Cross. "I didn't even see his fine ass." Usually she didn't fuck with boys younger than her ex, but Loyalty could definitely get it."

"He over there on the ground with the dice," Amber pointed out. She had spotted him soon as they walked in. Loyalty was her ex-boyfriend/first. "And you know he's from the 3rd."

"Awww, look at Amber keeping an eye on her first boo." Kendra teased.

"You better not let him hear you say that."

It had to be at least an hour before the boys broke up dice game, and started showing the girls any attention.

"What's up with y'all? Why you over here acting all stuck up and shit?" Double Cross said dropping across Portia and Amber's lap.

"Boyyy, get off my fucking leg!" Amber yelled punching Double in the back.

"Get your ass up then. Let me sit next to my bitch." Double Cross said.

"I ain't your bitch." Portia mushed Double Cross in the face.

"Don't get your ass beat." Double grabbed Portia by the hair and yanked it.

"Ouuucchh." Portia yelped, leaning her head towards the pull to lessen the pain.

"Man, y'all please don't start this Ike and Tina ass shit. Damn!" Amber rolled her eyes, getting up from the couch. She had to sit on the arm of the love seat, because all the seats were taken.

"You can got in my lap, Amber." Slim offered catching her off guard.

Amber looked at Jazzy to see how she felt about it. Even though Slim wasn't her boyfriend, Amber knew her friend was digging Slim. Jazzy gave her a slick head nod. Amber still could see the disappointment in her eyes.

"'Come here, Kendra." Lil Tee said from across the room.

Kendra looked around for Loyalty, but didn't see him. Hopefully he done left, she thought, sitting in Lil Tee's lap.

"Come holla at me, Jazzy." Ced tried his luck.

"Boy stop! TSK," Jazzy dissed him rolling her eyes and turning her lip up. See Ced was the dude who hung around the cool crew, but wasn't talking about nothing. He wasn't getting no money, he wore everybody in the crew clothes and shoes. To them he was only a follower.

"How the hell y'all got lights in a bando?" Amber asked taking the blunt cut of Slim's hand.

"If I tell you, I'll have to kill you." Slim joked grabbing her waist, pushing his dick into her ass on the slick.

"I bet y'all don't wanna play truth or dare." Portia proposed wanting to be devious.

"PG13 or X-Rated?" Lance asked popping the top off a Corona.

"Ain't nobody thirteen in here?" Kendra replied rolling her neck.

"Who first?" Amber asked eagerly.

"This the way it is going to go. One person speak for each group. A different person after every turn. No more than two trues in a row." Portia laid out the ground rules.

"We're in." Double Cross answered for everybody, pulling a quarter out of his pocket. "Heads or tails."

"Heads." Jazzy spoke up for her team.

Double Cross tossed the coin in the air. "Heads! Y'all won." Double Cross announced, catching the quarter in the palm of his hand.

"Truth or Dare?" Kendra asked.

"Truth." Ced answered, The girls mugged him and rolled their eyes at him. They already felt like he didn't belong in the game.

"Is it true that all y'all dumb asses dropped out of school just to sell crack?" Kendra decided to start the game off right.

"Nawl, dumb fuck. Loyalty still in school. So is Ced, Lance and

Lil Tee." Slim retorted getting pissed.

"Oh, that just make two of you stupid fucks. Where is Loyalty anyway?" Portia asked. Before she could turn her head around, Double Cross slapped her in the mouth.

"Next time umma knock your mutha-fucking teeth cut. Don't ask about no other nigga while you sitting next to me." Double Cross grabbed the bottom of her jaw.

"Man, come on with that lame shit. We trying to have fun." Kendra snapped on Double Cross.

"Shut the fuck up. Truth or dare?" Double Cross asked, letting Portia's jaw go."

"Punk ass bitch." Portia hissed.

"Dare." Amber boldly answered.

"We dare y'all to show them titties." Double Cross smiled.

Y'all with it?" Amber asked the crew. Everybody nodded their head. They got up and stood side by side.

"One, two, three." They all pulled their shirt's und bras over their breast giving them a quick flash.

"Now call turn." Jazzy said fixing her bra back. "Truth or dare?"

"Dare." Lil Tee spoke up for his crew.

"We dare y'all to show that dick." Jazzy said causing all the girls to start whistling and clapping.

"Iight. Give us thirty seconds to prime up." Slim quickly accepted the challenge.

They sat there quiet, as the boys pumped their wood through their pocket.

"Time up, Time up! Show that dick." Jazzy exclaimed. "Y'all line up.

"Y'all niggas close your eyes." Slim told them.

"I bet three hundred. I got all y'all beat." Double Cross bragged.

"Bet." Lil Tee said.

"Y'all shut up and pull them dicks out." Amber urged them, ready to get an eye full.

"One, two, three." and the snakes came out.

"Gaaaaawwwdad." Portia put her hand over her mouth.

"Owww weeee, Ced!" Amber couldn't believe little lame ass Ced had all that in his pants,

"Double, baby, you lost your money." Portia looked down the row at all the dicks. Even her cousin, Slim. He know he got a fat one on him, to be so skinny, she thought.

"Damn, Ced. You got that gator tail in your pants." Kendra could feel her pussy getting wet.

"Man, who the biggest between me and bruh?" Lil Tee asked wanting to win the bet. That lil three hundred could go with his re-up.

"Lil Tee, I don't think it's a twelve year old in this world with a dick like yours, boo." Jazzy said honestly. The boy had a big dick.

"Y'all about the same size. Double is a little longer and Lil Tee is a little thicker. But, Double, it look like you tried to piss out an apple, baby boy. How the hell you be getting all that in you, Portia? Ow Lawd." Kendra couldn't take her eyes off all the dicks.

"Okay, y'all can put up." Jazzy told them, unable to take the torment any longer. Truth or Dare?" Lance asked.

"Truth." Amber had to spare the crew from getting hit with the unexpected. She knew after what they had made them do, they would come back with some overboard shit.

"Lame ass." Double Cross cut in. He just knew, he was about to see all they pussies.

"Is it true, y'all wanna fuck something?" Lance knew it was plenty ways to get where he was trying to go. He wanted to get his dick wet.

"True." Amber answered

"Then what we waiting on?" Lil Tee asked.

"For y'all to make a move." Kendra licked her lips, while looking Lil Tee in the eyes. She was ready to suck him dry.

"What kind of moves getting made? Y'all lame ass niggas leaving a nigga out." Loyalty asked, popping back up from nowhere.

Kendra's heart dropped to her stomach and her face fell in her lap. When she looked up and seen her first cousin, coming back in the room from the hallway. Right when it was about to go down, she was too blowed.

"Where you been, bruh? You missing the fun." Lance told him. Out of all this time, he'd just realized, Loyalty had disappeared before the dice game ended.

"I was in the kitchen. Y'all got the music up so loud in here, the junkies been coming to the back door. "What's up though?" Loyalty pulled off his Enyce sweater and laid it on the back of the recliner. The coke fumes had gotten into the fabric while he was over the stove, stretching the thirty-one grams of coke, he had won from Double Cross.

"Truth or dare, Loyalty?" Portia called him out. She hated he missed out on the dick show. She was dying to see if the size matched the swagger. Because if it did...Ump, she thought.

"We dare y'all to pick the girl, who y'all really been wanting to fuck. Be all the way real." Portia said in anticipation.

She wanted to fuck Loyalty. She didn't give a fuck how Double felt about it. He wasn't her boyfriend.

"I want Kendra, You cool with that, bruh?" Lil Tee said looking at Loyalty. Everybody knew how Loyalty was about his cousin, Lil Tee wasn't trying to let no pussy come between him and his nigga.

Usually, Loyalty wouldn't allow anyone that he fucked with to holla at his cousin. But he wasn't even going to trip on Lil Tee. Kendra was fifteen- Older than him- and Lil Tee was only twelve. The youngest of the crew. And him and Double Cross was his closest potnahs out the crew, so everything was cool on his end. Kendra was already fucking, he couldn't stop that. She just wasn't about to be running around the hood fucking old niggas and shit. Maybe Lil Tee could sit her ass down. Lil Tee might have been the youngest, but that didn't mean he wasn't a player. The young nigga was twelve going on twenty, fo' real.

"I want Jazzy." Loyalty said shocking everybody in the room. They could've swore, Loyalty and Amber still had something going on.

Jazzy almost fainted when Loyalty called her name. She didn't even think he knew her name. She didn't even look Amber's way. The swap has definitely been made.

"I want Portia and Amber. But I want Amber more." Slim said trying to fuck with Double Cross. The nigga was always frontin, talking about Portia didn't have him fucked up. But every time a nigga say Portia name he get mad. Like, he knew Slim and Portia was cousins, he would still get mad.

"Shut your nasty ass up." Portia told her cousin.

"Slim, don't try to tear me up." Amber said remembering what she had just seen.

"Come on, Portia." Double Cross said not falling for Slim's bullshit. He already knew what it was.

Everybody got up and started making their way to the area it was going to go down in. for the people who didn't catch one of the two spare bedrooms- with a mattress on the floor- they had to play the living room sofa. Since Lance and Ced didn't get a pick, they had to sit on the front porch and catch the traps. Which was better if you asked the hustler, but you know at the present moment they were thinking with their small head, so they were blowed.

The lights was turned off and the music was turned up to the max. Jazzy followed behind Loyalty through the dimly lit hallway. She was looking down at his fresh white and gray Air Max 90's, as she walked behind him. She admired his swagger. There had never been a time, she'd seen Loyalty and he wasn't dressed to impress.

Just by the looks, she could tell the washed Enyce blue jeans were brand new, along with the gray Enyce sweater he had discarded. Now he was rocking the matching gray long sleeve Enyce t-shirt. That too was brand new. Even the authentic New York Yankee fitted her had on was brand new.

"Don't just stand at the door. Come sit down." Loyalty told her after noticing she'd stayed standing in the doorway.

Jazzy was feeling so confused. She was damn near on the verge of a panic attack. She didn't know what to do. She didn't know if Loyalty wanted her to come on to him first or what. Shit, the ice had already been broken. They had asked them, who they wanted to fuck, Jazzy thought. But the question was *'why did he pick her though?'* Kept resounding inside her head. He had led her into the kitchen, she was still trying to find a comfortable spot to fuck in. they should've just got straight to it. How the hell was she going to initiate sex with him, and he was sitting hunched over the kitchen table with a round light brown slab of something on a glass plate in front of him, cutting through it with a straight razor.

"What the hell is you eating?" Jazzy curiously asked, staring at the plate, as she sat across from him.

"I'm not eating this, crazy. This is crack." Loyalty chuckled expertly chopping the cookie down to nicks and dimes.

"For real?" Jazzy exclaimed, leaning closer to get a better look at the drug that she heard so much about. Lately, that's all her and her crew been talking about. It had them curious because so many proplr they knew was smoking and selling it. They just wanted to know what the hell do it look like? Now she was looking at it, she was trying to figure out, how did they smoke or snort what looked like a piece of tile?

"Yeah, fo' real. Haha!" Loyalty laughed at the astonishment he seen on her face. The funny thing about it, she had the same look on her face that he had the first time he seen his pops cutting up.

"I thought it would be powdered up, like baking soda. How the hell do they smoke a rock?" Jazzy could be real nosey when she wanted to know something.

"It's baking soda in here. When it's powdered, that's cocaine. That's what people snort. Crack is like dried bread. If you put a flame to it, it'll produce smoke. Crackheads put the rock in the tip of a shooter- which is only a glass pipe with brillo in it-and hold a flame to the rock. And they inhale the smoke as they pull it through the shooter." Loyalty dropped two dimes inside of an orange button bag.

"Wow. That's crazy." Jazzy couldn't help but to imagine her mother in a crack house, with the glass pipe set between her lips.

"Why you be fucking so much?" Loyalty asked catching her off guard.

"What kind of question is that?" Jazzy snapped.

"The kind of question I ask. If you don't know, you don't have to answer. You can't tell me what you don't know." Loyalty was grinning, as he put the small bags stuffed with crack rocks inside a sandwich bag.

"I don't fuck a lot. Tsk." Jazzy smacked her teeth and rolled her eyes, denying the accusation. That was the only come back she could conjure up.

"How many niggas you done fucked then?" Loyalty non-chalantly asked.

"Like four or five." Jazzy lied, all of a sudden feeling ashamed of her promiscuous behavior. This was the first time a dude ever came at her on some shit like that most of the time they were too busy adding to the number.

"I already know if you say, you only fucked four or five dudes I gotta multiply that by three." Loyalty stated honestly. He knew she was lying without taking a breath, he could name ten niggas who she'd slept with. Even without being privy to her sexual partners, her eyes still would have gave away the lie.

"You trying to judge me?" Jazzy asked sounding like she was on the verge of tears.

"Hell nawl! I'm trying to fuck you." Loyalty said confusing her.

"Well, why you asking all these questions? Just do what you do." Jazzy said, finding her voice again.

"See that's why I gotta multiply it by three. Just because I want to fuck you don't mean you suppose to let me. I haven't even earned your body." Loyalty flipped the script on her again. In the handbook his POPS had gave him, he was at the chapter titled "Psychological Warfare." He was practicing the art on Jazzy.

"I wasn't going to let you." the attitude was back to erase the embarrassment. Jazzy felt like Loyalty could see right through her. She wanted to pull out of the conversation, but the way he was just kicking the nonchalant attitude, he was leading her through a maze. He was the Puppet master and she the Puppet. Any second now, she was going to tell him, her deepest secret.

"Iight. How much money you got?" Loyalty asked her tying the sandwich bag in a knot.

"I don't have no money. You going to give me some?" now that was one thing she did not lie about. No telling when someone was trying to bless you, she thought.

"Now that's crazy. You running around here fucking all these young niggas who getting money, and you broke. Uh huh. I thought you was smarter than that, when I heard you was only fucking with niggas who was getting money, I thought you was smart. But I see you just another dumb head. I guess you on your Brandy shit you just wanna be down." Loyalty looked at her shaking his head.

"Who the fuck you think you is?" Jazzy was getting heated with Loyalty.

"Your boyfriend," Loyalty replied with a wide boyish grin on his face.

"You not my- " Jazzy's words get stuck in bee throat when she realized what he had just said.

"Here, keep this at your house in a safe spot. Don't let nobody know you got this. You know how to keep your mouth close, don't you?" Loyalty asked, pushing the sandwich bag full of break down towards her.

"How much you gonna pay me?" Jazzy was always down to make a dollar.

"I really wish you had a different way of viewing things. Why you keep requesting pork chops after I just offered you lobster? You gotta look at the bigger picture, Jazz." Loyalty mildly scolded her for her simple way of thinking.

"What?! I'm doing what you asked me to do you the one who just called me a dumb head. I'm your girl now, so I gotta stay fly. Matter of fact I gotta stay flyer than you. So, I gotta stack some money so I can get some fly shit." Jazzy replied smiling.

"If you my girl, you don't have to worry about nothing. I got you. You gotta open your eyes. What you want the bank or an account?" Loyalty asked.

"The bank." Jazzy replied.

"Well, I'm the bank. I gave you a chance to invest in the banks but you asked for an account. If you wanna settle for less, then get naked. I will give you a couple pennies to start your account." Loyalty said playing with her mind.

"Stop fucking trying me. Quit coming at me like I'm a hoe." Jazzy retorted.

"How the fuck am I trying you? You just was about to let me fuck you for free. Now I'm trying to put some money in your pocket, I'm trying you. I just don't get y'all broke ass young hoes," Loyalty shook his head bagging up more crack.

"Who you calling a motherfucking hoe?" Jazzy raised her voice. This nigga really got me twisted, she think, he think he about to just sit here and disrespect me.

"Why you cussing? I'm talking about you, though and the other young hoes like you. You know the ones who want high mileage on their pussies and no deposits in their pocket. Y'all really be on y'all "Broke Forever" shit. Loyalty wasn't letting up on her.

"I don't care about money. Fuck money. I'm young, what the fuck I need money for?! I didn't come back here for you to talk down on me. You can-"

"You came back here for me to fuck you - fuck you for free. But now I'm tryna give you a couple dollars for the pussy and you get mad. You a dumb hoe. Come On, lets fuck." Loyalty looked at the message that had just came through his phone, and laid it back on the table.

"Why you even picked me? Fuck you!"

"I know you want to fuck me. You a hoe. That's what hoes do."

"Man, leave me-" Jazzy burst out crying before she could get her last words out. She was trying her best to act like Loyalty's words wasn't getting to her-but they were. It wasn't really what he was saying, it was more the truth behind what he was saying that was getting to her.

Loyalty got up and walked to the other side of the table and sat beside Jazzy. He put his open palm beneath her face and caught the tear that was dropping from her eye. "You the baddest bitch I ever saw." In the handbook Grandman had wrote: "At the highest peak of your game. You will take on a wife. Never take a "readymade" hustler wife. What fit the next man, is not for you. Only time it's tailored, is when it's made specifically for you. Break it down, then build it back up. As you re-build, keep your eyes open for flaws. Sometimes imperfections or the only perfections you will find within a woman… and the lesson went on. Through his observation of history, he knew just the slightest misstep with a woman, had been the down fall of many great men (hustlers). That wasn't going to be him.

"You not acting like it." Jazzy said sniffling.

"You gotta respect yourself before I can. You still my girl right?" Loyalty asked.

"Do you want me to be?"

"Is you going to be down for me?" Loyalty went in his pockets and pulled out his money. "How much money do you want?"

"Please stop doing that. I don't-"

"Chill. I'm not on that. I'm proving to you that money don't mean nothing when it come to my girl."

"I don't want your money. I'm just going to be down for you."

Loyalty placed the money in her lap. "That's two thousand. Put it with the work. I'm serious about you being my girl."

Jazzy closed her eyes and sighed. "Look, you know, I done been with a lot of boys. All of them been my age, though. If you going to be my boyfriend, you got to let go of the past. I swear on everything I love, I will never cheat on you. I know how to be a good girlfriend. And I will keep my mouth closed about our business."

"What you mean let go of the past? I never was holding on to it. I don't have nothing to do with your past. I wasn't back there. We right here. In the present. This where we're going to start. Just because you done made a few mistakes, doesn't mean you can't recover from it.

"We're still young and at risk. Long as we learn before every number counts, everything is all good. I got you, though. Remember if the game ever flip on me, you don't flip on me. I took the chance on you. I seen it in you first. I took the chance. Win, lose or draw – I'm taking the chance. Never forget Loyalty. And I mean that in two ways. Do you know what loyalty mean? And I'm not talking about my name, I'm talking about the word that defines me.

Jazzy juggled her mind trying to find a definition for the word Loyalty. She couldn't so she said, no don't will you teach me?

Loyalty gave her the run down on everything. He schooled her on the pitfalls and tumbles of the game, prepared her mentally for the bad times that came before, during and sometime after the good times. "Loyalty is deeper than love…" he told her breaking down every little thing. And it was history from there. Loyalty took her from a young hood rat to a black princess. She even started to gain some hips and ass. Loyalty had her frame blossoming from all the good fucking and eating. No longer was she eating at McDonalds, Wendy's, Big Chic, and Johnny subs five-six times a week. Loyalty had her in Apple Bees, Outback steak house, Red Lobster, Ruth Chris, and several other hot spots, as if they were their second home. For two high school students, they were definitely gaining bragging rights.

"Ump, them was the days, Jazzy thought, coming back to reality when someone bumped into her chair.

"My bad." a young white dude apologized.

"You good. Damn I forgot I was still in the library," she said to herself, getting back to her studying.

Boy meets girl/Girl perfect woman Jazzy's phone started ringing. She hurried up and hit the ignore button. She could've sworn, she had turned the volume off before she came into the library. She quickly put her phone on silent. She'd just get back at the caller after she finished studying.

"Loyalty, Loyalty, Loyalty," she mumbled flipping the page of her textbook. "What would I do without you, boy?"

Chapter Nine

L oyalty popped out his room and went straight to the front of the dorm, and grabbed the dust mop, so he could see who was in the booth, seeing that it was Ms. Black, he nodded his head at her. She cut her eyes to the left and turned her back to the other side of the booth. He knew that was the signal, that Sgt. Lewis was in the mop closet.

Just to check and see who was still in their cell awake, he pushed the dust mop around the dorm a couple times. In prison, you'd think locked up with a bunch of killers and gangsters, you wouldn't have to worry about niggas gossiping about another niggas business, like Wendy Williams. But boy, these niggas was worse than a bunch of project bitches at the hood's beauty shop.

This had become Loyalty's routine every night that Sgt. Lewis worked since he moved to the north side, in the dorm that Sgt. Lewis was the Supervisor over. A couple of weeks after Sgt. Lewis had approached him, he had finessed the unit manager to move him off the south side, only reason he waited so long to move, was because he had to wait for his little brother, Don Haiti, to get out the hole and moved into the dorm with him and Gunna. He wasn't about to move and leave Gunna in the dorm by himself. Nawl, a nigga wasn't mobbin like that.

"What took you so long, black boy?" Sgt. Lewis said as soon as Loyalty slipped in the mop closet, and pushed the door closed

"I had to make sure nobody was watching. Damn, come here, girl, you smelling all good and shit." Loyalty grabbed her arm and pulled her to him. Unlike his little brother, Legend, Loyalty was a real relationship type nigga. He was just one of them niggas, who was just in love with being in love. Don't get it twisted though at the first sign of flaw, he'd cancel a bitch, like Nino did.

"'You not going to get your stuff first?" she nodded her head towards the net bag in the mop bucket. She allowed Loyalty to pull her into his arms, wrapping her arms around his neck.

"After I'm done with you." he said palming her round ass. "What all you bring?"

"Ten phones, two touch screens, and the weed. Don't ever get no strong ass shit like that again. I'll bring the rest of the stuff when I come back Friday. I missed you." Sgt. Lewis moaned, kissing on his neck.

"Oh yeah? Prove it." Loyalty squeezed her ass.

Sgt. Lewis pulled away from him and started unbuckling her belt. She unbuttoned her pants and pulled them below her twenty - nine inch waist, exposing her forty-four inch hips.

"I ain't got no panties on." She said in her sexy voice, poking out her glossed bottom lip. Loyalty didn't waste any time. He whooped that nine out, like he was Quick Draw McGraw. He walked up behind her, with his dick in one hand, stroking it back and forth. "So that's how much you miss me?"

"I bet you ain't about to hit me with that tap out." Sgt. Lewis giggled, looking over her shoulder at Loyalty, with her ass in the air, as she gripped the handles of the buffer.

"How much?" Loyalty grinned, sliding his bare dick between her soft thighs. He gripped both sides of her hips, pushing his dick in her with no hands. He stroked slowly, only pushing half of his dick inside of her. And he already had her speaking Chinese. He couldn't even front, the pussy was so good, he damn near had to pull out twice. Loyalty didn't know how she did it, but every time he fucked her, her pussy was virgin tight.

128

"Owww...fuuuccckkk." Sgt. Lewis looked over her shoulder, and watched Loyalty, as he watched his dick go in and out of her wet pussy, she bit her bottom lip and held it between her teeth.

"Don't look like that." Loyalty said looking in her eyes. She know she be making some mean fuck faces, Loyalty thought, as she sexily bit her bottom lip, letting it go as the "fuck" rolled off her tongue. That was definitely one for Jada Fire.

Sgt. Lewis spread her arms out further on the buffer handles, spreading her legs apart, she bucked her ass back on Loyalty, causing his whole nine to sink in her pussy. She dropped her head between her arms, and went to working her ass muscles in a way Loyalty, never seen before.

Loyalty had to step back and get a firm stance, and a better grip on her small waist. She was throwing her ass from side to side, and clapping her ass cheeks up and down at the same time. Before he finally got control, she nearly threw him out of the pussy three times.

"You can't handle this pussy, luh bwoy." Sgt. Lewis lifted her head up from between her arms, and looked back at it. She started giggling, dropping her head back down. Her long – now sweaty – black hair was hanging wildly over her face. Stepping up to the challenge, Loyalty waited until she bounced that ass up, and pulled half way out of her, catching that ass in the air, he rammed his dick into her gut. Sgt. Lewis screamed a little too loud. Before she could get control, Loyalty went to drilling that thick nine inch dick in her, like a Jack rabbit. He had her moaning so much, she had to bite down on her work shirt.

"Who pussy is it?" Loyalty demanded to know, as he dugg deep, pushing all nine inside her.

"Oh God this is your—youuuurrss…It's yooourrrsss!" she yelled cumming all over Loyalty's dick. He still was pounding in and out of her pussy relentlessly, she had went from holding the buffer handles to being bent over at the waist with her hand's on the floor. He had her in the three point stance.

"I'm not pulling out," Loyalty groaned as he felt his dick explode inside her wet paradise.

"Oww, baby daddy," Sgt. Lewis giggled with her palms still flat on the floor, along with her feet. She had her knees locked, as she made her ass clap around Loyalty's dick.

"It's hot as fuck in here." Loyalty slapped her ass, pulling his limp dick out of her creamy pussy. He was dripping sweat. The sex session had the unventilated prison closet steaming. Even Sgt. Lewis blue shirt had a wet ring, going all the way down to her chest.

"Us together, what you expect?!" she put her pants and boots back on, she checked her watch, while tucking her shirt back into her pants.

"It's time for my break. I gotta go wash up. I love you."

"I love you back. Don't call my phone until like five this evening. I gotta get some sleep."

Sgt. Lewis wrapped her arms around his neck, one last time, before she was away from him for two days. Standing on her tip toes, she sucked his bottom lip into her mouth. "I'm going to miss you."

"I already know." he said brushing his lips across her nose. Sgt. Lewis kissed him one more time, before walking towards the closet door, peeping out first.

"Babe, you'll never be able to catch them. They in the dark standing to the side. You even got some looking from the floor, through the crack at the bottom of the door. You might as well go on out," Loyalty said, knowing no matter how careful you were, there was no way to get around the chain gang neighborhood watch crews. Long as their eyes didn't turn into lips, Loyalty didn't give a fuck what they seen.

"Iight. I'll get at you later." Sgt. Lewis walked out of the closet, but instead of going straight out of the dorm, she made her rounds to play it off. Loyalty waited a couple minutes, allowing Sgt. Lewis time to leave out of the dorm, before he crept out of the mop closet, with the black trash bag, wrapped in a towel inside of a net bag in his hand. He rushed to his room and put the weed and phones up in his hiding spot. After the contraband was secured, he grabbed his shower stuff, and headed across the top range in his Jordan shorts and Jordan shower shoes.

"Damn, it's already 3AM," Loyalty checked the clock hanging on the hard brick wall, in the front of the dorm, He threw his beige Polo Ralph Lauren beach towel over the rail that was holding the shower curtain up. Loyalty loved taking a hot shower in the wee hours of the morning. Besides Sgt. Lewis, that was another reason, he had to be a third shift orderly.

Loyalty threw his Polo briefs and tank top, along with his Ralph Lauren Polo pajamas on the rail with his towel. He walked in the shower and sat his soap dish inside the soap holder that was built into the cement wall, He walked out the shower, after pushing the button to cut the water on. Leaning on the top range guard rail as the water warmed up, he looked towards the booth. He chuckled to himself when he noticed that Ms. Black had turned her chair towards the shower.

"Freaky ass hoe want a nigga to jack," Loyalty mumbled to himself, stepping inside the shower once the water cut off. Stripping down naked he decided to play with Ms. Black.

Loyalty pulled the shower curtain back, just enough for Ms. Black to see inside. He made sure he had the curtain, where only the officer in the control room could see inside. Before doing his thing, he made sure none of them faggot ass niggas on the right side of the dorm could see him. That was one of the main reasons he didn't jack in the first place. He wasn't about to let no nigga get a slick glance at him. You never know when one of them bitch ass niggas was looking out the corner of their eyes. If it was one thing Loyalty was no nonsense about; it was that homosexual shit. He could care less what another muthafuckah did, but that kind of shit wasn't apart of him and his circle. But on solo mornings like this, when the doors were still locked, the coast was pretty much clear. Soon as Ms. Black seen that Loyalty had the shower curtain cracked, she turned the bright booth light on, so he could see that she was watching him. Ms. Black knew how the jack game went. She knew the man got off on the fact, that the woman was watching him masturbate. She understood the sexual gratification a man could get from that. Shit she got off on watching the dick.

This bitch be talking about, her and Taliya (Sgt. Lewis) is like sisters, Loyalty thinks, I know I can fuck this hoe. This shit just like the streets. He locked eyes with Ms. Black and stroked his long dick back and forth, making sure she seen every inch of him. He could see the way, she kept rubbing her crossed thighs together.

Damn, I was just supposed to be playing with this bitch she got a nigga geeked all the way up, Loyalty thought, pulling the shower curtain back a little more. And just to think, he just came out of some pussy not even thirty minutes ago.

Ms. Black came from sitting behind the control panel to the dorm room window. She grabbed the Windex and a couple paper towels and started wiping the window. But she wasn't studying that window. Only thing she was trying to get a clear view of, was that big black dick in Loyalty's hand.

Lord knows, if I could find a way, I will give Loyalty some of this pussy, she thought. Fuck how anybody feel about it. Especially Taliya, what she don't know, won't hurt.

Ms. Black wanted to put her fingers inside her pussy so bad. But she would have to wait until Loyalty finished. She'd just go in the bathroom and play in her gooey pussy. She had already came twice by rubbing her clit between her thighs. This boy know he got some stamina, she thought, knowing he had just fucked Sgt. Lewis. Let me get an officer down here with me, who doing dirt. I'm going to fuck Loyalty's brains out, she immediately went in the booth bathroom, after watching Loyalty bust inside his hand.

"Ahhhh." Loyalty groaned, catching the nut inside his hand. He closed the shower curtain with his fingertips. I gotta get up out this muthafuckah, he shook his head, standing up under the water, after washing the cum off his hand. I suppose to be on the streets. Seven years in, he still couldn't believe he was in prison. This shit was surreal.

Chapter Ten

"Oooh fu-fuucckk…yeeesss!" Legacy screamed out as Legend leaned her over her sixth floor balcony, with his dick buried deep inside her womb. He was driving her crazy, knocking his mushroom shaped dick head up against her G-spot. This was way too much for her, after being celibate for sixteen months.

"This what you wanted to say, huh? Talk to me while I beat this pussy up." Legend demanded with a blunt hanging from his lips, as he dug deep into Legacy's wet box. He held onto her shoulder with one hand and her waist with the other, Legend was grinding into her hard, but gentle. He was trying to knock that pussy out the park.

Legacy refused to let Legend just handle her, like she was some inexperienced little girl. Never mind the fact, she had only fucked one person her whole life. Triple Cross was a beast when it came to putting that dick down. So even though her number was low, that didn't mean she didn't know how to work it. She had to push Triple out of her mind. She knew what she was doing wasn't right, but she couldn't help herself. Out of the four years she'd been with Triple Cross, she had never cheated on him; not even thought about it. Now all her faithfulness was gone out the window. Thanks to the fucked up luck of meeting her aphrodisiac; Legend.

As Legend threw that dick in her guts, she caught it and threw that pussy back on him. There was no doubt about it; he was a Legend. But straight up and down, like six o'clock; she was the Legacy. She had to make sure, he knew she stood for what she stood for.

"Oh God, Leeggeenndd." Legacy purred like a kitten, as she started to bust like an Uzi.

"You love me, Legacy? Tell me, you love me! "Legend had a grip on both sides of her waist, pounding in her so hard from the back, she was knocked on her tip toes every time he pushed inside of her.

"Legend, I-I-I…"

Legacy jerked awake, snapping out of the too realistic dream. She immediately threw the satin Fendi sheets from her body, and jumped out of her bed. She clicked her lamp on, half expecting to find another body in the bed. It was empty. She let out a deep sigh of relief. "I'm tripping for real." Legacy said rubbing her fingers through her hair, as she looked at the side of her bed, that hadn't been slept on in sixteen months. Her eyes bulged when they came across a wet spot, located where she'd just been laying. Legacy automatically ran her hand down the center of her boy shorts.

"Oh my God," Legacy gasped, when she felt the sticky mess in between her thighs. "Aww," she moaned when her hand brushed across her sensitive clitoris.

Legacy stepped out of her boy shorts, and stripped the one day old sheets from her bed. This was the third erotic dream she'd had about Legend, in the last two weeks since she first met him, at the kick back. The crazy part about it, she hadn't even seen or talked to him since that night. They didn't even exchange numbers. Just a simple conversation, with a trace of flirting, now he was dominating Legacy's thoughts and dreams. Day and night he was on her mind. It was like something- some kind of spell had been put on her. She had to shake this shit. Dude really had her trippin.

Legacy turned the water on inside the Jacuzzi styled tub. She poured some strawberry scented oil inside the water, along with some wild peach bath bubbles oil. Sitting on the edge of the tub, she stuck her arm down in the water and twisted it around.

"This is all I need." she lowered herself down into the water, and leaned her head back into the soft cushion with her eyes closed. It didn't even take a full second, soon as her eyes closed the same visuals from her dream, played through her mind so vividly. She still couldn't believe it was all a dream. The shit was seeming too real.

After soaking in the water for an hour, Legacy got out and rubbed down in her light scented strawberry body oil. Since she didn't have nothing planned for this rainy Saturday, she slipped on a pair of baby blue boy shorts with the cute little pink bow at the front, with a tank top, she never realized how boring, being a regular square citizen was, until she retired from her sixteen month drug career, two weeks ago. Back to her same boring life: karate, school, swimming. She couldn't even add 'spending time with her boyfriend' to the list, because his crazy ass was locked up.

Legacy grabbed her I-Pad and went into her living room. She turned on her fireplace and curled up on one of her floor pillows. After checking out the latest 'Hip Hop Weekly" magazine, she went through her eBook collection, trying to decide what she wanted to read, while he was forced to be awake at two something in the morning. She strolled Pass over one hundred eBooks, before she decided the read the new book by GOLD 'No Heart No Love' She was so in love with the characters out of this trilogy.

"Oh hell no!" Thirty minutes into the book and she was already engrossed by the story. She didn't know what it was about reading that made her love it so much. It was just like people who loved music. They don't know why they can't do without their I-Pod playing, or their earbuds into their phone. There probably was nothing to figure out. They loved good music; and Legacy loved a good story. To her there was nothing better than the breakdown of real emotions. Even when a book was labeled fiction, the emotions were still real. That's what a book was; a person's expressing their inner emotions.

GOLD be having a chick all in her feelings. He sure know how to make a woman feel like street dudes are the best dudes in the word. Fuck around and make a good girl go bad, Legacy said out loud, getting up to go answer her phone.

"I'm coming." She said in a sing song voice, slow jogging to the back of the condo, thinking it was Triple Cross calling. He be getting on the dumb shit, when she don't answer the first time he called.

"Hello." Legacy snatched the phone without checking the caller I.D.

"LG, what it do? I need you like yesterday. Please don't break my heart." One of Legacy's old customers, Mike-Mike said.

"Damn, bruh. It's over with like Miley and Liam. You know if I could, I'll do it." Legacy repeated the same words, she'd been saying for the last two weeks.

"Fuck! I got a dumb jugg too. I got these dumb country Alabama niggas about to pay thirty-eight-five a piece, for some bricks," Mike-Mike talked reckless over the phone.

"39.5? How many they trying to cop?" Legacy asked purely out of curiosity. She knew the game was fucked up on the prices right now. But 38.5.?! God damn! She did a quick calculation in her head. If she was still moving bricks, she would get two from her connect for sixty bands, and then she would make that seventeen band profit. But that was an "If." All that was a thing of the past.

"They want a fucking ten piece!" Mike- Mike said, getting all hysterical.

"Hol' up. You saying, your people want to get in the game for ten whole minutes? And they scoring 38.5 PER game?" Legacy asked, trying to make sure she was hearing him correctly.

"That's exactly what I'm saying." Mike- Mike confirmed. The line went silent for a few seconds. He knew, he had her thinking about it.

"You sure they don't eat donuts or lay in the bushes?" Legacy couldn't believe a nigga was that anxious to get some work, he'd pay nearly forty a key. He had to be the Feds or a jack boy.

"Positive, the only reason I won't take the fool off, is because the play is on my uncle's face. Holmes already done gave me the check. But I'll get back at you. I gotta find this chicken dinner." Mike-Mike sighed frustrated.

"Mike-Mike, you got the whole check right now?" Legacy spoke slowly to make sure her every word was understood.

"C'mon, LG. You know I don't play when it comes to that paper. I wanted to bring this move to you, because I already owe you sixteen bands, but I need to make this jugg." Mike-Mike said. "They paying me twenty-five just for plugging them in."

"Give me thirty minutes." Legacy hung up. She had forgot all about the money Mike-Mike owed her. When she retired from the drug game, she had chalked up the money left in the streets. It didn't hurt her. She had paid Triple's lawyer forty- five thousand bucks in full, and she still had sixty and some change put up in her safe. For the last two weeks, she'd been debating on what kind of old school she could get, that would crush Legend's. Because she'd already decided, that's what her cut of the drug money was going to.

Fifteen minutes later, Legacy sat on her bed with the money out her safe, stacked up in front of her. As she sat in the middle of the bed Indian style, she was contemplating what her next move was going to be. Right now she was in a conflicting position. When Triple first asked her to do this, she made a promise to God that she would stop, before she even started, but that promise was made, before she experienced the allure of the game. Before she felt her first adrenalin rush from counting that blood money. Before that inferior feeling of being untouchable, after the police pull beside you at the red light and you got that blow on you, all he do is nod his head and pull away. That shit is too much to ignore. But she had a decision to make: God or the game.

"What it is, Spirit?" Legacy asked her old Plug, after unconsciously dialing his number.

"What up, ma? Long time no hear." The young African responded in his thick West Indies accent.

"You know how shit goes in this game. Aye, what it'll cost me for ten whole nights?" Legacy jumped straight off the cliff head first. Fuck all the small talk. She didn't even care about the fact she never copped more than two-three bricks from Spirit, since she'd been shopping with him. But that shouldn't matter. All that counted was the fact, since they had met at the Hot 107.9 Birthday Bash, all her business had been legit and consistent.

"Twenty- eight a night." Spirit surprised her by giving her a response without hesitating.

"My face clean?" she took another leap out there, and asked for ten keys on consignment.

"Meet me at the flea market on Metropolitan." Spirit hung up in her ear. That just proved to her what she had read in one of GOLD'S books was true as fuck. *The boss always hung up first.*

Legacy sat froze in spot for a couple of minutes, trying to come to terms with what she'd just done, she lifted her head to the sky and said, "Sorry God, I lied. But please give me one more try. Just this last flip, I promise." Legacy hoped God had found it in his heart to forgive her. At the end of the day he was the creator of all. He knew the nuisance of selling drugs was just like using it.

She stuffed the money back in the safe at the back of her walk-in closet, and hurriedly got dressed in a white Gucci fitted sweat suit and a Pair of white Gucci sandals. She was back in her Bella persona. For the first time in weeks she felt up-beat and excited…and wasn't spending her every minute thinking about Legend. She grabbed her Gucci shades and rushed out the door.

Chapter Eleven

(a week later)

Legend strolled around downtown with his ever present spliff lazily resting between his index and middle finger, the smoke rising through his long fingers, stinking up the air in his immediate presence. He put the blunt between his lips and pulled the smoke into his lungs.

A couple of the shoppers cast sideways glances at him, like it was uncommon to bump into a person blowing weed in public. Shit, Miley Cyrus just fired up a joint at the podium of the award show, he thought, wishing he could catch up with the sexy twerking white girl. That shit was crazy, the whole America was smoking weed. The lower class, the middle class, the upper class, the young black boys from the hood, the white kid sitting in the front desk, even the fifty year old "Home Economics" teacher was blowing trees. The only difference between them and Legend... he was addicted.

Reluctantly, Legend stubbed his blunt out and dropped it in the big ash bucket, sitting outside the Unique Boutique, so he could enter the store and do some light shopping. Nothing major. Maybe a couple of t-shirts. At least three times a week he was going to make a trip to Unique's. Out at all the boutiques, Unique's was his favorite. From time to time, he fucked with the Louis Vuitton Boutique down the strip. And he was known by name at the Ralph Lauren, Yves Saint Laurent, and the Dolce & Gabbana Boutique on the other Side of the strip. But Unique's was his spot. They had all the fly designer jeans, t-shirts, and shoes. Basically Unique was just an expensive urban fashion store that offered the top designer brands.

"Legend, what up, boy?" the store clerk, Lala, asked in her sexy New York accented voice. That was another thing about Unique's; they hired all the young freshman females from the college, the other boutiques had old white women or some feminine ass white dude.

"SuP, Lah? What y'all got new?" Legend eyes roamed over the four-eleven petite dark beauty. He wanted to fuck Lala, but she was too much of a tease. He wasn't with all that flirting shit. She was one of them broads who would hug up on you at every Kick back, but soon as it was time to come up off that pussy, she got to freezing up. He didn't have time for all of that. It was too many bitches fucking to be chasing one who wasn't.

"Let me finish with this guy and I'll be right with you." Lala advised him following an older white man up the glass steps, heading to the second floor of the boutique where the more casual clothing was located.

Legend went ahead and started looking around the store. He already knew he was being watched. A young black man standing around smelling like weed, in a store where the cheapest item was nine hundred dollars. Yeah, most definitely the eye in the sky was on him. But he didn't give a fuck. His money was plastic just like the white folks.

"You found something you like?" Lala cheerful voice sounded from behind his back.

"Aye, I want that shirt. How many of them y'all got?" Legend turned around to face her, while pointing up the wall at a black and white Armani t-shirt with a picture of Jay-Z on the front, with the words, "I'm Black" going over the top of the picture, and the words "Born to Change the Game" going under the Picture.

"Which one? The Jay-Z one?" Lala asked grabbing the silver hook that was used to grab the items high up.

"Yeah." Legend scanned the section to see it there was anything else he wanted from up top.

"That's a one of one. You might as well get the whole outfit." Lala was on her tip toes, trying to get the shirt and she still couldn't reach the shit.

"Why? What all come with it?" Legend asked standing behind her enjoying the view of her little plump poking out.

"Because, yo, this shirt by itself cost thirteen hundred. The whole outfit is only two grand. It comes with the pants. I know some fly kicks you can get with this." Lala was still trying to reach the t-shirt.

"Iight. Give me the whole outfit. Man, you need some help? You're midget ass." Legend asked stepping closer to her.

"They put this shit maaadd-" before she could get her whole sentence out, Legend was lifting her 120 Pound, 4 feet eleven inch frame up in the air by her waist.

"Get that other shirt too. Both 2x's." Legend sat her on his shoulder. Other shoppers was looking at them laughing.

"I know your sizes. Yo, let me down before you get me fired." Lala said with the items on the hook.

"Long as I buy everything on that hook, you won't get fired." Legend slid Lala down his body. When her ass got by his hard dick, he pushed into her and slid her down his full length slowly. He could of swore she was pushing back on him. She just didn't know that was the easy way to get her little eighteen year old ass tore up.

"Ump. You mad craazzyy, yo," Lala seductively said looking at him through her black frame Chanel glasses.

"Where the parts?" Legend ignored the way she was looking at him. She kept playing, she'd be fucked by the end of the week.

"I got to measure you for them. Come over here you want the shoes, I was talking about?" Lala was a real little energizer bunny. She was already at the counter holding the measurer.

"What they look like?" Legend held his arms in the air, as she wrapped the measuring around his waist.

"Some black and white Lanvin Woven Nubucks. Stop looking at me like that. I'm going to put some room." Lala giggled.

"I was about to say. Not too much room though. I don't want them baggy-fitted comfortable and loose. Yeah, give me the shoes." Legend turned to the side, so she could get the length.

"Yo, close your mouth. I know you don't wear Armani baggy." Lala playfully put the measurer down the middle of his pants and laughed.

"Not just Armani. You don't wear thousand dollar Jeans hanging off your ass. What you laughing at?" Legend looked down to find out what was tickling Lala she was holding the measurer to his dick.

"Haha. You." Lala said wrapping the measurer back up.

"All you had to do is ask. That's nine the long way." Legend bragged, walking up to the counter. He had to hurry up and get up out the store. He could feel his weed light about to flick on.

"Whatever, yo. I hear you talking. Nine and a half for the shoes, right?" Lala asked over her shoulder, already headed towards the back, so she could grab the shoes.

"Yeah, give me two pair. One in a ten." Legend decided to get his Pops a pair also.

"You haven't even seen the shoe, you just don't agree to buy a pair of twenty-seven hundred dollar shoes, you don't even know what they going to look like. What if you don't like them?" Lala plopped the two shoe boxes on the glass counter, beside the two t-shirts.

Legend shrugged nonchalantly, "It don't matter. I probably never wear them anyway. I got a million pair of shoes."

"Well at least look at them. I like em, yo." Lala pulled one of the shoes out of the box.

"They official." Legend said barely paying attention to the shoe, as he pulled his LV bill folder out his pocket.

"You're so spoiled. $9,600.93. Your pants will be in, in about a week. I'll just let you know when they come in." Lala bagged the two shirts two pair of shoes separately.

"Fuck! My American Express card is in the car." Legend put the bill folder in his pocket, and pulled out a wad of nothing but hundreds. He counted out one hundred, one hundred dollar bills and laid them on the counter.

"400.07 is your change. Damn, why this couldn't be one of them, keep the change, moments. Give me your number." Lala demanded as she handed him his change.

"For what?" Legend was looking through the glass at the designer shades that was on display.

"So I can let you know when your pants are coming in." Lala responded.

"You don't need my number for that. I'll just stop by." Legend grabbed his bags off the counter.

"Man, give me the number, yo." Lala said rolling her eyes.

"Tell me why you want it." Legend wasn't with an them lil girl beating around the bush games.

"Give it to me and you'll find out." Lala snared in her thick New York accent.

"I'm not with all that lil girl shit. 678-977-1656." Legend couldn't wait to fold her lil ass up. He definitely was on a mission to fuck all the freshman's.

"Yo, just because I'm eighteen, don't mean I'm a little girl. There isn't nothing little about me, but my body." Lala replied.

"Your crews be on some little girl shit- Birds of a feather, flock together. Legend retorted leaking into her-fake gray eyes.

"Yo, that's your fault, b. You be wilding. I got nothing to do with that. You got to keep that thingamajig in your pants. Everybody can't handle it." Lala already knew why he was calling her crew, little girls. But that was them not her. He brung that shit on himself. Nobody told him to be sleeping with a crew of homegirls at one time.

"Can you handle it?" Legend asked being serious. He wasn't with all that playing on his phone shit, her little crew was doing. That was the con of fucking with freshman hoes; some of them still acted like high school bitches.

"If it go there. I'm a grown woman, boy." Lala smiled.

"It's going to go there. Get at me though." Legend was about to walk out the store, but Lala stopped him.

"You forgot your change." Lala held up the seven scent.

"You said, you wanted to keep the change. Keep the change." Legend walked out the door.

"Hey handsome." An older woman in a business suit said walking pass him.

Legend winked at the white woman, and kept on pushing. These were the kind of things that kept Legend from settling down. Walking around, just dying to be fucked out by a young nigga. And if nobody else didn't do it; Legend was going to fuck them.

He threw the bags in the trunk and got in the car. Today he was driving around in his mother's Range Rover. Since he had to get it washed tomorrow, he decided to ride it around for the day. Plus he had to pick up his newest whip in a couple of hours.

Legend fired up a fresh blunt, looking through his phone, trying to find someone to follow him to pick up his car from the shop. He tried to call Daph, but her whack ass didn't answer. She probably was in her feelings again. Right when he was about to dial another number, his phone started ringing in his hands.

"Sister-in-law." Legend answered for his big brother, Loyalty's girlfriend.

"Ain't shit. What you got going on? I'm surprised you're at Z's. All the bitches down here. You slipping, bruh. Haha." Jazzy teased her little brother-in-law.

"I'm sick of them broads at the college. I'm downtown. I got to pick up my car from Wendall's. What's up? You fucking with me?" Legend was already headed towards the campus. He knew Jazzy wasn't going to turn him down.

"Damn, lil bruh. I'm about to go back to class. What time you gotta pick it up?" Jazzy asked sounding sad. She hated to let Legend down.

Through the years they'd really formed a real big sister little brother relationship. Back before Loyalty was getting money on the inside, Legend would look out for her, out of the paper his parents used to hit him off with, for allowance. There had been plenty of nights, when the tears wouldn't stop flowing and she was feeling lonely, with no one else in her corner, she always had Legend.

"It's all good. There isn't a certain time. I just wanted to catch him before he closed at three. What time you get out of class?" Legend asked.

"Four o'clock. Hold up, bruh." Jazzy started talking to someone in her background.

"Look, my lil home girl said, she'll take you. Just meet her at Z's." She said trying to talk over the noise in her cafeteria.

"I'm in ma dukes Range. Who your home girl? I hope not Ebony dog face ass." Legend half-joked.

"Don't do that. You wasn't saying that when you was all in her. But nawl this someone else, you don't know her. Why you in your mamma car?" Jazzy asked.

"She still was ugly then. I fuck ugly hoes too. Everything but fat hoes and white hoes. Man, you know I be having to wash her truck at least twice a week." Legend pulled onto the campus coming from Maple Street.

"Boy, you out of control. How much, Mrs. Carter, paying you for that? Another ten thousand on your weekly allowance. Your spoiled ass." Jazzy sometime wished Loyalty would of played it straight, and been out on the streets living like Legend. She didn't know one hood nigga who wasn't hustling to get where Legend had started at. And just like Legend, Loyalty was supposed to be there without all that extra shit. But pride was a silent killer. And whether Loyalty wanted to admit it or not, he had laved his pride to kill him.

"I wish. For ten bands, I'll wash them bitches every day of the week. Aye, I'm coming around the curve. Old girl gone have to drive ma dukes car back for me. When you get out of class? I gotta give you the stuff for Loyalty." Legend almost forgot about the package he picked up from Uncle Sherman, this morning."

"I told you at four. But cool, we're walking out now. Spare my little sister too, boy. I been hiding her from you." Jazzy already knew when it came to females, Legend was a beast. She thanked God, she got the other brother. She was surprised, Legend, didn't live in the hearth department.

"I'm not studying your little friend. I'm out here. Come out." Legend pulled up to the entrance of Z's and sat idle, and enjoyed another blunt. He tried to put his phone in the cup holder, and ended up dropping it on the floor board.

"Damn, why, I missed lunch?" Legend was shaking his head as a gang of females poured out of Z's. He was disappointed in himself, when he counted thirty-seven bitches he hadn't fucked.

"Ain't no way all this new pussy running around here like that. Who the fuck I been fucking?" Legend thought. Just then a group of Kappa's came out the door. Out of the group of seventeen, he counted three he hadn't fucked... and tea of them were fat.

Legend let the window down, When he Seen Jazzy coming out with another girl behind her. He really couldn't tell where she was, due to the fact, she had on a pair of large sunglasses.

"Oh, shit please don't tell me, this is your brother -in-law." Legacy blurted out, taking off her sunglasses.

"Oh my God." Jazzy threw her hands in the air.

"Don't tell me, you done fucked my lil suh already, Legend?" she sighed shaking her head.

"Hell Nah, crazy." Legend chuckled at Jazzy's outspokenness.

"Aye, I didn't even know you knew Legacy. What up, Legacy?" he smirked, placing the blunt back between his lips. He hadn't seen Legacy since that night at the Kick back. God damn, she was looking like an angel in all that white, he thought.

"You don't know me." Legacy said giving off plenty of attitude. But her stomach was doing back flips. All that running she had been doing, only lead her to the exact person she was running from.

Jazzy looked back and forth from Legend to Legacy and a smile spread across her face. Just standing near the two young spoiled tweens, she could feel the undeniable attraction between the two. Just to be honest, they made a perfect picture. Something like a young Jay-Z and Beyoncé. Aww, what a cute couple they would make, she thought. But that would never happen. Her brother-in-law was a male wore. And Legacy was in love. It still was a good show to watch. Legacy was being so stiff on Legend. That really amused her. She couldn't remember ever seeing a female treat Legend like an average. She didn't know what Legend had did to Legacy on their first encounter, but whatever it was, it didn't sit right with Legacy.

"Alright, y'all kids play nice. Unlike you two dweebs, I can't afford to Skip a class. Call me later, lil bro. Love you. Be careful Legacy. Haha." Jazzy rushed aft laughing to herself, she could tell by the look on her face, Legacy wanted to change her mind. Jazzy couldn't let her brother be left on stuck. She'll be alright, she thought. There was no doubt in her mind, Legacy was completely loyal to Triple. And there was no nigga who could take Legacy away from him. But if he wanted to keep it that way; he better keep her away from Legend Carter. Because if a nigga's bitch pop up on his radar, he going to fuck her.

"You ready?" Legend asked.

I know Jazzy didn't, Legacy thought. "Nope."

"Fuck you mean?" Legend didn't know what the fuck was wrong with this broad.

"What the fuck I said!" She snapped back.

Chapter Twelve

I recognize your fragrance (Hol 'Up) you ain't even gotta say shit/I know your taste is a little bit, mmmh, high maintenance/Everybody else basic, you live life on an everyday basis/with Poetic Justice/If I told you that a flower could bloom in a dark room, would you trust me..

Only reason I'm in this truck right now, is on the strength of Jazzy, legacy kept saying over and over in her head, as she sat on the passenger side of the Range Rover. From the very moment she got in the car, she been pretending to be captivated by her phone. But that was only a front. It was taking everything in her, to fight the urge to stare at Legend. They always said, social media was the best escape from the real world. So Legacy went to sending out Twitter posts in rapid succession.

"This nigga I'm with got me feeling some type of way. I'm 'bout ready to put his name on my rear end #NoLicensePlate #Don'tAskI'mNotTellin #I'mJustBeingHonest

Legacy re-read her last Twitter post over again, trying to figure out, what had made her post that. Whatever it was, it had her page going crazy everybody wanted to know who the hell she was with. Every time they asked, she just retweeted her previous hashtag, #Don'tAskI'mNotTellin.

She had to admit, the ride wasn't going how she thought it would go. For some foolish reason, she thought Legend would be trying to spit game at her the whole way there. But it wasn't nothing close to that. He hadn't said a word to her, since they pulled away from Z's. It was kind of like, he had forgot she was even in the truck with him. Out of her twenty year, she had never been insecure as an ordinary broad.

Fuck how he view you, Legacy's conscience tried to convince her, you got a man. But that shit wasn't working. Fuck it, she finally allowed her eyes to ream towards the driver side. Legend was leaned on the door, with his right hand on the steering wheel, with what had to be his fifth blunt clutched between his fingers. He was smoothly bobbing his head to the sounds of Kendrick Lamar. Before she could roll her eyes away from him, he had briefly glanced her way when he switched hands on the steering wheel, so he could hit his blunt.

"I know you be driving your parent's cars." Legacy said trying to regroup from being caught staring.

Legend hit his signal light, preparing for his upcoming turn. "You done seen me in three cars. Two of them were mine. If you knew about me, you would keep your mouth closed."

"Why is you so rude? You're the first mamma's boy I've met, who doesn't have any manners." Legacy retorted.

"Why is you so annoying?" Legend exhaled the O.G, making his turn.

"Excuse me," Legacy couldn't believe he'd just tried her like that.

Annoying?! I don't even talk e-fucking-nough, that little comment had her but nobody ever called her that.

"Why wouldn't you tell me your name?" Legend switched the conversation up. He was using a technique he'd learned from the player band book, his Pops made him read from the age of seven to seventeen.

'Knock a woman's mind off balance, so she'll trip. And before she fall, you catch her. She'll remember the catch. Not the fact, you were the one who originally caused her to lose balance... the words played in Legend s mind, as if he was reading them over again.

"It don't matter. Don't you know it now?" Legacy replied in her soft sweet voice. Something in her wanted to press him for elaboration on his *annoying* comment, but something stronger made her want his acceptance badder than an explanation.

"It do matter. I asked you, you never told me. I can't really determine if it's your name or not, until you tell me out your own mouth." Legend pulled some more smoke into his lungs.

"Yes, my name is Legacy. Is you happy now?" Legacy raked her fingers through her hair.

"Nickname or real name?" Legend asked.

"My freaking real name. Is Legend your real name?" she rhetorically asked.

"Yeah," he replied. What's your middle name?"

"Hmmm. It seem like you're trying to get to know me." Legacy couldn't hold the smile in.

Shares in Twitter lust became available at twenty-six dollars. What you think the IP will be?" Legend asked switching the course of the conversation again.

"Probably a billion .Maybe 1.2 billion. IDK, you the one who know all this investment stuff. But dang, I didn't even know the stock had came open for it. That would be a good investment." Legacy was thinking about hollering at her mother about buying a couple of shares.

"That's the same thing people thought about MySpace? If you would of invested in Myspace." Legend pointed out an example of how things could go up and down.

"Depending on how early an investor I was, it would at been a good investment. At the early to mid-stages, I would of gained major profit before the company bottomed. Did it bottom?" Legacy hoped she was sounding as relevant and logical, as he was.

"If you was my adviser, at what point would have told me to pull out?" Legend grinned at the way his question sounded.

"Before I got- never mind. Haha." Legacy laughed. "But probably as soon as I seen the way Facebook was sprouting. What would you have done?" Legacy asked.

"That really makes sense. But I would of bought me. A pound of weed, and smoked until I forgot about investing in anything but some cigars and a lighter." Legend joked, as he turned down the road heading to Wendall's all service car shop.

"Yeah, right. I bet you was in all the extra after school programs. What school you went to? I went to Rosa Parks Academy. You know the all-girl school in North Carrollton. You smoke too much." Legacy was becoming so comfortable, her mouth was just running. She didn't even realize "The catch" had actually been the beginning of her "Fall."

"You still fuck with your dude?" Legend noticed the way she had attempted to slide in his personal space so he pulled out and switched it up on her.

"Why you want me to tell you all about me, and you won't tell me nothing about you? That isn't how it work." Legacy for that question. There wasn't no truth or lie in her answer.

"Get the best of you." Legend quoted half of one of Jay-Z's bars, leaving the other half in his head.

"But I never put my all in." Legacy surprised him, by finishing Jay –Z's bar from Mya's Best of Me remix.

"Really?" she rolled her eyes at him.

Hell yeah. Look I'll be right back." Legend parked the truck at the top of Wendell's. He didn't want to drive down the dirt road. He'd just got the truck washed.

"I'm getting out too." Legacy opened up her door about to get out until she seen it was a dirt road. "I'll wait."

"I know that's right." Legend laughed at her closing the door.

Legacy sat in the truck patiently waiting for Legend to return. Her sorority sisters were blowing her phone up trying to find out what dude was she with. It was getting so ridiculous. She had to tell them she was only joking. Just doing something to make Twitter exciting. They wasn't going for it though. Even Jazzy had offered her two cents by posting: Really?!@IAmLegacy I told you to #BeCareful

To get all the attention off at her, she text Jazzy, and told her to delete her post. Jazzy had asked a couple questions. But she was way off with her assumptions, she was jumping to conclusions for real. When she asked her, what she thought about, Legend? She kept it all the way real, and told her, that she was attracted to him in every way. But she was loyal to Triple Cross. All Legend was, was a good look...a damn good look he was. Being in the kind of relationship she was in, Jazzy, saluted what Legacy had said, Real bitches don't jump ship.

"What up, Mr. Wendall?" Legend stuck his hand out for the man who maintained all his cars.

"How you doing. Mr. Carter? I didn't think you was going to come today. Follow me." Wendell shook Legend's hand talking a mile a minute.

"'You know I love my cars." Legend ducked his head, stepping out the small office buildings following Wendall to the car shed.

"I already know. You're just like your daddy and brother when it comes to them cars. I remember how your brother, Loyalty, use to do it. What that was 05...Wendall trailed off, trying to remember.

"Yeah,'05. That boy brought me a different box Chevy or Cutlass to fix up every other month. But here goes your baby!" Wendall snatched the cover off of the eighty- six Monte Carlo SS.

"You're an animal with this shit Mr. Wendall." Legend walked around the car totally smitten by the beautiful work of art. "Fuckin right, he thought. He had put together another show stopper. The white paint on the SS had so many clear coats on it you literally would expect your hand to be wet after you touched the car. The black checker board racing flag that was flying from the front of the car (in a light fade) to the tail of the car (getting darker) looked just as wet.

"You see how I did your roofing? This the first time I've did a panoramic top like this. Instead of taking metal dividers out, I just ordered some chrome ones. They'll coordinate with your rims and the steering wheel," Wendall explained.

Legend ranned his hand across the glass top. He had to do this to them. Wasn't no way around it. From the very moment he heard about a nigga taking the original top off of a hard top, and replacing it with the clear glass, he had to be one of the first around his way to do it. Legend stepped back and admired the whole car. The custom made twenty-four inch chrome out racing wheels, he'd copped from Baily's Rim shop, was hitting just right.

"I dipped your motor in chrome also. It's showroom ready. I put the four-hundred big block in there. You got the stall kit, the snatch kit and positive retraction. The interior just like you wanted it. The white leather race car seats, black trim, chrome gear shift in the floor. Wendell slammed the hood down.

"I gotta be the hardest in the garage." Legend bragged looking down the line at the other cars that was still under the covers.

"In the Chevy market I got to give it to you. But I got a couple muscles that's killing it. Matter of fact I'm working on a GTO for your Pops, completely restored." Wendall took his rag and wiped his prints off of the hood.

"Oh yeah? Let me check it out." Legend wanted to see what Grand had going on. Whatever it was, it had to be official. Because his pops didn't even ride old schools any more. That fool stayed in foreigns, like he was in another country.

"He told me, not to show you. Ha! But I got to get back to work, kid. What you putting together next?" Wendall dropped the keys in Legend's palm.

"I don't know. Ol' head about to make me get a Mustang. How much I owe you?" Legend pulled out his mother's checkbook.

"Your father took care of the expenses." Wendall said waving him off as he walked out of the garage leaving the door up.

Legend let the Lambo doors up on the SS and got in the car. "I feel like Jeff Gordon in this muthafucker." he said letting the door down, cranking the car up. He tapped the gas lightly causing the engine to growl. The car jumped like a pitbull trying to get off the leash.

"Where the fuck is this boy at?" Soon as Legacy said that, she seen a glass top SS, driving slowly up the hill. Now whoever that is just took first place. Sorry Legend." Legacy couldn't take her eyes off the car that appeared to still be soak and wet. Due to the glare of the sun, she couldn't make out the face of the driver, she wish she was creative enough to put together a whip like the one she was looking at.

"Why you staring at me with your mouth wide open like that? Don't tell me this car make you feel some type of way too." Legend pulled up beside the truck ginning with a blunt hanging from his lips.

"You make me feel some type of way," Legacy replied honesty. She had never been afraid to speak her mind, so she wasn't about to start today.

"That's what you been wanting to say. I can make you feel a lot of different ways." Legend wasn't missing the chance this time- he went in for the kill.

"I got a boyfriend, Legend." Legacy could hear the regret in her own voice.

"What that gotta do with us fucking?" Legend boldly responded.

"What you- I know-" Legacy couldn't even get the words out her mouth she was so stunned. She couldn't believe Legend had come at her like she was some action. "I'm going to act like I didn't hear that. But you really got me fucked up."

"Don't act like you didn't hear it. Look, follow me to my house." Legend dropped the car into gear.

"I'm not going to your house. I'll follow you back to the campus." Legacy hopped over to the driver seat.

"What sense does that make? Just follow me so I can drop my car off. Then I'll take you back to the campus." Legend wasn't in the mood to be going back and forth with this girl.

"I told you what it was. I'm not following you to your house. I don't know you like that. You could be a rapist or something." Legacy knew she was being difficult for no reason. But he shouldn't have tried her like he did.

"I had on a pair of seventeen hundred dollar bifocals and still missed ten of you. You trippin. You talking to a nigga who forget bitches." Legend retorted with venom on his tongue.

"Nah, it's impossible for you to miss ten of me. Because there is only one of me. And the only reason, you forget bitches is because you fuck with worthless bitches." Legacy came back.

"Just drop the truck off at my momma's office. You know where the Carter's Visual Advertising firm is at? The tallest skyscraper in the city you can't miss it. It's uptown. She'll take you wherever you need to go." Legend crunk the music and floored the gas pedal.

"Little spoiled fuck!" She yelled, shaking her head and laughing to herself. She crunk the truck up and started to follow behind Legend before he got too far away. No wonder he get all this shit, she think. His people own the biggest Advertising Firm in this area. "Little boy don't even know, I move bricks for real." I'll drop a kilo on your head boy, she playfully thought.

Chapter Thirteen

(Weeks later)

Triple Cross stepped out of the barber shop brushing the little pieces of hair off his pants. This was his second the streets, after sitting in the county jail for 17 months awaiting trial. Thanks to the lawyer, Legacy had snatched up for him, he had got acquitted of all charges after his nine day trial. He was definitely thanking the game God for the blessing. Lord knows he wasn't trying to see the pen… like a needle in the hay stack.

Now, that he was back on the turf, all them same niggas who was stiffen him, while he was in the county, were the sane niggas who was kicking all that Damn, I'm glad you beat that shit, lil bruh. Hit my line if you need something, shit. You already know how them fuck niggas play it. But it was all good, Triple had a game plan.

Riding around the block, bumping lil Boosie, Triple smoked camel after camel, and peeped the scene. Not much had changed since he'd been gone. A couple new cars here, some new freaks where the old ones used to be, a few niggas up who used to be down. But other than that ain't shit changed. But shit defiantly was about to change. And you better believe, Triple about to play cashier.

After riding around the whole black, he finally made it to his hood the third ward A.K.A The Nolia. It seemed like forever since he'd been in his stomping grounds. A smile instantly spreaded across his face, as he read the words that had been spray painted over the Magnolia Gardens sign. Only the killers survive.

Them was exactly Triple's sentiments, where the "Killers" had been sprayed "Strong" had been crossed out.

Only the strong survive, Triple thought shaking his head. Back in the days that use to be the motto of the hood. Some shit them old school niggas were living by back in the 70's, 80's and 90's. It was a new era now. The 90 babies was slowly but surely taking over the hood. And in the process of doing so, they were establishing new rules.

In this new era, you wasn't nobody until you kill somebody. Fuck all that strong shit. Strength wasn't no fucking Survivor Kit this wasn't boxing, bullets didn't have a designated weight class. Big small, or tall - you fuck around and get caught under that gun, your strong ass was going to be on first name basis with the reaper that's why in Triple's eyes it was killed or be killed.

Triple was the true definition at being a product of his environment. Everything about him was Third Ward. To him the world wasn't no bigger than the third. Out of his twenty-one years, he'd never resided anywhere else. This was where he was born and raised. His mother was from the first section of the Third, and his pops was from the second section (AKA the middle) of the third. But him and his older brother was raised in the third section by their grandmamma. So, although they were born in the middle, Cutter Homes (A notorious projects in the third section also known by Cut throat City) had adopted them like they were there. But you might as well say they were. They had moved out there when they were still in the single digits.

A lot of older people mainly his grandma often tell him, when his mother was still alive he was a different person. But who wouldn't change after some shit like that? It wasn't no feeling inside of Triple. He'd lost his pops to the streets, his mother was a victim of AIDS, and he lost his brother to the gun. What the fuck did he have to be happy about? The world had been so cold to him at a young age, he didn't have no choice, but to freeze over. He wasn't crying about it, though. Two tears in a bucket: It was the life they chose.

With his forty in his lap and a camel between his lips, he cruised through the 100-400 block of the 'Nolia, bobbing his head up and down to Boosie. To another set of eyes the scene he was viewing would be viewed as adnormal; but to him the scene was one of mystic beauty. And he wasn't saying that because it was scantily clad women parading up and down the strip, trying to peddle their product. Nawl, it was beautiful to him, because this was home, this was how you was welcome into the Nolia. They did say the first impression was the best impression.

The 100-400 block (AKA the first section) was where his momma was from. This was her stomping ground. His mother had did everything under the sun in the first section. She'd sold pussy, pimped other hoes, robbed tricks, and set up a coke trap. Most people thought that his mother had contracted HIV from selling pussy, but that wasn't true. She had contracted the virus from being raped.

He still could feel the rage in his heart, just thinking about the day his mother told him the story in her weak voice. From that moment on he'd developed a hate so deep for rapist. Hitler's hate for the Jewish couldn't even match up to it. This single story would be the cause behind him and his brother first body at the youthful age of 10 and 14.

Back in the days the first section use to be a real hoe stroll, controlled by the pimps. But now it was a little different. All the pimps had been chased out of the Nolia by the new generation.

In the eyes of the 90's baby's the pimps was viewed as easy licks, so it sorta became a trend. Whenever a nigga needed some paper, they'd just go to the first section and rob a pimp. You already know after a while shit started to augment and the pimps started to strike back. It didn't take but for one young cat from the middle of the Third to get shot by a pimp, for shit to go from this to that. In a blink of an eye pimps started coming up missing. A lot of them was found slumped behind the wheel of their hog.

The beef with the pimp's was one of the things that marked the beginning of the 90 baby's terror on the Third. Being more into the hustle back then, Triple had missed out on catching some free bodies...but, boy would that change.

Other than the demise of the pimp's, everything was still the same. The hoes was still on the stroll, but they were doing their own thing. Triple was glad the pimps had been barred from the hood. In his eyes Pimp's was the lowest of the lows. Nothing but a lazy ass nigga who can't get it from the mud, so he played on women's weakness for his come up some called a hustle, but he wasn't agreeing with that fuck shit.

Triple observed the scene as bitches paraded up and down the strip and out of cars, and up and down the strip of the many hoe houses that lined the busy strip. Still to this day the first section was the section of the whole Third that got the most traffic. Mainly because this was the only section of the Third, that allowed people from outside the Third to come to the Third. Any other part, you better have a G-Pass. But all day and night, women and men from all walks of life crept through the first section and cop a little satisfaction. At any given time you could come through the first section and cop you a raw dime. Or of it float your boat, you could get both.

See just like the first section was a pussy and trap, it was also a powder trap. That's why it was nick named 'the P Stroll' because that's all was sold in the first section. Pussy and powder. Triple remembered the times, him and his lil cRew would take the cut from Baisley all the way up to P-Stroll. This would be after one of them nights they'd been done hit one of their older brother's stash, and had a couple of hundred to their name. Young with the hot nuts, the first thing that came to their mind, was going to the P-Stroll and get some pussy. They wasn't no more than eleven or twelve back then. You could do a survey around the Third, and ask every young nigga who they lost their virginity to, and I bet you ninety -five percent of them say some bitch off the P-Stroll. That was the good thing about prostitutes, they didn't care about age.

Crossing over to the 500 - 900 block (AKA The middle) it was a different scene. This was the zombie land and the name was self explanatory once you seen the dope fiends all over the place. Some was even on the side of the road in a nod. And a couple feet away, you could find one trying to find a vein. This was the home of the Herain. Didn't nothing get moved in the middle but that boy. This was the section he was originally from. The middle had produced a lot of rich niggas. Niggas that was known for getting money anyway, but that was mainly off of the middle's reputation.

Back in the days, there use to be some apartments called, Shatter Place. This was the section his Pops was from. Through the blessing of the ol' head who use to run the hood, his parents had ranned Shotter Place with an iron fist. Shotter Place had produced some official niggas. But then them fools wasn't getting any respect from the new generation. Maybe a couple of the ol' heads. But the other niggas who was running around screaming that OG shit wasn't getting no respect. The old Shooter Place had been burned down in Ninety-one. Young niggas coming we these days didn't wanna hear about what use to be. Only thing a nigga knew about Shatter Place was it was the spot to find some easy pussy. The new Shotter Place was filled with young hoes living on section eight.

In the 'Nolia (Third ward) all that "I done did" shit don't mean nothing. Trying to get a 90 baby to hear that shit was like talking to a deaf man, they wasn't trying to hear about nothing they didn't witness. Reputation got your ass nowheRe. Either you was doing it or you wasn't plain and simple.

Finally making it to the 1000 - 1400 block (AKA, 3rd and Grand) Triple started to feel completely in his comfort zone. This was his part of the hood. This was the third and final section of the part of Magnolia Blvd that ranned through the Third Ward (Magnolia Gardens) The Third section was the heartbeat of the Nolia.

When you heard of the third section of the Nolia, you thought of two things: death and being cut throated. 3rd and Grand had a reputation that went everywhere they went. And that mutha-fuckah even showed up in places they never went. You can go to another state and niggas still knew about 3rd and Grand, soon as you tell 'em you from Carrollton. The first thing they going to ask you is, is you from the Third Ward and when you tell 'em you is they gon ask about Grand and Cutter Homes (AKA Cutthroat City) the most infamous and dangerous projects in the whole city. Niggas and bitches from Third Grand was arrogant and didn't give a fuck. And they made sure you knew it.

3rd and Grand was the home of the most official ol' heads in the whole city. As a matter-of-fact the third section was named after one of the ol' heads. 3rd and Grand. The 3rd represented the third section. The third ward and Grand represented the Ol' head, Hundred Grand. If the third was the heartbeat of the hood, ol' head, Grandman was the heart and soul of the whole city. Plus a nigga called it Grand, because when the ol' head was still running the hood, everything was grand for real.

Now days shit was different on 3rd Grand. Whereas back in the days everybody was all about their paper. Now niggas wasn't trying to keep count of nothing but their bodies. You wasn't nobody if you didn't have no bodies. Hands down 3rd and Grand held the Nolia down 3Rd and Grand was the reason police didn't come through the Nolia in single patrol cars. And even when they came through deep, it still was going to be shots fired, so the police really must wait to catch you coming out of the Nolia. Till this day it was niggas posted up on the block, who'd been on the run for two-three years. Long as they stayed in the Nolia, they would stay free.

Triple beeped the horn at a couple of niggas standing on the corner of Clairmont & Magnolia Blvd, as he pulled through the entrance of cutthroat City (Cutter Homes) they didn't know who he was, due to the five percent tints on his baby momma's black Acura.

"I gotta get some more fucking camels." Triple mumbled taking the keys out of the ignition, tossing the empty box of cigarettes in the passenger seat. Tucking the glock forty, after putting one in the chamber, he got out of the car. He knew he couldn't get caught slipping. Even though he had love in his hand, it was some niggas who hated him also. Triple didn't play fair. It was anybody can get it with him. He didn't give a fuck if it was a nigga from the third. If a nigga had it, and he wanted it, then he was going to get it.

Triple Cross was a tall, skinny, brown skin nigga who looked seventeen instead of twenty-one. His lack of facial hair made him look a lot younger than he was. Triple had a mouth full of solid gold teeth. A lot of people said he resembled the deceased New Orleans rapper, Soulja Slim and that was a crazy coincidence, because Soulja Slim was his favorite rapper. That was the reason his hood had nicknamed him, Magnolia slim. Him being from the Nolia, being tall and Slim, and a certified cutthroater like the Magnolia Slim (Soulja Slim), the name fitted him perfectly.

See the Third ward was a community that consisted of about fifty- five blocks. The correct same of the neighborhood was Magnolia Gardens. Back in the 80's the ol' heads just had started calling the hood the Third Ward. That was around the time they had put the city on the map as the murder capital. At first they had stated calling the hood baby New Orleans. But a nigga had took a trip to the Nolia aad seen what was really going on. One trip to the Third Ward Of New Orleans and it was a no brainer. From that day forward the hood was dubbed: the Third Ward.

"I send this out to the dopeman (yeah, I miss you) who bumping this in Federal Prison, I got no love for these bitches..." Triple walked out of the candy lady's apartment rapping, with a grenade juice in hand. He strolled through the bricks with no worries. He knew some niggas from the hood was salty about what happen to Ken-Ken and Lil Earl. Only thing he could tell them about that was, Nigga get out your feelings.

"Hey Triple!" a group of females chimed as he walked pass the park. Triple Cross finished chewing the Salt and Vinegar chips, and took a swig at his juice.

"What's good? Fuck you looking at me like that for, Shant?" he asked the girl who was sitting on the swing mugging him.

"You didn't see my text message last night?" Shant asked.

"Hell no." Triple Cross lied. He had seen all sixteen of them mutha-fuckers. He wasn't trying to fuck Shant on his first night out. He didn't even want to fuck Legacy, but he had to fuck with her. He owed her that much, after she had helped get him that lawyer. Plus she had stacked up a little cash for him. Now he was on some diffcrcnt shit. It seemed like jail had boasted his pussy rate. Especially with the grown bitches.

Shant rolled her eyes at him. "You's a fucking lie."

"Iight." he shrugged his shoulders. "Call me later tonight. I'm tryna see you. You fucking with me?" Just because he didn't want to fuck her the other night, that didn't mean he wasn't trying to fuck her tonight. Shant lil thick ugly ass had some good pussy.

"Where you gone be at? Cause I'm not about to be blowing your line up. You got Tasha for that." Shant retorted with a half attitude.

"Just call." Triple said walking off. The bricks was booming. But that wasn't nothing out the ordinary. Cutthroat city was the biggest projects in the whole entire city. Every second of the day it was something going on in the bricks.

"My nigga, Slim, what it is?" Fat Chris greeted Triple, soon as he stepped in the breezeway.

Triple dapped Fat Chris and Ghost up. "Shit. What the fuck you got going on?" he walked up a couple of stairs and sat down.

"Shit." Fat Chris pulled a vial out his pocket, serving a fiend. "Tryna get this fucking paper."

"Nigga, I'm glad you whooped that case. These crackers was counting you out, Slim." said sparking up a blunt.

Triple kicked his leg out and put his Pistol and Phone in his lap, so he could be more comfortable, Ghost and Fat Chris was his niggas from way back. Just like him they both were from The Middle, but had migrated to 3rd and Grand as an adolescent. Back in the days it used to be him, Ghost, Fat Chris, and Double Cross against everybody, when they all moved to 3rd & Grand, they had to fight every day to prove themselves. It didn't matter that they were from the Nolia. They wasn't born in the third section.

But shit had changed for them when they clicked up with a couple of youngin's from 3rd & Grand, who name was carrying weight. Plus the ol' head Grandman had taken a liking to Triple Cross. That is all it took. Back in the days Grandman was like a fad in the third. All he had to do was say, "Be," and it was. Still to this day ol' head Grand still had the same clout in the whole City, he just wasn't using it anymore. Ol' head was on some Corporate shit. You didn't see Grand unless you went through the business district of the city, or if you just so happen to venture downtown to one of them five star restaurants, you're liable to see Grand and one of his business associates sharing over-priced steaks.

Now days shit was different. The young niggas ranned the Nolia. Most of the Ol' heads had left the third for a nice spot on South Beach. It was a few who was still dropping the work in the third, but most of them had passed the torch. All of them old mother-fuckers was stuck in their ways, and the game had changed. So instead of changing with it - they moved away from it.

"You already know how that shit be." Triple spit over the rail, landing a glob of spit on the door of someone's apartment. "When Lil Reek get out?"

"I think bruh got about thirty more days." Fat Chris replied.

"Niggas hate to see a real nigga on top. But when that rat ass nigga, Troy, touched down they threw a fucking block party.

"Aye, do y'all got any more of that last shit?" a fiend cut in on Ghost.

Fat Chris pulled the vials out his packet. "What you trying to get, Amy?"

"I just want a blast." Amy scratched her arm, pulling some crumpled bills out her sock.

Triple phone started vibrating in his lap. It took him a minute to realize it was ringing. Watching Chris and Ghost make that hand over fist money, had him recollecting on the days he used to be right there with them, sharing the traps. His hustling days seemed like something from another lifetime, he'd gotten so deep in the taking game.

"What you want bruh?" Triple answered rudely.

"Excuse me!?" legacy soft voice boomed through the speakers.

"Man, I ain't trying to go through all that what's up?" Triple retorted, instantly feeling aggravated.

"What the fuck you got an attitude for, Triple?" Legacy snapped. She didn't know what the fuck was wrong with Triple, but he had been acting funny every since he'd gotten that money from her.

"Because you keep calling my fucking phone. I already know you don't want shit." Triple snapped back.

"It doesn't matter what I want. I'm your girlfriend. Or have you forgot about that?"

"Iight. I'm on the phone now. What up?" Triple asked.

"I thought you was coming over today? I miss you." Legacy said.

Triple held the phone with his shoulders, plucking a camel out the pack. "Give me a light, Ghost."

"You need to stop smoking them Cancer sticks." Legacy said hearing him inhale the smoke.

Triple flicked the ash and blew the smoke out. "Aye, umma call you back later.

"Why you keep trying to rush me off the phone? Damn! What's up with you." Legacy yelled.

"Man, get off my line with all that." Triple was stiff on all that emotional shit. "You must be on your period? All that PMS-ing." He mumbled.

"Bring me something to eat." Legacy asked.

"You got a car. Go get your own food. I'm in the hood."

"And what that suppose to mean? You act like there isn't a thousand fast food restaurants in the third ward. Just say you don't want to do it.

Legacy was really on the verge of giving up on this shit with Triple. "I'm gone." Triple ended the call.

"Aye, who that pulling up in that white 750 Li?" Fat Chris looked out the breezeway.

"Oh, that's yo boy Toot. Potnah done caught a grip."

Triple sat back and watched the dread headed man step out the BMW, draped in Linen threads and diamonds, this be the same Cutter Homes, he thought, as niggas and bitches flocked to Toot. I know shit ain't changed this much.

"Niggas must not be cut throating anymore?" Triple asked. Wasn't no way Toot was pulling up in Cutthroat City like that.

"Yeah, he was from the bricks, but that shit never stopped nothing.

"Bruh, you must done took your ear from the streets? Toot got the whole Third behind him, Dude putting everybody on. Shawty, showing love for real." Ghost said.

Fat Chris just smacked his teeth. "C'on man. You just saying that cause you working for that fuck nigga." Fat Chris didn't fuck with Toot, But he wasn't no gunslinger. He wasn't no hoe either. He just was a hustler.

"You walking for that soft ass nigga, Ghost?" Triple asked in disbelief.

"Quit trying me, Chris.'" Ghost snapped. "Hell Nawl, I don't work for nobody. Bruh just be fronting me the work.

"Same difference. You working, nigga." Fat Chris pressed on, not letting up.

Triple shook his head. "He must be giving you a double cup? You know buddy is pussy.

Before Ghost could respond, Toot stepped through the breezeway with a bag slung over his shoulder and his phone glued to his ear. "Look, get that shit together. I'll be through later on." Toot ordered before disconnecting the call. When he noticed Triple Cross sitting on the steps, his heart skipped a beat. He didn't even know the young nigga was out. He played it cool though. But in his heart, he hated Triple. He knew that nigga was guilty on the murders of Ken-Ken and Lil Earl. And like a real bitch ass nigga, he was hoping that Triple got fried on them charges. Now he was contemplating putting a ticket on his head. But he knew he would have to go out of the Third Ward to get that done. As much as they hated him, the Nolia loved Magnolia Slim. But the young nigga was a fucking problem.

"Triple, what up, Lil bruh?" Toot asked wishing he would of left his jewelry in the car. Plus he had two hundred grand in the Louie bag slung across his shoulders. He knew it wasn't too many niggas that would try him in Cutthroat City -Well on the Nolia period. But he knew Triple was one of the select few who would. Triple didn't have a conscience. No matter who you was, who you knew or where you were from -Triple Cross would get at you.

Triple could smell the fear on Toot. For a minute he was pondering should he lay the nigga down in the breezeway. He already knew it was some work in the bag. But them seventeen months in the county had him doing a little more thinking. Fuck that he wasn't trying to see the bing again. True enough he loved the robbing game, but that shit carried too much time. He had to switch the game up. Instead of taking the money, he was about to apply pressure for it. The press game didn't carry a bit of time.

"You already know, big bruh. I'm playing it cool, cause these suckers got me hot, ya feel me?!'" Triple replied.

"Fuckin right. You good? Why you didn't hit a nigga while you was in the county. Toot fronted, knowing damn well he'd rejected every call from Triple. He'd even changed his number.

This bitch know he was screening my calls. It's all good, umma let 'em think he playing me. "BRuh, you know a nigga don't be trying to call nothing but some hoes. Hell nawl, I ain't good. Ain't shit in my pockets but some lent. You fucking with me?" Triple played his position. This was part of his press. Ask but really demand.

Toot looked at his phone. "C'mon, what kind of question is that? You know I'm fuckin with you you lil bruh. Aye, Ghost, you done with that last package?"

"Hell yeah. I'm ready to re-up. I got the paper up front. I'm good on the front tip." Ghost said.

"Say no more. Just give that paper to Lil bruh. I'm about to get it Ready for you. What up, Fat boy?" Toot knew Fat Chris didn't fuck with him, but he didn't give a fuck. It was all because Toot was fucking one of the same young hoes, Chris was fucking.

"You tell me." Fat Chris responded stiffly.

"I got you." Ghost said.

"I got that lil paper on me now."

"That's what's up. Aye, just get at me, Triple." Toot took off towards the back of the building. This would be his last time using this spot. Everything in the spot would be moved before night fall.

"How much you owe him?" Triple asked Ghost. "Who the fuck he fucking with in the back?"

"I cut him five bands. Here." Ghost went in his pocket and counted out the paper. "He fucking that hoe Missy."

"Noooo!" Triple exclaimed. "'Don't she got a baby by Ken-Ken?"

"Hell yeah. And Mylito from High street, you know how we do." Ghost informed.

"Fuck them High Street niggas. I thought lil Ken-Ken was Toot mans and them." Triple stated sarcastically.

"You know how a nigga play when it comes to them hoes. What is up with old girl you had moving work for you?"

Triple stood up, stuffing the Money in his baggy LRG jeans, and putting the glock back in his waist line. "Fuck that hoe bitch. Umma get up with y'all fools later." he dapped them up and walked out of the breezeway.

Chapter Fourteen

‘These young niggas thought, I fell out the loop/Cause the last time I hopped out coupe/I hopped out in a suit Grandman leaned the pot to the side, trying to stretch the yoyo as far as he could. It had been so long since he had an egg beater in his hand, it felt kind of funny. But that unusual. Soon as he seen the work locking up, he took a fork and hit in the middle. He did that to kill the air bubbles.

"Look at this nigga, Jay, frontin, tryna take my shine, I ain't say this verbally, just had some shit on my mind plus um puffin on like a O more than I use to puff, it got me taking some advice from people who ain't use to stuff, it got me taking advice from people who ain't use to stuff. They got me feeling like I'm the one who move the stuff, while he ride around in brand new coupe's and stuff, they had me practically hating his guts as he approached, Jigga, what up?" Grandman rapped along with Memphis Bleek's verse on Jay-z's "Coming of Age part 2", as he dropped the coke and baking soda in the pot.

He took his egg beater and whooped the now foamy substance, until it fell flat. This was Grandmans element. He was at his best at times like this. This was what he was made for. If he couldn't do nothing else, he could take a sixty-two to one-twelve. Everything he ever wanted in life he got it from the pot. Everything his family ever wanted in life, he got it for them from the pot. Even when he retired from the dope game, he still used what he got from the pot to build his unbreakable empire.

Now here he was, back in the pot. But now he was here for a different reason. It was no explanation why he-a ten million dollar nigga (in cold cash) with a net worth of fifty-two million- was back slanging bricks. His logics was his logic. He needed something and he knew how to get it. Simple as that.

Grandman had planned this, before he actually did it. He had everything mapped out from day one. He knew he couldn't slip. He had too much to lose. The main name of the game was calculation. Adding, subtracting, multiplying and dividing his every move. Making sure everybody around him moved to the same beat. Long as you sealed every crack there was no room for mistakes.

Holding the pot in the sink, Grand now splashed cold water into the pot, so the fresh water could push the dissolved coke and Baking soda to the bottom of the pot.

Grandman had been at this all day. He'd left home this morning with his wife thinking he was about to clock into one of his many businesses. She just didn't know. He was clocking in alright. But this was the business she would never know about. His wife would go crazy if she knew her husband was locked up in a stash house full of dope, money and guns. The niggas from the Third ward would go crazy too. But both of them would be two different kind of crazies.

"Speaking of the devil," Grand smiled seeing his wife face pop up on the picture ID. He went head and finished what he was doing, before be answered the phone.

"Carter," he answered teasing his wife. He knew she hated when he answered his phone professionally for her.

"Don't Carter me. Lolette checked him. "What are you doing? Is you bringing me dinner?"

Grandman checked the time on his Rolex. "Damn, it's almost six o'clock why you still at the office?" he had really lost track of time. I guess cooking up ninety- two ounces could be real time consuming he thought.

Lolette started snapping orders to someone in the background. "You must be inside a room with no lights or cable?"

Grand looked around at the kitchen that contained nothing but boxes of Baking soda, triple beam scales, wrapping bricks, the wrap from unwrapped bricks, and a CD case full of Jay-Z CD's sitting on top of a little CD player.

Other than that, his wife was on point.

"You wouldn't believe. But what's going on?" Grand asked, dropping the work inside of large Ziploc bags.

"The LGBT is attacking us behind the "No Homo" comment Legend made at the E.K.A.C event last week. It's all over the news. Two companies have pulled out on us already. They're saying we're secretly raising our son to be homophobic. This shit is stressing me. I guess I'm feeling the wrath because I'm at Central Office of the Carter Advertising Firm. You need to come down here," Lolette had turned instantly hysterical.

Grand scratched his head trying to make sense of what his wife was telling him. He couldn't be hearing her correctly. Something wasn't right. "You joking, right?"

"When have I ever played about something like this? The LGBT is trying to get all of our businesses boycotted."

"What?! Who the fuck they think they fucking with? Them cross dressing muthafuckers better get the fuck out of my way.

Serious shit. What the fuck they mean, we're secretly causing our son to be homophobic? Ain't no secret about that shit. What we suppose to do? Raise him to openly accept gays? Fuck NO! That's not what the bible teaches.

"Matter-of-fact go through our employee roster every mutherfucker you run across who sexual preference is under question fire that mutherfucker. I don't give a fuck how long they been working for us. X that muthafuckahá! What's the dude name that work at Carter's International?" Grand was fuming

"Who are you talking about baby? It's three hundred and sixty-two people employed through Carter's International" Lola knew her husband was pissed off.

"Fuck it, fire every suspect mutha-fucker who work there. Especially the marketing director. Yeah, that's who I'm talking about. What's his fucking name?

Terry-Jerry - Kerry." Lolette searched her brain for the dudes name. She knew exactly who her husband was talking about. He did act a little too feminine.

"I don't give a fuck! Cancel that mutha-fuckah. And make it known that I'm firing every gay mother-fucker who work under the Carter brand. Pussy mutha-fuckers." Grand was pacing back and forth in the kitchen. He had to take deep breaths before he exploded.

"Calm down, babe, we can't abandon our professionalism. I know you going to handle the situation however you see fit. But lets continue to react rationally. whatever you decide to do I'm behind you. Lolette said.

"Beside me. Never behind me." Grandman did in a much calmer voice. He ranned his hand over his face and sighed. "Look, double up on advertisement for the E.KA.C event.Triple up on every thing that got to do with the Carter brand. I don't give a fuck if you go over-board on everything. Put together a give-a-way. Where is legend?"

Lolette felt a lot better now that her husband was in the picture calling all the shots. "Say it and it's done. I haven't talked to Legend. He probably somewhere stoned. Blind to the world and it's many troubles, you know your son.

"Call him, Aye, lets" he was interrupted by the beeping of his line.

"Aye, this one of our financial advisers. I'll call you soon as I end the call."

"Love you, I'm about to piss off the world for you."

"It don't matter. We're already rich we can do what we want to do our empire is unbreakable. I love you back. "Grand replied.

"I know, I know. But we gotta be smart, so we can stay rich, that's the only reason I'm being cautious. You just don't know, a war with gay people cost a lot of money. Hehehe." Lolette giggled.

Grand walked we to the table that was stacked with money and kilo's. "Don't worry about money, babe. We can lose every thing today, and we'll still be millionaires for the rest of our days on God's green earth you believe in me, don't you?"

"Isn't twenty-four years proof enough for you? you don't have to convince me you can do it. I've seen you do it. But go ahead and handle your business. Call me right back."

"Say no more." Grand went through his recent calls and dialed his last missed call back.

She think she done seen me do it, Grand think as the phone ring. She ain't never seen me buy a quarter to eight just off of the wrist game. Long as I got my hands we gon be Rich Forever, baby.

"Matthew Francis." A preppy voice answered.

"Matty, what's going on bud? This Carter." Grand was all business now.

"Carter, where the hell you been, man? The whole world is looking for you. We took some major hits today. Matty sounded more hysterical than Lolette.

This muthafukah might be a sissy. Cause he definitely sounding like a bitch, "Heyy I had to have a sit down with some brick masons. I'm working on laying some bricks on my new foundation. Heard I got some drag queens trying to tear my old one down. Tell me something good Matty." Grand played with his words. Speaking a lingo the lilly white boy couldn't understand.

"Tell you something good?! Man, we lost 2.5 million dollars in ten minutes." Matty exclaimed, throwing a stack of papers across the room.

"2.5 Million?! Spheww." I gotta triple up my re-up next time, Grand thought. Somebody taking a size at us huh?"

"A bite at us? More like they biting the hell out of us. We gotta do something!" Matty said.

Grand wanted to laugh at Matty. It's nothing we can do. It's stocks and bonds. When you get into the business you got to be prepared to lose some, as well as win some. Who knows, maybe in the next ten minutes we'll gain 5.5 million. It's your job to make the right moves to get as back up. No matter how much we lose, you still going to get paid.

"TSK. I'm not going to get paid, you go broke. And the way the LGBT is calling for your blood- Carter blood-you'll be broke before the week is out. You got to get your son to make a public apology. That's the only thing I can see." Matty suggested.

"You can cancel that. My son is not about to apologize to a group of confused, misguided, morally neglected people. I don't see nobody apologizing to the fifteen year old kid who got a life sentence on his first offense. Or what about the girl who was a victim of rape? Oh, and lets not forget about all the kids who are born into starvation. Why the LGBT isn't pushing for apologies For Trayvon Martin? Oh because he wasn't a queer. They better re-consider, they got me misconstrued. I don't bend, break, or fold. Keep doing what you doing, Matty. Remember we're the ones who still clutch our nuts. Just keep me posted via Email, we'll have a face to face beginning of next week." Grand was exhausted from the useless conversation. Plus he still had 2.5 Million to make up for.

Matty sighed. "Will do, Boss. Talk to you later," Grand laid his phone down on the table on top of a quarter bird (Nine Ounces of cocaine/252 grams of cocaine) and next to a Desert Eagle (.50 cal)

"Yo" Grandman answered the phone on the first ring. "Young Mego, what's good?"

"I just copped a new Bentley, Ol' head. I dropped that handle. I'm handling foreign things now, bruh. Fuck up with you? This new hog head cost me a hundred K (100 thousand) thirty rows of V.V. S.S in my A.P. shouts out to Hundred Grand. I know you still on your hundred grand shit." Mego responded dressing the lingo up so good it coud be nominated for an ESBY award.

Grandman unzipped the leather Gucci duffle bag and started stuffing the bus with tightly wrapped kilo's of cocaine.The vibe was still so deep in his veins, he automatically picked up the coke talk. This was his native tongue. Although he was fluent in Spanish, French, Patois, Arabic, Kreoyle, and several other languages. He couldn't speak nothing as good as he could talk that chicken talk coded language when speaking about coke transaction over the phone. Language is used to elude any outside ears that could be listening in on the conversation. And it was also used to avoid a conspiracy charge.

To the naked ear it sounded like Mego was just talking some fly shit. But the real translation of what Mego was saying was. "I'm done with my re-up. I just dropped a quarter million off at the spot. And I found a plug on the EURO'S, so I dropped that other quarter million in your foreign account. Front me thirty keys of raw cocaine. Plus umma buy a hundred. You still front a nigga what he want it if he buy a hundred or better, right?"

The whole foreign exchange thing was a new move Grand was using. He made this rule for a very detrimental reason. Anybody could come to him with a half a million in U.S currency. But any nigga who had made it that far in the dope game, to where he was spending a half a million on his re-up and the only money he'd ever seen was American... then he was a man with limits. And niggas who lived within the boundaries was a nigga who would eventually become confined. And once he become entrapped he would become weak for emancipation, because he'd lived within the limits so long, he'll miss what he was being taking away from...cause he ain't did nothing with it. It's impossible for a nigga who ain't did shit to see the bigger picture.

Grandman was only dealing with bosses. Niggas who knew their reach was limitless. He wasn't about to catch a case fuckin with some stupid niggas who got money and went crazy. Them type of niggas worshipped money. Them type of niggas always had a price. They wanted the fame. Grandman didn't have time for that type shit. His attitude was, "you got a million dollars and you still in your home town year around?" Get out my face. A million dollar nigga with no passport? You gotta be on an undercover operation.

Grandman was taking risk with niggas who knew that money was only the escape route to a better destination. He was fucking with niggas who passport had been bleed on every time you traveled out of the country, Your passport got stamped) He was fucking with niggas who ordered their re-up, not picked it up. Whoever said you couldn't buy dope with your black card?

Grandman filled the second bag up and tossed it by the kitchen door along with the first one.

"Where you at?" Grand asked.

"I just touched down in Ireland." Mego replied. Grandman fucked with niggas who re-ed up from a different country. Niggas who moved keys without ever touching the piano. Every nigga on his team got shit done just by pressing a button.

"I got a watch with no diamonds, that cost a buck- fifty. Small head and the plastic band. I love my new Rolls Royce Wraith. How could you not be in love with a car that cost 300K? But for some fucking reason I can't stay out of my Phantom, maybe because the grill is mean, and the driver is the same color as the car. Did you dig that new Katy Perry song?" Grandman let the dressed up coke talk roll of his tongue with ease. (Translation; say no more. I got you a hundred and fifty keys. They wrapped small and tight in plastic. Look, this out of love, I'll give you 300 keys on consignment.Or you can get 400 keys. It's going to be laced in the grill of the car. A white person going to bring it to you. It's going to be a sophisticated looking white female.)

Mego was a young hustler, who'd Grandman had put under his wings, back in the days when he was still waist deep in the game. When Mego first started rolling for Grandman, he was only thirteen years old and slanging sacks of weed in his Jonesboro South neighborhood (a project in the zone 3 area of Atlanta) now look at him. He was making boss moves.

"Yeah, I fucked with it. But umma let Juicy J stay on that track. I'm gone, right. Just catch a diamond." Mego ended the call. (Translation. I'll take the 300 keys I'm good on the four. And just send the work to my bitch spot.)

After packaging all the work up for the rest of the people he had waiting on him, he locked the stash spot up. His right hand man, Marley, would be through to get the birds ready for the highway. It was the end of the day for him. He had to see what the fuck was going on with his son and wife. He could careless about all that other shit. Fuck the LGBT. Fuck the money. Fuck everybody and their feelings. All he cared about was his family.

"House of Beauty. This is cutie." Lolette answered the phone in vivacious manner.

Grandman chuckled, "I must get the wrong number. I was trying to call House of Booty and catch up with Judy." he joked push starting his Ferrari 458 Italia.

"Aha. In your dreams." Lolette responded.

Waiting for the garage door to rise up, he put the car in reverse. "Not even in my dreams. What got you feeling all elated?"

"Oh nothing. Where you at?" Lolette tossed her purse in the trunk of her M3 Beamer. "I'm missing you."

"I'm on my way to the office. But it seem like you got everything under control." You talked to Legend?" Grandman backed out of the garage letting the door back down. "I miss you back." he added.

"I was about to say, Lolette giggled. "No I haven't talked to him. He won't answer. You tried calling him."

"Nawl. He ain't answer for you, I know he ain't going to answer for me. I'll catch up with him later. You want me to bring you something to eat?"

Lolette maneuvered through the parking garage, talking to her husband on the car speaker. "Don't come to the office. We'll deal with that mess some other time. Let's meet at a secret location and pretend we're twenty-one again."

"Lets just meet at home, we're not twenty-one anymore. We're forty-five," Grandman teased. "You going to cook dinner?"

"You are such a lame, old man. All you want to do is sit in the house." Lolette put her large designer sunglasses on, as she pulled into the evening traffic. "No, I am not cooking. Have your chef do it." She joked.

"Meet me at the clear-port." Grandman said seriously.

"For what?" Lolette asked. "And I'm forty-two, sir."

"We're about to go to St. Tropez," I don't know who the fuck she calling old, Grand thought,

"What?! We can't just pick up and leave. We're in the middle of the business quarter."

"Ight then. Don't be kicking on that forever young shit. Is you cooking dinner?" Grandman called her bluff.

"Yes darling. I bet I'll beat you home." Lolette challenged.

Grandman sat at the light. "What's the bet?"

"Make it light on yourself. I got access to your bank accounts." Lola retorted. Damn, this light need to hurry up and change, she thought, drumming her finger on the steering wheel.

"You beat me there, I'll cook dinner for the next month." Grandman proposed.

Lola smacked her teeth. "TSK. Quit being cheap. You win. I'll buy you a Rolex."

"Big face rollie, solid gold with the vvs's, platinum with diamonds... whatever, I got ten of those. You gotta come with something better," he told bis wife.

"Two pinky rings. One black diamond. One blue diamond. Deal or no deal?" Lola wasn't planning on losing, she was just upping the ante so her husband would. She knew his weakness was pinky rings.

"Deal. If you beat me there, I'll buy you a new Hermès Birkin bag."

"It better cost fourteen racks, Bye." Lolette clicked on him.

"I'll see you at the finish line." Grand said outloud. He tossed his phone on the passenger seat, pressing the button to let his top down. Now that he was off the phone, he crank the music up.

♪ *Say hello to the bad guy/They say that i'mma bad guy/I come from the bottom/Now I'm mad fly/They say i'mma menace, that's the picture they paint/They say a lot about me/ Let me tell you what i ain't...* ♪

He smashed down on the gas, as Jay-Z smashed the track.

Too Be Continued in '*THE LEGACY CONTINUES*'

- **Scarred & Broken BY GOLD&JANELL Coming Summer 2022**

Chapter 1

Rocket was slouched back in the English white upholstery of the matte black Hell Cat, with a blunt of white runts clutched between his dark lips, as he bobbed his head to "Treacherous" by Lil Durk. Taking a deep drag from the blunt, Rocket grabbed the steering wheel and lifted up in his seat.

"Damn," he murmured when the wad of currency and .45, that was rested in the lap of his sand brown Gucci cargo pants, hit the floor; he had completely forgot he had put the shit in his lap. Scooting his seat back he retrieved the cash and strap from the floor of the car.

Opening the center console, he placed the dirty wad of unorganized U.S. currency inside it and closed it back. Increasing the volume of the music, sitting the gun back in his lap, Rocket got back in his zone.

♪ *...This shit Treacherous, this shit Treacherous, this shit Treacherous, this for the savages, this for the savages, this for the savages...* ♪

Boop, boop, boop...

An unexpected knock on his passenger's side window snatched his attention away from the screen of his iPhone X. Turning the music down, Rocket pressed the button to let the passenger's window down.

"What up, Kathy?" Rocket asked the fiend, already knowing the motive behind her approach.

The scrawny woman outside of his car cocked her head to the side, kissing her teeth. "Chile, don't be asking me no stupid questions," Kathy rolled her eyes. "Do you still got that white shit you had?"

"Yeah," Rocket grabbed the Glade sandwich bag out of the cup holder, that was filled with slabs of crack cocaine. "What you tryna do?"

Kathy tried to open the car door, but it was locked. "Open the door."

"Man, you ain't about to get your funky ass in my car," Rocket retorted, still untying the sandwich bag. Kathy was staring at him with the long face; he didn't give a fuck, though. He didn't have any compassion for no crack head.

"I got a 50," Kathy pulled the crumpled bills out of her dingy bra. "Gon' and bless me, Rocket," she said, dropping the money on the passenger seat via the slightly opened window.

Rocket left the money on the passenger seat while he expertly broke one of the slabs in half, with his index and thumb nail. He gave both pieces a quick glance, eye balling the weight. He was just making sure he could get four dimes out if either slab. "Here," he let the window down a little more.

"Hol' up, boy!" Kathy exclaimed, quickly snatching the slab out of his hand. She looked out the corner of her eyes, trying to make sure none of the other junkies had seen her purchase. "I'll be back, Rocket. You gon' be right here?" She was already in motion, as she threw the question over her shoulder, headed in the opposite direction.

Rocket put the rest of the crack back inside the bag, placing it in the cup holder until the next trap pull up. He finally decided to reach over and check the greasy bills that Kathy dropped in the window.

"Junkie ass bitch," he shook his head after counting the money. Kathy had shorted him 10$. He was going to let her slide this time; and the only reason he was going to do that was on the strength of her bringing money his way all day. He knew the short would come eventually.

"Fuck it," Rocket hit the push start, bringing the engine to life. He didn't immediately pull off, he had to respond to a couple of text messages from his girlfriend, Nicki. He sent the messages out then put the car in drive. It was time for the night life.

After a couple of hours the money started to slow down, and the begging started to speed up. Rocket knew it was time for him to go then. He went home and took him a shower, entering his night mode phase. By the time he got back in traffic it was after midnight, so he headed directly to the club. It was this new club they had just opened up off of FIB that everybody had started fucking with. Although he was under age he knew he wasn't going to have a problem getting in.

Rocket was a seventeen year old golden child with everybody and everything he decided to do. Known around the country as the nation's best high school basketball player, the number one recruit of the classes of 2020, possibly 2019 if he decided to reclassify. It was more of the same with football, except he was the number two player and recruit when it came to the Quarter Back position.

Although Rocket was talented and very gifted, he still was more focused on his illicit activities. The only thread that was holding him to the cloth of education was a promise he made to his mother before she was killed. It was a struggle every passing day, but Rocket's word to his mother was his life; he refused to break the vow he gave his mother's resting soul. Sometimes it was hard for him to balance the two, but some how managed to pull it off flawlessly. It wasn't like he was in the streets for no reason; he had to help lighten the load for his three older sisters.

Being the youngest child–and only son–of an African-American woman, who went against the odds and did whatever she had to do to provide for her four children, and support her deported husband, taught Rocket family values and gave him a strong set of morals and principles; add that with being the only son of an Haitian immigrant that was so determined to be with his family–after being deported back to Haiti–he escaped the poverties of the third world country on a twelve person boat. Risking his life at sea all in the name of love and loyalty, that was the foundation of Rocket's Lion's heart, honor, ambition, perseverance, determination, persistence, and commitment.

Rocket had a keen perception of what it was to fail and prevail. That's why his whole mentality was built on an "I will not lose" philosophy.

Rocket's mother met his pops during one of her Church's charity trips to the Capitol city of Haiti, Port-au-Prince. The story behind their romance was kind of inscrutable. Even with Rocket hearing the story a million times he just didn't get it. All that was limpid to him was the basics: first came his sister RyRy, unlike him she was born in the States. Then his father was deported, causing his mother to leave her the young daughters with their grandmother while she spent time with her lover in Haiti. That's when Rocket was planted in his mother's womb. Right there in the slums of La Saline.

Due to the pregnancy, Rocket's mother ended up staying in Haiti until after his birth.

It was more to the story, but that was too much for Rocket. He just started the timeline at 5 years old when everybody was together in the States and his parents were married. That simplified the whole thing. To him that was the beginning… and the ending came January 12, 2010. His parents were on a trip back to Haiti, enjoying the month that Haitian independence came.

Rocket could still remember the emotions that flowed through him when he learned that his parents were victims of the earthquake that claimed an undisclosed number of lives throughout Haiti. It took him a long time to learn how to cope with the tragedy that struck him at such an young age. In the years following his parents' untimely death is when Rocket lost his NBA and NFL dreams, developed a "fuck sports" attitude… and gave his heart to the streets.

For a teenager, Rocket was well beyond his years. He carried himself with dignity, pride, and exuded the hubris of a man of respect. With no father figure around, Rocket took to the drug dealers and rappers to get the lessons he needed as a man. His other three siblings were all females, so he couldn't learn how to be a man from them. There were certain things he learned from his older sisters, but mainly the lessons he got via them was through their drug dealing boyfriends; especially his oldest sister's ex boyfriend, Chenard.

Just like every young dude that jumped off the porch early, Rocket had already experienced a lot of pit falls and tumbles of the game. He could tell the street stories, that personally involved him, starting at the age of ten; but that's not when he started his street career officially. In his eyes, it didn't start until he got his first bomb; that was at the age of 13.

At the beginning of his drug dealing career, Rocket didn't care about nothing but staying clean, giving his sisters and girlfriend money, saving money was the last thing on his mind. Who really expected him to be? He was young, popular, and had a pocket full of cash. He was getting money before he was old enough to get his learner's license, so you know the future and stacking for a rainy day was the last thing on his mind. He was caught up in the ghetto's lime light. The money was coming fast, so he spent it faster. He made sure his sisters stayed straight, and he helped Rikae and Ramona with the bills. After that? Everything else was for the wind. Fuck how many older hustlers he hung around with; He was on his young hustlers shit.

Now, though? Rocket was really getting some money. After scratching the surface for so long he had finally elevated to a new level. It was a long time coming for him, but he was on the move for real for real. He had it all aligned now. He was reing–up with his own money(no fronts), and he was doubling or tripling his paper on damn near every trip. Unlike when he first started hustling, everytime he flipped, he tucked and stashed. He wasn't big Willie status yet, but he was pacing it. He wasn't in no race or competition with nobody. He was rocking his shades night time–literally–when it came to seeing other hustlers. No matter the level they were on. Rocket was in his own lane; fuck another nigga's paper; he was too busy counting his own.

Pulling up in the parking lot of the club, Rocket cruised around looking for a parking space in the front of the club. When he realized that he wasn't going to find one in the front, he settled for one in the center. He really want worried about nobody fucking with his shit. Niggas through the city knew what was up with him. He shot bullets just as well as he shot 3pointers.

Killing the engine, Rocket got out of the car. He checked his phone once more before putting it on silent. Once he got in the club he wasn't going to be able to hear shit. Concealing his strap under his shirt, Rocket proceeded towards the entrance of the club.

"Hey, Rocket," a scantily clad, light skin female called out.

Turning his Atlanta Braves hat to the back after putting his long dreads in a ponytail, "what's up with it, Daysha?" He responded, openly looking her up and down.

"I'm just chilling. I haven't been seeing you around," Daysha said. "Don't you think you need to be at home resting for school?" She teased, flirting with the lanky, handsome teenager.

"Probably," Rocket shrugged, giving off his signature nonchalant demeanor. He was way past the school jokes; that was so last, last, last, last year. Ever since he was 14 years old he'd been hitting major clubs, his face wasn't new to the scene. Even before he got his weight up he was rolling with the heavy hitters. The bitch just don't know how to approach a young don, Rocket think to himself.

None of this shit was new to Rocket: the money, the cars, the clothes, the hoes, the attention, etc. He'd seen it all before. The only difference now was the element of his game. The whip on chrome rims? That was his now. The money? He had all four pockets full, he had it in a shoe box at his spot, in the sock draw in his sister room, and it was some ducked off at Nicki spot.

Something that never changed–was Rocket's player demeanor. Way back before he was getting it he'd been smashing whatever female he set his sights on. But now? Sheesh! It was a different level. It seemed like every groovy light skin, butter-pecan, and Godiva chocolate chick, who used to "luh bro" him back in the days, was note throwing the pussy at him. At first that shit caught him off guard, but he was starting to adjust to the street fame.

I'm just coppin' a quarter brick and hoes already treating me like the brick man, Rocket think. I can't wait to see how these bitches act when I actually start getting 4-5 of them thangs.

Daysha had her eyes on Rocket. She wanted his dick in the worse way. She'd been knowing luh Rocket since he was playing peewee league. Back then the only thing that was on luh Rocket's mind was making it to the league on the pro level.

Standing at 6'4", 205 pounds with a smooth grade of dark chocolate skin, Rocket was a favorite amongst the ladies. His natural charisma was one of the things that drove the females crazy for him, but his long dread looks commanded alot of attention. Plus he was just cool as fuck. To females Rocket was a fun time; they knew his heart was with Nicki for life.

"Damn, Daysha, you already half-naked," her friend, Tarika, said. "If you want to give the young nigga the pussy, just tell him. Don't be holding up the fucking line, freak hoe."

Daysha shot her friend a bird. "Fuck you stank ass bitch," she rolled her eyes. "And I know you're not talking about nobody being naked," Daysha added.

"Both of y'all hoes need to shut the fuck up," the other friend Amber chimed in.

Rocket just shook his head, laughing at Daysha and her crew. This was the something he was used to. No matter what hood, what zone; this was Atlanta. He already knew how Daysha and her crew got down. A couple of his older partners use to be fucking on them. Let the hood tell it: they were some sexy, fine ass sack chasing hoes, that were trying to suck and fuck their way to high class thot status.

To Rocket? They were just like him—attracted and addicted to the allure of the game. Action, the squeeze, nat-nat, whatever title came they chose to put on an "ambitious" female; Rocket didn't see nothing wrong with the way they decided to pursue their happiness. He refused to judge them. Maybe them older niggas did, but that wasn't his motion. He was from a different era, a different generation, what them girls were doing 10-15 years ago that shit wasn't his business.

That shit tripped him out how everything one of them older niggas from the hood seen him fucking with one of the older bitches, that was from around the way, the first thing they go to saying was " luh bruh, she ain't talking about shit." Rocket didn't give a fuck what she was talking about—he just wanted to fuck on something. When it came to anything 21 and older, Rocket wasn't trying to hear about that past shit.

"Let me get y'all IDs," the little ratchet chick said, smacking her gum.

Everybody started sliding their IDs through the slot. Rocket didn't have an ID to slide, so instead of an ID he pulled a bankroll out of his pocket. Immediately every female in line eyes were on him, praying for their way to be paid.

"Aye, I got you a 50," Rocket removed a $100 bill from the wad and returned the rest to the pocket of his G-star raw jeans. "I ain't got no ID, though," he pulled another $100 bill out of his pocket, without pulling out the whole bankroll this time. " This for them three," he motioned towards Daysha's crew, sliding the cash through the slot. He fucked with them just on the strength of them being from the hood.

Without hesitation the woman working the window accepted the money. Shit, she thought, this an easy $130 for me. "It ain't that serious, hunni," she rolled her eyes, stamping their hand with the 21 and older stamp.

"Thank you, Rock-Rock," Daysha smiled, calling Rocket by his childhood nickname, as they headed in the building.

Rocket chuckled. "C'mon, man," he said, stopping at the see security check line. "It's Rocket, ya dig? I ain't no luh nigga no more."

"Ump," Tarika was gone on the Molly, so the facial expression she gave Rocket told it all, but she only said, "we done heard," although she had that blunt 'I want to fuck you' face on.

"Since you heard, act like you know," Rocket gave a nonchalant retort, rubbing his hairless face with his open palm.

Tarika licked the bottom of her top lip with the tip of her tongue, then seductively biting her bottom lip saying, "Give me a chance, and I will, baby."

"Bitch, you talking about me," Daysha said, rolling her eyes.

Rocket was looking over the heads in front of him, trying to see who the security guard was. He was hoping it was his mans, because he wasn't going in the club without his strap on him.

"...You good... damn, girl, where you get all that ass from?"

Rocket relaxed when he heard the voice of the guard. It was his boy, Big Riden, from Allison.

"... Troy, my nigga, go ahead... now I know your name gotta be sunshine, because you're definitely shining, baby. Your first drink on me," Big Riden talked shit and flirted the whole time he did security checks. "I know you ain't got no panties on under that tight ass dress..."

"I don't," she replied.

"Shidd, don't tell ah nigga, show ah nigga," Big Riden replied, causing everybody to start laughing.

There was a couple more people on front of Rocket, Tarika, Amber, and Daysha. While they were waiting for the line to move, Daysha took advantage of the wait. Stepping back a little, Daysha pressed her fat ass into the crouch area of Rocket's G-star Raw jeans. Right on cue Rocket grabbed her waist and pressed his dick between her cheeks. His dick got hard immediately. Daysha looked over her shoulder at him, and smiled.

Daysha was 28 years old, 11 years older than Rocket, but she wasn't thinking about no age. Rocket was still in high school–he was legal, though. She was just like the other older women that was fucking or trying to fuck on Rocket; she didn't see the same little boy she watched grow up. All she seen was a full grown man... and $$$ signs. She remembered when Rocket had first jumped off the porch. He was fucking with this older hustler from Thomasville projects, who fucked with his sister. Daysha used to be fucking with Chenard, too, but Rocket's sister was wifey.

Way back then Daysha knew that Rocket would be that nigga. Everybody really expected him to stay focused on sports, but things changed when his parents died.

"Shawty, what the fuck going?" Big Riden got excited when he seen his young nigga.

"My boy," Rocket slapped hands with Big Riden.

"Keep your nose clean," Big Riden warned, knowing Rocket had that fye on him.

Rocket put two fingers to his forehead and saluted. "You already, my nigga," he replied, getting ready to step through the single door that lead to the double doors.

Tarika stopped Rocket before he went through the double doors. "We trying to leave with you tonight," she told him, t reaching up under Daysha's mini-skirt

"Teheheehhee," Daysha giggled when Tarika's fingers slid inside of her wet pussy. "Mmmmh," she moaned. "Quit, girl, before you scare my luh baby away," she took Tarika's fingers out of her pussy.

"Y'all out of control," Amber commented, shaking her head at her friends behavior. Usually she would be down with her team, but not this time. She just couldn't bring herself to look at Rocket like that. He was still "luh bruh" in her eyes. On top of that his big sister, Ramona, used to be her best friend back in high school. That was probably the reason she couldn't stop thinking of him as 'Rock-Rock' no matter how much money he was getting. Damn, Amber think, he is growing up to be sexy as fuck, though.

Tarika put the same two fingers, that she just took out of Daysha's pussy, in her mouth. " I'm trying to let him know what's really going," Tarika stuck her tongue out, showing Rocket her rainbow colored tongue ring.

"This bitch gets no more Molly," Amber said.

Rocket's dick was harder than a Flintstone newspaper at the thought of fucking on Daysha and Tarika at the same time. Out of all the fucking he'd done–he still haven't had a threesome. He really wanted to smash Amber, but she still was on that 'luh bruh' shit. He really believed she was scared of his sister, Ramona.

"We going to see what's up," Rocket played it cool. He was a player for real; he wasn't letting no female see him sweat over no pussy.

Tarika blew him a kiss. "You do that, Rock-Rock," she said, trying to play on his ego.

Chapter 2

Taylor sat at the red light, tapping her finger on the steering wheel of her tan 2018 Nissan Altima, moving her body to the beat of "Wildest Dreams" by Taylor Swift.

"Dang," complained to herself, "the light isn't going to ever change," she checked her Apple watch.

Soon as the words escaped her lips, the light changed.

"About time," she pushed her foot down on the gas, moving along with the late night traffic. "Uh, " she expressed when the traffic once again slowed down.

I should of just took my ass back home, like I started to do, she thought as she switched lanes again.

Taylor was seriously contemplating turning around and saying " fuck! The last minute trip to North Miami" to see her son's sperm donor. The only reason she didn't abort the trip, that she had come from Tampa for, was because her 3 year old son was still on the backseat talking about seeing his buster ass daddy. If it wasn't for that, she would of been turned around… or at least that's what she kept telling herself at this moment.

Right in the midst of thinking about her baby daddy, her phone started ringing. With her eyes still on the road, she grabbed the phone out the cup holder.

"Why do you keep calling me, Travis?" She answered, making sure he knew he was really on her nerves. "What, what, what? What the fuck do you want, man? You already know we on the way, dude. Tha fuck!" She snapped, but her soft accented voice took some sting away from the harsh words.

"See who that iz at da doe', dawg," Travis instructed one of his workers before he offered a rebuttal to Taylor's belligerent address. "Who da fuck you thank you talking, Tay'?" He questioned, holding the phone to his ear with his shoulder, as he laced his weed with cocaine before he rolled it.

"You, nigga! The fuck," she retorted. "Now, what the fuck you want? You blowing my phone up for nothing. You don't want shit, Travis."

"If you seen me calling, why da fuck yo' luh stupid ass didn't answer?" Travis questioned.

Taylor sighed, shaking her head. *Why do I even deal with this disrespectful ass dude?* She hated that Travis was a piece of her past she couldn't just move on and forget about. Taylor could only imagine how these 3-4 days about to go.

"Travis do you have any common sense? If you see I'm not answering, why the fuck keep calling, guy?"

"Man, keep all of that white folkz shit in Tampa," Travis dismissed her prior insult. "I ain't 'bout to going back and forth witcha," he said, as he weighed up some work for his people. "Whea you at?"

"I'm in Broward, man," Taylor just gave him his answer, so he could get off her fucking line.

"Fuck you doing still in Broward?"

"I had to stop by the ugly to holla at family," Taylor replied, sarcastically. "That was rhetorical. Don't you think?" She grinned.

"You need to hurry up and get here," Travis told her, "I need you to handle something for me."

"I'm not moving none of your"–Taylor paused when she realized why Travis was so persistent about her coming to Miami in the first place. "I should of knew your lame ass had ulterior motives. That's why I don't fuck with you now."

"Man, shut da fuck up," Travis retorted." That's fo' thuddy-five, dawg," he said, handing his people the work. "I owe you siddy-five grams. Er'thang I got over here iz wrapped up. Im'ma bless you, dawg. Hol' me to it."

Taylor just held the phone, listening to Travis make his drug transaction. "Stupid ass, it's 'four hundred and thirty-five' and 'sixty-five'," she corrected, knowing he heard her.

Travis ignored Taylor and continued to handle his business. "This da whole bag?" He asked, not in the mood to count the stack of money.

The customer in the background said, "everything good, bruh. That's the whole chcck. I'm up and out."

"Bye, Travis," Taylor said. "I'll see you when I get there."

"Cool," Travis wasn't studying Taylor right now. " Just hurry up, Tay'."

"I'll get there when I get there,"Taylor retorted, hanging up the phone.

Taylor got off on her exit placing the phone between her thighs. She grabbed the steering wheel with her left hand, rubbing her right palm over her natural, long, black hair.

"Ma," Trevor, her son, called from the backseat.

Taylor looked at her baby via the center mirror. "Yes, baby," she answered sweetly.

"Is you mad at daddy?" Trevor asked.

"No, baby," she replied. "I'm not mad at your daddy."

"Then why did you call him a "stupid ass"?" Trevor's little baby voice was so innocent, Taylor couldn't even get mad at him for cursing.

"It's just a figure of speech, baby," Taylor explained. "What I tell you about repeating my words, Trev'?"

"I'm sorrryyy," Trevor apologized. "Can you turn the music back up?"

Taylor just smiled, as she augmented the volume of the music, obliging her baby boy's request. She was just so thankful that she was blessed with her son. There were times when he was her only reason for living. Anytime she needed a charge up the orisa sent the energy via her baby boy.

Taylor was an 18 year old, single mother, that was currently working her way through her senior year of high school, and juggling two part time jobs. She really didn't have to work as much as she did, but she wanted to make sure her and her son didn't need nothing or anyone, but each other. She had a support team, she just was the type of woman who liked to lean on herself.

Travis was a buster, but she couldn't lie and say "he didn't do anything for his son", because he did whatever, whenever. It was just difficult for her to deal with him. Travis was a major figure in the Miami drug game, and he had four other kids by four different women. On top of that: Taylor was his youngest baby mother, so you know how that went.

Over the last couple of years, Taylor had started to work on her character, image, and self-respect. She remembered two years prior she was running around Miami still chasing behind Travis. She was so naïve at the time. If she knew what she knew now back then... She would of never allowed an 18 year old drug dealer, with 3 kids already, get her pregnant at 14 years old. But it was a lesson and a blessing.

Taylor was starting to understand that life was full of lessons; some you learned from, some you didn't... But you lived with all of them.

Every obstacle Taylor had to overcome was reversed, and now she used them as a source of strength and motivation. One of the main things Taylor had to when she decided it was time to change– she had to get out of Dade county. The city wasn't doing nothing but draining her youth, innocence, add dimming her light. She was from Lil Haiti, but she grew up in Carroll City, Miami.

In her hood everybody was looking for a come up. It didn't matter how they got there, they just had to get there. The females were scheming on the dudes together, then when one came up and the other one didn't–they scheme on each other. The dudes weren't any better. Her hood was crazy, dangerous, and contagious, but she loved it.

From the beginning, Taylor's mother wasn't too fond of the fact her 14 year old daughter was pregnant–by an 18 year old drug dealer. She tried everything in her power to keep Taylor out of the cycle of the streets, but that was kind of hard to do when you resided in one of the worst neighborhoods in the city. Taylor's mother had been down that same road before; and it didn't get her nothing but headaches and a whole lot of heartbreaks.

Seeing that the cycle was becoming deeper, Taylor's mother said "enough is enough", and packed up and moved her daughter out of Miami. She bought a house in a quiet suburban neighborhood in Tampa, FL; and they both started over new. That ended up being the best thing she ever did as a parent.

Taylor was the only child of two Haitian immigrants–who migrated to the states in the early 80's–but she was born in Miami. Her father was killed when she was only two years old, so she really didn't know much about him. She really didn't have many family members in the states, but the Haitians in South Florida were very tight knitted. She did have some family that stayed in Georgia, but she hardly ever got to see them, outside of when they came down for the major Haitian holidays.

Her cousin, Dynasty, was like her big sister. That was probably the only person in this world she trusted with her secrets and life. She had a lot of respect for her. She was really on her grown woman vibe. That was one person Taylor wasn't ashamed up admit she wanted to be like. Dynasty was the definition of beauty and brains.

No debate, hands down Taylor already had the beauty thing down packed. She was almost perfect when it came to her facial features, pearly white teeth, and bodily assets. With smoky-eyes and lithe, Taylor was the kind of beauty that was a walking advertisement. Her personality is what made her addictive. She was funny, charming, passionate, down-to-earth, and smart.

You would think Taylor was the identical twin of Taral Hicks (Keisha from the movie Belly). Their skin complexion was exactly the same, Taylor looks were just a little more exotic and her derriere was bigger and rounder. Another thing that separated the two was Taylor's infatuation with red lipstick.

In her new life, in Tampa, Taylor was reinventing herself. The whole sack chasing, legs in the air, young thot persona was out the window. She was completely kicking the preppy Haitian girl swagg. That Cardi B/City Girls ratchet shit was played out for her. Nobody in Tampa knew of her past, and she liked it like that. Even with the new persona, Taylor still had all type of dudes lusting after her. They were all naïve to the fact the 5'10" Haitian bombshell that they were categorizing as an angel–was really a nightmare dressed as a daydream.

Taylor pulled up in the matchbox at midnight with her tinted windows rolled down. Just riding through the apartments she was beginning to feel nostalgic. It had been over a year since their migration to central Florida, so she was kind of anticipating the love she was about to receive from her people.

The Matchbox was a beige, squared-up apartment complex that sat off of Honeyhilll Drive on 199th street. The two floor establishment was the only projects in this particular area, so you know the overflow of killers, robbers, and dealers was in abundance. To say the least; there were a lot of killing and drug dealing going down in the Matchbox. Only the wickedest survived for real in this hood… The weak was prey in the jungle.

"Oh! Hell nawl!" A short, thick red female, wearing booty shorts exclaimed as soon as Taylor ejected herself from her vehicle. "I know that ain't you, bitch!"

Taylor just shook her head, as she removed Trevor from his car seat. "Chill with that ghetto ass shit, Ashley," she told her homegirl from way back.

"Oh," Ashley rolled her eyes, "you Hollywood now?"

"Yeah, right, bitch," Taylor kneeled down and rolled Trevor's pants legs up one time, so he wouldn't be walking on the back of his Ralph Lauren Polo jeans. "If anything, I'm South Beach."

"If that's the case, I guess your ass still Carroll City," Ashley tooted her lips up, "because the only time your ass been across that bridge is to steal them folks shit."

Taylor laughed. "Fuck you, trick. Fuck you," she slammed her car door close.

"Look at my luh nephew," Ashley said. "He getting so big and handsome."

It was almost 1 in the morning and the Matchbox was bursting with activity-like it was the middle of the day. There were niggas posted up, smoking weed, shooting dice, and fucking with the thots on one side. Then on the other side; you had niggas distributing crack cocaine, heroin, weed, pills and Molly… And there were half-naked females all over.

"Don't forget about bad," Taylor added. "This luh nigga bad as fuck. The other day, he done jumped on this luh boy and took his big wheel."

"You already know that's how y'all crazy ass Haitians come out the pussy," Ashely half-joked.

"Pussy! Pussy! Pussy! Pussy!" Trevor started chanting, pointing at Ashley's bulging vagina area.

Taylor followed Trevor's hand, her eyes falling on Ashley's camel-toe. "Boy!" She exclaimed, popping his arm lightly.

"Oh my god," Ashley giggled. " This too much pussy for ya, luh Trevor. You gotta catch up with me when you get a little older, baby."

"You got a fat pussy," Trevor retorted, smiling.

"Trevor!" Taylor hissed. "Don't make me beat your ass. Keep trying to show out, I'm going to beat your ass out here."

"Don't be doing that boy like that, bitch," Ashley said. "Your hot ass need to watch what you be doing around him."

"I don't be doing shit. That's that shit he be getting from his buster ass daddy," Taylor responded. "I'm about to get all in Travis shit about that, though. What the fuck been going on, though, Trashley?" She switched the subject, accosting her by one of her childhood nicknames. "You still running around being a little skizzer?"

"Never that," Ashley rolled her eyes. "Skizzer be them broke bitches. I keep a bag. You know what's going on. What you got going on? You and your mom done took the show on the road. I know y'all up there tricking with them Scientologists in Clearwater," she joked.

"Stop playing," Taylor smacked her teeth.

"What's up, Tay'?" A dude interrupted them.

Taylor looked over her shoulder. "Ain't shit, Snap. Tell me something good. I know you know where the pot of gold at."

"I'm looking for it as we speak," Snap shifted his attention to Ashley. "What's up with your people, man?"

Taylor shrugged her shoulders. "I don't know. What's up with her?" She reversed the question.

"Ashley don't fuck with ah nigga, Taylor," Snap replied.

"Tsk," Ashley rolled her eyes, kissing her teeth. "You don't fuck with yourself, Snap."

"Look, I'm not Cupid," Taylor said. "I'm just about to let y'all discuss whatever it is y'all need to discuss."

"Naw," Ashley grabbed Taylor's arm. "We ain't got nothing to talk about."

"Well, Snap, take your nephew up there with his daddy for me," Taylor said, helping her homegirl with the curve.

"C'mon, luh Travis," Snap said.

"No," Taylor shook her head. "His name is 'Trevor'. Your jerk ass brother didn't sign no birth certificate to have a junior."

Snap didn't even comment on that one. "Sayless, Taylor," he lead Trevor up the stairs to his little brother's spot.

Taylor waited for Snap to clear the area before she asked, "what the hell y'all got going on? I didn't know you was fucking on Snap."

"Tsk," Ashley kissed her teeth. "Don't nobody fuck with that use-to-be ass nigga. When he first got out of prison, I gave him a quick shot of million dollar"–

"More like twenty dollar," Taylor teased, going in her Chanel clutch.

"Thinking he was gon' end up back on top–I heard you, too, bitch–but the nigga fucked up all the cash that the hood gave him," Ashley explained. "Now he want some charity pussy."

"How the hell he did that? Travis ain't fucking with him?" Taylor asked incredulous, expertly applying her Revlon super lustrous lipstick in Rich girl Red.

"Tah," Ashley offered a sarcastic expression. "Not on consignment. Travis ain't just fucking with these niggas like that. Buddy really playing for keeps out here. He getting money for real now, Taylor, but he still on the dumb shit."

Taylor sat on the hood of the car, declining a blunt from one of the occupants of the area. No matter how long she stayed away; she was still Miami. "I'm good, Chank," she didn't smoke anymore, but she definitely didn't smoke weed she didn't roll or see rolled. This was the dirty capital. "What dumb shit?" She wanted to know everything.

"Word on the streets he raned off on some zoes, that he was getting the work from," Ashley informed her.

"Travis raned off on some Haitians?" Taylor raised her eyebrows. "I couldn't have just heard you right?"

"Yeah, you heard me," Ashley nodded her head up and down. "Your dude is tripping. It could just be a rumor, though. Everybody just went to running their mouth about shit, after Travis killed them three dudes."

"Three dudes?" Taylor furrowed her brows. "Haitians? Travis killed some Haitians?" *I knew I shouldn't have brought my ass down here,* she thought.

Ashley rolled her eyes to the top of her head. "Hell no!" She giggled. "Some niggas from the swamp(Overtown). Travis got shot, too. I think three times, but they say that fool was slinging that stick like a guitar."

At that moment Taylor realized how far removed she was from this shit. This same type of conversation used to turn her the fuck on; but now? It just showed her how much she didn't want this life for her son. "What do the Haitians got to do with that?"

"People saying that was the hit team, hunni," Ashley shrugged. "You know how the streets talk."

"You know who the dudes were? I'm talking about the ones he suppose to had raned off on? The Haitians," Taylor was in her feelings about Travis alleged dispute with her people.

"You remember them Atlanta Haitians that migrated down here?"

"Yeah," just as Taylor suspected; it was some Haitians that she knew personally. "You talking about Wes, Wrigley, and them? You know I fuck with all of them. Even the sisters."

"I know you do," Ashley acknowledged. "You know, after you left, Wes started making major moves. He was back and forth, but Haitian Trgeá held it down for him. That's who Travis supposed to got the stuff from."

"What he supposed to raned off with?" Taylor asked.

"They say it 50 bricks," Ashley knew all the gossip. "Like I said, it might just be a rumor. That's all I heard. This been 3-4 months ago, and he ain't dead yet."

"That nigga is stupid," Taylor didn't know what else to say.

"You know what it is," Ashley shrugged her shoulders. "He's 21 with the bag and he got his hood behind. We done seen this a million times. I still can't believe you let that nigga, out of everybody, get you pregnant."

"A mistake isn't a mistake if you learn from it," Taylor shrugged. "Things happen."

"Aye, Tay'!"

Before Taylor turned around, she already knew who it was accosting her. When she turned around her eyes landed on her baby daddy. He was coming down the stairs with no shirt on, brandishing a Dracko. He had on a pair of Balmain jeans, that was being held up by a Gucci belt, with a Miami Heat hat turned to the back. She couldn't stand her baby daddy, but she was weak for his demeanor.

"What da fuck you doing out here with this gossiping ass bitch?" Travis asked, stopping in front of the car.

Chapter 3

S oon as Rocket stepped through the main entrance of the club "Hard" by Saydam Hussain started blasting via the mega speakers. He had to blink a couple times to get his eyes adjusted to the darkness. The weed smoke was so thick, Rocket could feel it entering his system everytime he inhaled. Due to the fact he didn't get blunted very often, the second hand smoke was liable to get him high.

Just from a quick survey of the area, Rocket located a crowd of niggas that was from around his way posted up in one of the corner booths. Before he went anywhere, he surveyed the scene for a couple more minutes. It was a habit he'd acquired from Chenard, his oldest sister, ex-boyfriend.

Chenard was the first older hustler to take Rocket under his wings, teaching him the fundamental of the game. Back when Rocket was a kid, Chenard was that nigga in the city. That was before he caught a trafficking case and had to do a couple of years. When he got out from that bid was when Rocket started rocking with him. Niggas didn't expect Chenard to run it up so fast–but he did. With a new perception of the game, Chenard switched the game up on the second time around. He wifed up Rikae, he cut off all the leeches, and kept all the squares out of his power circle. Before Chenard got knocked by the feds three years ago, he was close to locking the whole city down.

Rocket hated how shit went down with fool, he had crazy love for dude. In his opinion Chenard was the realest nigga to ever do it out of his era. A lot of rules he played by, he learned them from Chenard. One thing Chenard always preached to him was to "stay aware of your surroundings."

"Excuse me, luh baby," Rocket said, trying to get by a group of females that were blocking the stairs. He had to get downstairs to the pool tables. He never played the dance floor long–he wasn't with that dark shit. Through the years, he'd seen a lot of niggas get did something fucking around on the dance floor.

The female turned around, ready to snap on whoever it was that had their hand on the small of her back. The music was blasting, so she couldn't hear what he had said. She didn't know the dude's name, but she knew who he was. She had seen him around with some official niggas. She held her tongue and stepped to the side. "My bad, boo," she said, smiling.

Rocket brushed past the chick, not hearing nothing she had said, heading down the stairs. Once he got to the level where the bar was located, the area was more illuminated. He pushed through the bottom level, stopping occasionally to exchange words with somebody from around the way. A couple females, that he knew, was trying to get him to catch the booth with them, but he declined. He was headed to the spot where all the hustlers congregated. Soon as he rounded the corner he heard:

"Hol' them dice!"

"Y'all niggas tighten up!"

"Bet a thousand, shoot a thousand."

"You ain't saying shit!"

The noise from the dice game was carrying all the way from the cut to the big area. This was an every weekend ritual for majority of the occupants of the dice game. Every nigga around the dice game was getting after the bag in some kind of way.

Just in time, Rocket thought to himself. This was right up his alley. He didn't even have to bend the corner to know who all was in the cut. The area before the back cut was being occupied by mostly females. That was far from a surprise.

"B-Rad, wazzam, foo?" Rocket slapped hands with one of the big dogs out of the zone 3 community Mechanicsville.

B-Rad laid the stack of money, he had in his hand, on the table in order to slap hands with Rocket. "Hell you got going on, Shawty?"

"Just pulling up," Rocket replied. "Strolling through, like a big dog 'pose to, ya dig?"

DeeMoney was on the ground, getting ready to shoot the dice. "C'mon, luh Rocket, with all that cool talking shit," he said, shaking the dice.

"Fuck all that. You better focus on them dice, holmes," 3dub Reggie said. "I done dropped $6k on that fuck ass point.

"Mean Gene, wazzam, unc?" Rocket nodded his head at Chenard's tight man.

"Quit all that crying, broke ass nigga. We got rap money now," DeeMoney retorted, shaking the dice high above his head. "Three hoes and a pimp," he let the dice go, snapping his fingers. Instead of a four the dice landed on nine.

"Hit the point, nigga," 24Lotto told DeeMoney. "What's going on, Rocket? You good, luh woe?"

"Most definitely," Rocket watched the dice.

Mean Mug dropped $500 on the table. "This nigga arm will go out before he hit that fo'. Who like it?"

"I like it," Rocket called the bet, pulling his bankroll out of his pocket. "What that is?"

"5," Mean Mug said, "it can be more, though."

"That's a rack," Rocket dropped the money on the table. "Anybody else don't like the four?"

"Huh?" B-Rad bobbed his head. "Y'all heard, luh bruh. My whole hood getting money... even my young nigga," he boasted.

"C'mon with all that talking, B," Eastside Dre said. "You bet something. We been getting money on the east."

"Bet something? Bet something?" B-Rad looked at Dre sideways. "That's what you said, 20k ass nigga?"

"You heard what my young nigga said," Big Brandon spoke up for luh Dre. Big Brandon was one of the big dogs out the east. He knew Dre was out of his league. He didn't even have the type of money B-Rad was playing with; he just had to save face for his hood.

"Whatever y'all niggas gon' do, y'all need to do it," DeeMoney said, "cause I'm about to shoot."

"50k all fifties, nigga," B-Rad dropped a stack, wrapped the long way, on the ground. "Y'all know what's up with ah nigga fo'real. I spent y'all niggas re-up on rubber bands and sandwich bags."

Dre scratched the side of his head. "Man, shiiddd, I'm straight on all of that."

Rocket chuckled to himself. "You wanna bet something small?" He smirked. "I got two bands on the floor."

"Man, I'm gone," DeeMoney rolled the dice. "Luh Joe!"

Ten rolls later, DeeMoney hit the four and six other points.

Rocket eased away from the dice game–after he raked up a cool $9k. He bought an ounce of kush, from YFN TrePound on the strength of him beating him out a few bands, and went and posted up in the big area of the pool table section. Whenever he was in the club, this was the place you could find him at. He loved this atmosphere. This was where all the real hustlers could be found… and the bad bitches.

What the fuck? Rocket thought. I know that ain't my girl.

"Aye, aye, aye," Rocket reached out, and grabbed Nicki's arm, trying to get her attention.

"What the fuck wron–" Nicki turned around about to go the fuck off, until she realized it was the person she was down here looking for: her boyfriend, Rocket. "Boy, I was just about to do you something," Nicki pointed out, her New Orleans accent still very thick.

"I ain't trying up hear that shit," Rocket let her arm go. "What you doing here?"

"We'll be by the bar, Nicki," Kayla said. She already knew now that Nicki knew Rocket was in the, she wasn't about to leave out of his presence. "Hey, Rocket. What's up with you, bro?"

"I'm coolin', Kayla," Rocket said. "You iight?"

"Yea, I'm good, bro. Bye, Nicki," Kayla rolled her eyes at her best friend. "Your lame ass," she joked.

"Fuck you, too," Nicki laughed. "You better not leave without telling me."

"You riding back with us?" Kayla asked.

"Naw," Nicki responded, looking up at Rocket. "Not if he acting right."

"She leaving with y'all," Rocket told Kayla.

"I'll call before we pull out," Kayla said before walking off.

Rocket sat on the edge of the table, busting down a backwood, with his long legs kicked out. He was debating on whether or not he should trip on Nicki for being at the club. Fuck that shit, he thought. He wasn't with all that arguing shit anyway. It wasn't no pressure; she was grown.

"Why you looking at me like that, Rocket?" Nicki asked, crossing her arms across her perky breast.

Rocket admired Nicki's petite frame, and her angelic face. The Rag&Bone skinny jeans had her derriere looking super plump and round. Hands down, Nicki was out of this world gorgeous. She stood at 5'6", she weighed about 120 pounds, no fat no where. She was the definition on 'slim thick'. She had natural hazel-brown eyes that went along with her brown skin complexion. Her hair was long with highlights, but she was rocking twist locks right now. He wanted her to dread it up, but she wasn't going for that.

Rocket and Nicki had been together for nearly five years now. Rocket was Nicki's first cut, and she was Rocket's first love. They were both very young, and they understood that, so their relationship hadn't suffered any real hardship, but what they had was still beautiful. You could tell they both cherished, loved, honored, and respected recorder each other.

"Soooo," Nicki pursed her full lips, "I just get the silent treatment?" She asked, stepping between his legs.

"I was waiting on you to answer my question," he said, breaking the weed down inside of the cigar.

"I'm 18 years old and out of high school," Nicki rolled her eyes. "I need to be asking you under age ass, what are you doing in the club?" She teased.

"That's what's up," Rocket tried to get up from the table, but he couldn't because Nicki wouldn't move from between his legs. "Watch out, Nick'."

"C'mon with all of that, Rocket. Don't make me go crazy on your lanky, black ass in this club tonight," Nicki warned. "I'm not in the mood for your bull junk, Rocket. For real, for real."

Rocket ignited the tip of his blunt. "It ain't no pressure," he exhaled the smoke away from her face, "but if it was the other way around, you would be on some other shit."

"No, I wouldn't," Nicki rolled her eyes. "If you would gave me a chance to tell you, you would know I'm here with RyRy, Rocket."

RyRy was Rocket's 19 year old sister. She was the second youngest, right before him, but everybody treated her like the baby.

She was Rocket's baby girl for real, though. He spoiled RyRy like no other. She was his father's first child by their mother.

"Where Ry' at?" Rocket asked.

Nicki shrugged her shoulders. "I don't know. She probably some where with Octavos. When I heard you were here I came straight down here."

"RyRy a real lame," Rocket shook his head.

"Stay out that girl's business, Rocket," Nicki told him. "You must not be going to school in the morning?"

"You know I'm going to school."

Nicki checked the time on her phone. "Rocket, it's almost 3, bae," Nicki shifted her eyes. "You need to get some rest then. Let's go home," she tried to hide her grin.

"I'm good," Rocket wasn't going for that. "You can gon' and go home, though."

"You the one got football practice," Nicki shrugged, "not me. I just got half of a day at work," Nicki started swaying her hips. "I can party all night."

"You about to go home," Rocket knew he wasn't going to be able to get away Nicki without going with her, he still had to try to work his ones. "I'll be over there before you go to work."

"Man, please," Nicki kissed her teeth, rolling her eyes. "You think I'm going for that?"

"Going for what?" Rocket asked. "I'm for real, bruh. Soon as I handle all my business, I'm pulling up."

"Nah, I'm straight on that one," Nicki shook her head. "Sorry, my boy."

"What the hell you been doing all day?" Rocket wasn't even about to go back and forth about that with Nicki. She watched l wasn't going to budge.

"Nothing really," Nicki pursed her lips. "I was going to go to church with mama, but I overslept. That's all I been doing lately. Eating and sleeping. I don't know what's wrong with me," Nicki put her hands in Rocket's pockets. She easily found wads of money, but she was actually looking for his phone.

"Why you all in my pockets?" Rocket asked not attempting to remove her hands, though. He already knew what she was looking for. "You might be pregnant," he joked.

"You playing," she pulled the wads of money out of both of his front pocket, "I might be for real. How much is this? Let me get some money," she didn't wait for an answer, she just started peeling bills off.

"I don't know what you asked for," Rocket twisted the end of one of his dreads, watching Nicki peel off at least $2k, "if you wasn't going to wait for permission. You see what happened to Felicia for going in ah nigga pocket," he really was joking now, because he would never hit Nicki… or any other female.

Nicki rolled her eyes. "Boy, you know I'm the Debo of this relationship," she replied with a smirk on her face. "You must been back there shooting dice?" She asked, placing her money in her clutch, after putting his money back in his pockets.

"Yea, but I'm having paper," Rocket responded.

"Shut up," Nicki poked her arrogant ass boyfriend in the side. "I'm already knowing that. The money is just cleaner than it usually be."

"You observing everything else, have you took a pregnancy test yet?" Rocket nudged Nicki forward, gently, so he could get up from the pool table.

"Nope," Nicki brushed off the question. "You coming to my apartment after the club or naw?"

"Or naw." Rocket smirked.

"You're about to make me put a hit out on you," Nicki warned with a straight face. "Stop playing, man. I want some."

"I thought you wanted me to go to school," Rocket teased, knowing she was horny.

"What that gotta do with anything? You can leave for school from my spot… Like you always do," Nicki retorted.

Rocket stood in front of Nicki, looking down, placing his hand in her removable dreadlocks. " You gon' let 'em lock?" He tried to smoothly change the subject.

"Definitely not, I told you that. I'm not doing that to my hair," Nicki twisted her lips to the side. "You can forget about that. You got enough dreads for the both of us," Nicki pushed away from his body. "Now," she put her hands on her hips, " is you coming home with me tonight or not?"

"It's morning."

"Fuck what time it is," Nicki retorted. "Answer the question."

"I got like two and a quarter left," Rocket licked his lips. "I really wanna re-up today, ya dig?"

"Rocket, you can handle that shit later. Tha fuck. You're taking me home," Nicki told him, "and you're taking your ass to school, Rocket. You already know you can't miss no more days."

"I'm going to school," Rocket replied, slyly watching the ass of some chick walking up the stairs. "When I leave the spot, I'm coming straight to your house, I'll take a shower and be at school by lunch."

"You know coach is going to trip."

"I don't give ah fuck," Rocket shrugged. "I might not stay for practice anyway."

Nicki was about to get on his case, but she decided to let him have it. She just didn't understand Rocket sometime. He knew he could make it to the NFL or NBA easily, but he rathered run the streets–instead of run plays on the court or field. Sometimes she wanted to push him harder, but she didn't want him to think she was trying to force him to focus on sports; so she could benefit off of it. That was far from the case. No matter if Rocket chose the streets or sports: she has his back regardless.

"Alright, Rocket," Nicki sighed, " whatever."

"C'mon with all of that," Rocket pulled Nicki into his arms. "Why you always acting like a baby, bruh?"

"Boy, don't nobody be acting like no baby. You be tripping, bruh," she emphasized the 'bruh'. He knew she didn't like it when he called her that shit.

Rocket kissed her forehead. "Only because I know you'll catch me if I fall," he stated truthfully. "Can I catch up with Capo Nuke before he leave? Then we can go."

"I'm about to go find Ry and Kayla," Nicki said with a 'I'm about to get fucked on' smile on her face. "Don't leave me at this club, Rocket," she gave him a stern look.

"Man, I'm not even about to go through that with you."

"Yeah, cause I will totally fuck your shit up tonight. Your clothes, your money, your shoes, and all. I'll leave your work, though. Maybe that'll keep you from leaving me," she giggled.

"You out of control," Rocket just shook his head.

"You heard what I said," Nicki replied, over her shoulder, as she walked off.

Made in the USA
Columbia, SC
02 April 2022

58433553R00122